THE OUTSIDE MAN

Richard North Patterson

THE OUTSIDE MAN

WHEELER
PUBLISHING, INC.
ROCKLAND, MA

★ AN AMERICAN COMPANY ★

Published in Large Print by arrangement with Little, Brown and Company
in the United States and Canada.

Wheeler Large Print Book Series.

Set in 16 pt Plantin.

Library of Congress Cataloging-in-Publication Data

Patterson, Richard North.
    The outside man / Richard North Patterson.
        p. (large print) cm.(Wheeler large print book series)
    ISBN 1-56895-907-9 (hardcover)
    1. Southern States—Fiction. 2. Friendship—Fiction. 3. Large type
books. I. Title. II. Series

[PS3566.A8242 O9   2000]
813'.54—dc21
                                                                00-039870
                                                                CIP

For Jesse Hill Ford

Murder doesn't round out anybody's life except the murdered's and maybe the murderer's.

Nick Charles, from
Dashiell Hammett's
The Thin Man

We sail with a corpse in the cargo.

Ibsen

ONE

Perhaps the murders were fated when I met Kris Ann, then moved with her here, to Alabama. The move was a change of plans. I'd meant us to live in Washington. We never did, and so three deaths began waiting in the ambush of time.

Seven years passed, and then Cade handed me the envelope. It seemed like nothing at all. I'd come from a Saturday partners' meeting called to set new rates—nineteen southern Protestants and me at a long walnut table buffed so high I could see my face in it—trying to feel like one hundred eighty dollars an hour. It took some imagination. So when Cade caught me near the elevator and with a quick, chill glance at my blue jeans asked if I'd drop some papers with Lydia Cantwell, my only thought was to do that much for free.

Outside the morning was hazy from the smokestacks of our clients and the streets looked stale and a little hungover, like a room full of cigarette smoke after a long party. Behind my parking space the neon sign of a dingy department store murmured its fatigue in old-fashioned cursive letters. I tossed the envelope on the passenger seat and drove south with the top down through near-empty streets, then up and over a sudden barrier of green wooded hills until the city behind me dropped abruptly from sight.

Now the road curled downward past immense

stone houses sheltered by pine and dogwood and magnolia. The air became clear, damp and heavy, and the feel and blueness of it merged with deep lawns and the bursts of pink and white to create that violence of beauty you can find only in the South, in April. Behind me Birmingham sprawled in a valley of heat and smoke: squat steel mills the corroded color of rust, concrete highways, low-slung warehouses, sinewy towers of glass and steel, sweltering streets. But the road ahead was shady and still. A lone black maid in stretch pants straggled by its side as though on a treadmill to eternity, her slow repeated movements speaking of boredom in the bone and brain, days endlessly the same. I passed her, turning down a road that traced the winding path of a valley in what had once been pine forest, the wind in my face.

There was nothing ahead but shadows. I took the curves fast—shifting and braking, accelerating and shifting—as a smooth radio voice from New York eased into a mass murder, the oil crisis, and a Gallup poll in which three out of four Americans thought things were getting worse. "Speaking last night in Atlanta," he went on, "the chairman of the Federal Reserve Board warned that this country is threatened by permanent inflation which will change the lives of rich and poor alike...." But there was nothing I could do about that, except not smoke my first cigarette. So I didn't, and found myself at the Cantwells'.

Their drive began with a stand of oaks, continuing its gradual climb through magnolia and dogwood until it reached the crest of pines where the house loomed, a white brick monolith with gables and twenty rooms and the sense of weight that time brings. Seventy years before, Henry Cantwell's grandfather had brooded on the site, then built: over time ivy had crept up the walls, hedges had grown, a formal garden had come to surround the slate patio in back, and, finally, Lydia Cantwell's roses had lined the walk that led from the drive to the double door. I parked, taking the envelope, and followed it.

The grounds were shrouded in morning silence broken only by a few birdcalls and the rustling of pine boughs. The snarl of the buzzer when I pushed it sounded rude, and got no answer. But when I knocked, the door cracked open by itself.

I looked in, surprised, calling once. No one answered. I hesitated, then stepped inside.

The foyer faced a spiral staircase, with a sitting room to the left and the dining room opposite. Next to me was a low table. I placed the envelope there, turned to leave, stopped in the doorway, and then, turning back, picked it up again.

It was an innocuous manila, sealed only by two splayed metal fasteners that Cade's secretary had put through the hole in its flap, then pressed down to each side. I pried the fasteners upright and opened the flap. Inside was a typed document of sixteen pages. I riffled it, then read again, this time carefully. When I had finished I checked for missing pages, found none, and reread the twelfth page, twice. Then I placed the papers back in the envelope and took it with me to the sitting room.

It was sparsely decorated, mainly from the past. On polished end tables were porcelain figurines—a sparrow, Marie Antoinette—that Lydia had collected. From above the fireplace stared an oil of her father, framed by candelabra and looking vaguely distressed, as if he smelled smoke. The built-in shelf next to that held portraits of more dead ancestors and a larger one of Henry Cantwell, gray hair neatly parted. The papers in the envelope reminded me that Jason's picture had been removed. Then I noticed that Lydia's was gone.

I called out.

No one answered. I walked past the fireplace through the open door to Henry's library, filled with books: *Lancelot* by Walker Percy, some Aeschylus, much Faulkner and Camus, James Joyce's *Ulysses*, and leaning next to that with a bookmark sticking from it, *Crime and Punishment*. Often I would find Henry in a cardigan sweater, amidst his volumes: the most reliable friends, he'd once remarked, full of consolation. But his half-glasses were on the shelf and his chair was empty. I returned to the sitting room, stopped, and listened.

I didn't like finding the house unlocked, or its silence. Though in the seven years since, I'd been to the Cantwells' perhaps a hundred times, I could still hear the sounds of our engagement party, when the house had been

4

filled with people and laughter and the clink of a barman dropping ice in crystal. I'd begun awkwardly, conscious of Cade and worried that if I moved too quickly I'd slop champagne on the Oriental rugs. I had never met the Cantwells and, while Henry and Lydia were gracious, Jason watched me from one corner with a peculiar bright intensity, never coming forward. The chances of meeting a second northerner were nil and everyone else seemed to have money to burn, even Kris Ann's florid uncle who had backed me to the fireplace denouncing the Berrigan brothers. Then Kris Ann appeared behind him in the crush. For an instant her look seemed probing and uncertain and then, knowing I saw her, she flashed me the dazzling, flirty, self-mocking smile that was an in-joke between us—her southern-girl smile, she called it—until it warmed the darkness of her eyes. I'd felt myself relax, and after that I remembered the moment precisely: her smile, the room, and the sounds of the party—so that now it seemed too quiet.

"Lydia?" I called, and then went back through the foyer to the staircase, glancing toward the dining room as I passed.

I stopped there.

Lydia Cantwell lay sprawled behind the dining room table. Her eyes bulged and her tongue protruded from a smear of lipstick. Her throat was circled with bruises.

It was a moment before I knew that I had crossed myself.

I went to her then, kneeling. Her wrist was

stiff and cold to the touch. There was no pulse.

My limbs had gone numb and heavy. I stumbled back from her. Her terrycloth robe was pulled to mid-thigh and her legs seemed pitifully thin. Black hair straggled on the Persian rug, and I noticed, foolishly, that she had dyed the gray at her temples.

I felt a moment of awful tenderness, as if I should cover her legs. Instead I went to the kitchen and called the police. When I returned, my throat was parched and my mouth tasted bitter, like half-swallowed aspirin.

It was then I saw her picture.

It had been taken at a formal sitting and placed next to Henry's in the other room. Now it sat on the dining room table. Someone had stabbed out the eyes. I rushed back to the kitchen and vomited.

I raised my head from the sink, breathed deeply, and went back to the dining room. The envelope lay where I'd dropped it, by Lydia's hand. I picked it up and went outside. I didn't look back at the woman, or her picture.

The porch was cool. Above the roses a hummingbird hovered in delicate suspension, a picture from a Chinese vase.

I walked to my car and slid the envelope under the seat.

TWO

"Panic is the first enemy of the lawyer," Cade had once told me. So when the first police came—two uniformed patrolmen in a squad car—I tried to blank out everything but the envelope.

The young man rushed past me through the front door, slamming it behind him. The other stopped in front of me. He was short and paunchy, with pale blue eyes and a creased clown's face so sad it must have always seemed close to tears. "What happened?" he asked.

"I don't know."

'Sure." His voice was patient and unsatisfied. "Just how you found her."

I swallowed. "I got here maybe fifteen minutes ago, on business. Mrs. Cantwell's our client—" I paused, deleting the envelope. "No one answered, and the door was unlocked. That wasn't like her; she was a careful woman. So I stepped inside to check."

The door opened behind me. "Called in the body," the young man said. "Rayfield's coming himself. You'll want to see this."

His partner nodded and turned back to me. "You'd better come inside, Mr. Shaw." I didn't move. "Come on," he said, almost gently.

I followed him to the sitting room without looking at Lydia. He pointed me to a sofa across from the fireplace where I couldn't see the dining room or her body. "You'll have to wait here for Homicide," he said, and left.

"Jesus Christ," someone muttered. It was the older man's voice, coming from the dining room, low and close to tender.

"Look at the picture," his partner said.

There was silence. "We got a creep maybe—someone who'll do it twice."

"Might could be rape. It's funny—Rayfield was sending Watkins until I said her name, and then he decided to come himself."

"Look around you," the older man said. "She used to be somebody."

There was no malice in that, just fact and a little kinship, as though Lydia Cantwell had taken a great fall quickly and thus qualified for sympathy. My throat was dry.

The front door opened, there were murmured greetings, and footsteps near the body. A new voice—soft and flat—asked, "Called the medical examiner?" "Yessir," the older man said, and then two plainclothesmen walked into the sitting room.

The thin one had a neat mustache, wire-rimmed glasses, and the meticulous intense look of a demolition expert. But it was the second man who held my attention. He was perhaps fifty, with a large potato face and small cobalt eyes at once pained and bleak and totally absorbed, the eyes of a bitter saint. They lit on me, appraising.

"I'm Rayfield," he said and inclined his head toward the younger man. "This is Sergeant Bast."

I nodded without speaking. Four uniformed police came briskly through the front door with ropes, cameras, and sketch pads, headed for the dining room. The last one carried a black doctor's bag. "Ready to go, Lieutenant," he called.

Rayfield glanced over. "Rope it off," he ordered, and walked out.

The young patrolman appeared next to a vase of white chrysanthemums, watching me. I didn't look up.

"Feel her armpits?" someone asked. "She's room temperature."

Another said, "She's eight hours old, anyhow. They get this cold no way to tell for sure. Rape test's not much good."

"Do it anyway," Rayfield said. Cameras began spitting.

The impersonal noise of strangers—doors opening, footsteps, orders, slamming drawers—came to me like the sound of television through an open window. Someone clambered up the stairs. I lit a Camel, forcing myself to watch Rayfield as he backed into the sitting room. He was around six-two, thick-bodied and awkwardly careful of movement, as if trapped in his own skin. His suit and tie were just something to wear, his gray wavy hair was cut military-style, his stare at the Cantwells' furnishings abstemious and disapproving. He turned to me, asking, "You're her lawyer?"

"That's right." My mouth was acrid with vomit taste and I needed some water. Instead

I took a deep, harsh drag of cigarette smoke and stood.

Bast materialized with a note pad. Rayfield took out a black notebook and asked, "Mrs. Cantwell invite you?"

I noticed that his hair tonic lent him a not unpleasant whiff of the barber shop: the smell of my father. "Not exactly," I answered. "I was on the way home from the office."

"Then she wasn't expecting you." His flat drawl might have passed for witlessness if I hadn't lived in the South, or caught the sharpness of his eyes.

"I'm not sure—she'd talked yesterday with my father-in-law."

"But you didn't call her."

"No."

"Then why'd you come?"

"Private business. Law business, that's all."

"What was it?"

I shook my head. "I'm sorry, Lieutenant. That's covered by the attorney-client privilege."

Bast's eyes rose from his notes. "Give me the semen slide," someone said in the living room. Rayfield drawled, "She's dead now, Mr. Shaw," in a voice so flat and uninflected that his words held the barest trace of irony.

"Not just her. The family."

His eyebrows raised. "Dead?"

"No. Clients."

"Just who are we talking about?"

"Her husband, for one. Henry Cantwell."

Rayfield paused, head angled to look at

me as if revising some impression. His thumb began clicking the ballpoint. I noticed then that his hands were at odds with the rest of him: pale and delicate, with long piano-player's fingers, his nails fastidiously trimmed. In a monotone he asked, "You a friend of Henry Cantwell's?"

From the side Bast glanced hastily at Rayfield. "His friend, and lawyer," I answered.

Rayfield's pen stopped clicking. His tone was cool, accusing. "Where is he?"

"I don't know." Then it hit me that Henry might be dead or in trouble. It hit me hard, like sudden knowledge in a man not smart.

"What's the problem, Mr. Shaw?"

"Nothing."

"Then where is he?"

I turned to Bast. "There's an envelope under the front seat of my car—the Alfa Romeo. You'd better get it."

Bast looked to Rayfield. But Rayfield was staring at me, voice now taut as he asked, "Did Henry Cantwell do this?"

"Get the envelope," I repeated to Bast.

Rayfield kept staring. But Bast nodded and went through the front door. In the minute it took him to come back Rayfield said nothing, his eyes never moving until Bast gave him the envelope. He pulled the document, reading its caption. "Her will?"

"Her new will. She never got to sign it."

He flipped its pages as Bast read over his shoulder. He finished, said nothing, and started again, more slowly. "Take another smear," said someone near Lydia. I reached to stub my cigarette in one of her ashtrays, jabbing twice, before it went out. Finally, Rayfield asked, "Isn't there a son?"

I nodded. "Jason."

"But not in here."

"No. Not in there."

Rayfield looked up. "How old's he now?"

"Mid-twenties."

"Know where he lives?"

"Just that he goes to the university. Sort of a perpetual student."

Rayfield turned to Bast. "Better find the boy."

Bast left. Rayfield rolled up the will and began tapping it in his palm. He turned suddenly, walking toward Henry's picture until he stood in front of it. Without turning, he asked, "Who's your father-in-law?"

"Roland Cade."

Rayfield turned slowly back to me, eyes widening slightly before they dropped to the will. He stared at it in pensive silence, pen held to his lips. Abruptly, he said, "We'd better call him," and went to the kitchen.

The young patrolman still watched me. Police talked near Lydia. An awed voice said, "Take a man to do like that."

"Maybe a strong woman," someone answered.

I went to the window.

The sun had climbed, filtering through the pines in yellow shafts. Beyond the grounds, I knew people were living their same lives, and at the club couples were playing mixed doubles, or drinking. But I couldn't envision it. When Rayfield returned I was staring at nothing.

"You must be worried about Henry Cantwell," he said softly from behind. "Would that be like him, being gone?"

His tone seemed strangely kind. But when I played it back I heard a faint, tense undertone. I turned and said in a flat voice, "I wouldn't know."

Rayfield watched me for a moment, then looked down at the will again. "Mrs. Cantwell," he said almost musingly, "what was she like?"

I had no answer.

For me it had never changed from that first engagement party. Mercedes and long Lincolns had eased up the drive as Henry and Lydia greeted each new arrival. Poised and perfectly coiffed, she'd begun as my youthful notion of a great lady, except that I'd watched too long. Guest upon guest, the, precise same smile came and went without quite touching her eyes, and her hugs of greeting resembled acts of will. She seemed to play out the party like a role she knew expertly, which stifled her, real only in a quick turn of the head, one sudden worried glance toward Jason. And for seven years after, she kissed my cheek, remembered when we'd last talked and asked how I was, listening closely to my answer with her head slightly tilted—a minuet of courtesy which, when over, left behind nothing but itself. I'd wondered for a while, then just stopped. "She was our friend," I said now. "It's hard for me to talk about."

The older man from the squad car had appeared next to Rayfield. "No sign of forced entry, sir," he put in.

"Upstairs, too?"

"Yessir."

Rayfield seemed almost to smile without changing expression. "Mrs. Cantwell," he said to me. "How'd she get her money?"

"For Christ's sake, Lieutenant, we're not talking about some bird that crashed into a picture window. I *knew* her."

"That's right," he said bluntly. "Past tense. She's been strangled by someone who looks like he could do this again to some other friend of yours. That's why we're talking."

We stared at each other. "Her mother was a Maddox," I finally said. "Maddox Coal and Steel."

He jotted that in his notebook. "What about her father's side?"

I pointed toward the portrait. "Remember the Grangeville case?"

Rayfield turned to look. "The one way back, where they executed those two Negroes for rape."

"He was the judge who sentenced them."

Rayfield's face was devoid of expression. "You're not from here, are you?"

I knew where "here" was. "No. Cleveland."

"And Cleveland's where your people are."

"That's right."

I'd tracked his thoughts, so I wasn't surprised when he said in a flat voice, "Grangeville was a long time back," and shut the notebook. It was then that it struck me that he had asked almost nothing about Henry Cantwell.

"Clean her up," someone said. I winced, involuntarily, and then Cade walked through the door.

THREE

Cade stopped in the alcove to stare at Lydia Cantwell. No one spoke. Cade's head inclined in the attitude of patience, as if waiting for her to awaken. Slowly, perceptibly, the stiffness went from his back.

"Mr. Cade." It was Rayfield, standing next to me.

Cade turned, ashen, gazing for a moment with vague, frightened blankness as though jarred from sleep by a sudden noise. Then his black hawk-eyes settled on Rayfield until they seemed to glare at him from a face all surfaces and angles, like those of some great arrogant bird. Rayfield's pen clicked, once.

"We're in here," he said.

For several seconds Cade watched Rayfield, refusing to move. Finally, he limped toward us. World War II had left a pin in his hip and he moved with torso canted slightly forward, to ease a pain which seemed etched in the squint of his eyelids and the grooves running like scars from his nostrils to the corners of his mouth and then to the square of his jaw.

But his hair was still chestnut and his stomach flat: looking down at Rayfield, he seemed younger than fifty-six.

Rayfield held out the will. "You know about this."

Cade gave him a look of repugnance. "All I know is that an old friend lies horribly murdered in the next room."

"You did draft this will, though."

"Yesterday. I said that when you called."

"Then maybe you could tell me how that happened."

Cade shot me a hasty glance. "I'll need to speak with Mr. Shaw."

Rayfield tugged his ear in a distracted, impatient gesture, looking from Cade to me and back again. Then he nodded toward the door. "You can do that outside."

We left through the alcove. A white-coated man stood over the body. Lydia Cantwell's thin legs splayed crazily from behind him like the bottom end of a department store mannequin that had toppled backward. Her toenails were bright red. There was the faint odor of chemicals. I turned away.

We passed the old patrolman at the door and then walked through the roses, a line of police cars, and an ambulance, stopping by the magnolias at the far side of the drive. The blossoms gave a thin, sweet smell. Next to us sun burnt a shimmering patch of asphalt. The white glare of car windows cut into my eyes.

"You found her like that?" Cade was asking.

I nodded.

"Sweet Jesus," he said softly. A crow cawed. Cade's voice turned harsh. "What's he want?"

"I don't know."

"Then why in hell did you give them the will?"

"Because Henry's missing."

"You don't think Henry—"

"Not me. This man Rayfield. It wasn't a break-in, Roland. She let him in."

"Who? Jason?"

"Maybe. I don't know. You said once that Jason is a sick man."

Cade's voice was rough. "He's scum—for all I care they can electrocute him. But you're stripping the Cantwells in public. You know what the papers will run? That will, and the Cantwells' troubles with it."

"The will is evidence," I shot back. "And there are fewer Cantwells than there used to be."

Cade flushed. "What makes you suppose—whatever we might think—that Henry Cantwell wants us pointing at the boy?"

"What makes you suppose," I said tightly, "that Henry Cantwell's still alive?"

Cade's mouth opened in an odd, surprised expression. "Look," I told him, "I found Lydia murdered and Henry missing. Jason's supposed to hate them both. The will may be his motive. I had to turn it over. If Henry's in danger—if anything's happened—the police should be hunting for Jason. They'd better do that even if Henry's just gone fishing: Rayfield thinks whoever killed her may do this again. And if I hadn't given him the will, then

17

Henry's his suspect, and by noon every hick sheriff will be looking to bring him back in handcuffs for the six o'clock news—"

"Quiet." Cade's eyes fixed on some point over my shoulder. I realized my fists were clenched. I relaxed them and turned. Two uniformed police bore a stretcher covered by a white blanket between the roses. Only her outline showed. They carried the stretcher to the back of the ambulance and slid it inside. The door slammed. Someone started the motor. Then the ambulance backed slowly down the long drive and was gone. We listened as the motor sound faded and died, and for a long time after.

Cade slumped with his hands in his pockets. "Why quarrel?" he said softly. "It's done."

We stared at the ground.

"I can't believe this," I murmured.

He shook his head. "I've known her so long. And Kris Ann—it will be hard on her, too. I hardly know how to tell her."

The last was spoken almost to himself. I looked up at him sharply. "I'll tell Krissy."

Cade turned to me, arms folded, his face set as if fighting to hold silent. Abruptly, he broke away and called to the man at the door for Rayfield.

A moment later Rayfield appeared amidst the roses, striding toward us deliberately and without huffy. "You ready?" he demanded.

Cade reddened. "You'll want to know how that will came to be drafted."

Rayfield took out his notebook. "Go ahead."

Cade paused, breathing deeply, composing himself into a lawyer. "Mrs. Cantwell called me yesterday," he began, "to insist on seeing me. I said of course, and she came, around three. Our receptionist can confirm the time, if that's important. In any event, she sat in my office and asked me to change her will." Cade's voice seemed muted by a kind of buried sadness. "Her prior will favored her husband and son in equal measure. Now she wanted to leave everything to Mr. Cantwell."

Rayfield's pen skittered across the note pad, face tight with expectation as he watched Cade. Cade continued. "Jason Cantwell's a deeply troubled boy. He's had psychiatric counseling and fooled with radical politics. There are other things—I'm frank to admit I don't care for him. But Mrs. Cantwell refused to give reasons. I did see that she was quite agitated, to the point that her hands shook when normally she was calm and precise.

"It wasn't a long interview. I asked her if she'd talked with Henry and, when she said no, advised her to. I thought that was best—it was her money, all right, but Jason isn't just *her* son. She said she might, but that she wanted the will revised that day. It wasn't much trouble—just changing some paragraphs—so when she left, I had Miss Millar, my secretary, type it up. I decided to send it to Lydia at home and give her time to consider. If I'd had her come back for it, we could have witnessed the document and the thing would have been done. This way she'd have the weekend and perhaps talk with Henry. So I called her about five and said I'd send it out this morning." Cade stopped, exhaled, and said, "You know the rest."

It had been some moments since anyone else had spoken. Cade's voice had journeyed through calm and sadness in a near-hypnotic rhythm. Rayfield watched him.

"You should be looking for Henry Cantwell," I said to Rayfield.

He looked over at me strangely. "Any particular reason why you're this worried?"

"Look, dammit—"

Cade cut in hastily. "We're his lawyers, Lieutenant. That's all it is."

I spun on Cade, angry. He was watching Rayfield intently, hand half-raised between them. Rayfield stared back as if choosing his next words. He was interrupted by the whir of a motor. We turned, and then a black Mercedes loomed amidst the dogwood and drove into our silence.

The car stopped and a slight, gray-haired man got out, blinking as if he had stumbled from a darkroom. I hesitated, frozen by pity and relief. But Cade went quickly to him. "It's Lydia," he said.

Henry Cantwell's face turned tight and queer. Cade braced his shoulders. "She's been murdered, Henry."

Henry's features crumbled, slowly and completely, like ruined putty. He sagged in Cade's hands. "Henry," Cade urged.

His tone mixed sympathy and command.

Henry stiffened upright as Cade backed him against the hood. He stared emptily ahead. Then he curled and his face dropped into his hands. His shoulders trembled, and then hurt-animal sounds came from between his fingers. I wanted to go to him. But he didn't need my face to remember when he thought of breaking down. So I watched him: a banker in a three-piece suit, sobbing against the hood of his black Mercedes. Rayfield watched next to me, unnaturally still.

After a time Henry cried himself out. Haltingly, Cade walked him to the house, one arm draping Henry's shoulders as he limped beside him. Rayfield followed.

Two cops called to each other as they paced the rear grounds, finding nothing. I leaned against a magnolia tree, smoked one cigarette to the nub, and walked back to the house.

Rayfield was alone in the sitting room, staring at the closed door to Henry's library.

"Where are they?" I asked.

He butted his head toward the library. "In there."

"What happened?"

"I asked where he'd been. Cade pulled him into the library."

"What did you expect?"

Rayfield gave me a long cobalt look. Then he began watching the door again.

It slid open minutes later. Cade came first, and then Henry, following with a glazed expression.

"I'd like to be alone," he said to no one. Without waiting, he began to shuffle toward the stairway with the steps of an old man. Rayfield reached out toward him, mouth open as if to speak, and then his hand fell to his side and he watched Henry move away.

Henry stopped when he reached me. Without speaking he put his hand on my shoulder and looked toward the dining room. For a moment I felt his weight and Rayfield's silent look. Then Henry dropped his arm and started up the stairs.

I watched him climb as the shape of his future came to me. The quiet he had cherished here would build until it screamed. Gawkers would nose their cars up the drive, and people who didn't would claim to know him—or Lydia or Jason—and to remember some telling incident. And if the killer weren't found, someone, to liven up a party, would mention Henry: "He was always so quiet, so much to himself...." He reached the top of the stairs, and disappeared.

"You can have him at four," Cade was saying. "Assuming it won't be a media event."

Rayfield's lips were an angry line. "We'll do what's proper."

"Good." Cade was once again crisp. "I take it, you're through here."

The almost insulting slowness of Rayfield's look at Cade lent the lingering sense of some deeper, more obscure conflict than that between police and lawyer. "We're through," he finally answered. Leaving, he snapped,

"Check the neighbors," to someone at the door, and slammed it behind him.

Cade and I stood alone. "Henry's in no shape to be questioned," I said.

He gave me a gelid stare. "Do you think I like this? But it won't help him to wait and suffer. This way the police will grant us some consideration."

"Not Rayfield. There's something wrong about him."

"Yes. He's a policeman."

I ignored that. "A couple of times I wondered if he knew Henry somehow, or you."

"Why would he?" Cade said disdainfully. "Henry's not a criminal, and I'm not a criminal lawyer."

"That's a second thing that bothers me. We should bring in the Danelaw firm, someone who does this kind of work."

"Henry wants us, not some knit-suited showoff." I sensed Cade trying to regain initiative lost in the matter of the will. "You needn't participate if you think that's such a mistake. I haven't asked you to."

We faced each other. Unspoken were the last four years of tacit avoidance, the finding of work with other projects and partners, other clients than Cade's. "Henry's my friend, Roland."

Cade shrugged dismissingly. "Meet me, then. Just don't upset Kris Ann."

There was nothing more—no instructions, confidences, or requests for help. Cade began pacing the sitting room. I said goodbye, got in the car, and drove, past the black Mercedes and away from Cade, the pines, the silent house, the chemical smell of death.

FOUR

I reached the street of oaks and sloping lawns and white-trimmed Georgian homes before I knew what I wanted.

Kris Ann's Audi—a gift from Cade to match his own—sat in the rear garage. I parked beside it, walking through the backyard and between the house and the overgrown lot next door until I reached the front porch.

Kris Ann stood beneath the green canvas awning in the way she had, straight like a dancer from her hips through the small of her back. She whirled at the sound of footsteps, black hair flying out and away. Then she came to me. I felt her breathing and the wetness of her face.

"Your father..." I began.

Our eyes met and held. As she leaned back I grasped her hand. We went upstairs in a kind of torpor. Undressing, no one spoke. We made love with silent intensity, each without looking at the other. Stiff desperate fingers raked my back, she cried out, and was still.

Afterward she wept, her face turned from me. I held her until it was done.

"Krissy..."

She turned to me suddenly. Her eyes were deep and black and brilliant, and seven years had touched only their corners. But in the puffiness beneath them, the slackness of shock still in her face, was the first shadow of age to come. Softly, she said, "What had he done to her?"

"Does it matter?"

"It matters to any woman. But to Lydia..."

Her eyes shut. I could almost see her imaginings: Lydia Cantwell, strangled as close from sex as she was now. Afternoon sun through the leafy tangle outside our window glinted in her hair, thick and soft as I touched it. She shook it free. "It's like I can feel it." Her voice turned low and angry. "Where was Jason?"

"I don't know."

I felt the line of her body stiffen. "He could do this." She slid away from me, rolling on her stomach and pulling the bedsheet over her shoulders.

I bent to kiss her, then stopped. "Maybe a drink—"

She shook her head. "You can. But not me. Not now."

For a moment I watched her. Then I put on a robe and went downstairs.

It was the maid's day off. In the dining room one of Kris Ann's silk blouses lay on the cabinet which held her mother's gold-dipped silver and a lopsided clay ashtray with "I love you" scratched on it by a small retarded girl to whom she taught art. Next to that was the liquor. I poured some Bushmills, neat, and took that and the blouse upstairs.

The bed was empty. Kris Ann stood in front of her makeup mirror, brushing her hair in a dispirited ritual of something to do. Her skin was tawny and her back straight and slim, with smooth hollows beneath her shoulder blades. My father's wolf-face appeared behind her in the mirror. She leaned back. "When I was little, Adam—after Mother died—Henry and Lydia would take me to the symphony or the ballet, like *The Nutcracker* at Christmas. I'd sit between them and she'd explain the stories. And Henry—"

"I know."

She stopped brushing, her reflection grave as she watched mine. "Adam," she said quietly. "Daddy's been a lawyer for a long time."

I nodded. "And Henry's my friend."

"Daddy's friend, too."

"I think I can help."

"But how much help will it be if Henry ends up in the middle, between Daddy and you? How do you suppose he'll feel then?"

"I'll watch out for him. You know that."

She was still, staring into the mirror. With sudden anger she flung a perfume bottle at her reflection. It shattered with the glass. I grabbed her shoulders as shards scattered on the dressing table. "Baby—I'm sorry..."

Her shoulders sagged. "Worthless." Her voice was almost dead now. "I can't *do* anything."

"There's Henry."

Finally she nodded. "We can stay with him, if he needs that."

"I'll find out." I picked up the drink and finished it in one swallow. "I think you should go to the Kells' until I get back from the police. Call Rennie and I'll drive you there."

"I'm okay, now. Really."

"It's not just that. The police think whoever killed Lydia knew her and might do this thing again."

She looked away. "It was Jason," she said harshly. "I can feel it."

"Whoever, Krissy, it was bad. Let me drop you."

"No. I'll lock the doors." She didn't look up. I hesitated, watching her. "Honestly, I'll be all right. I just want to be alone. I can't face anyone yet, that's all."

I didn't move. Then Kris Ann raised her head in the cool, prideful pose I recognized as Cade's. Softly she finished, "You'll be late, Adam."

I let her go.

I went through the house checking locks and windows. When I had done that Kris Ann put on a robe to walk me downstairs. At the door she shook her head, as if trying to dismiss a dream. "You need to do this, Adam. Even with Daddy there."

"Even so."

I touched her cheek and she shivered.

"Poor Henry," she said.

27

FIVE

As I drove to the police station, it came to me that my talks with Henry Cantwell had begun on a day like this.

It had been a bright spring afternoon, my first months with the firm. Our tax partner had left early to play golf and asked me to drop off Henry's returns. When I got there, late afternoon was falling on the Cantwell place like a gentle mood, muting its colors yet lending them a strange richness that was almost dislocating. So I lingered a moment before pressing the buzzer.

A light-skinned black woman with Indian features answered and led me to the library without a flicker of acknowledgment. But Henry rose from his chair with a bright, surprising smile.

"It's good to see you again, Adam. How long has it been?"

"Almost since the wedding, I think."

"Too long." He gave me a firm handshake and gestured toward the window. "Is that as nice as it looks?"

"I've seen nothing quite like it." I gave him the papers. "While I remember, Grayson Fox said to be sure and sign these if you want to keep out of jail. I take it that's a joke."

He made a rueful face. "I forgot last year," he explained wryly. "Lydia tells me it's premature senility."

I grinned. "Then it's catching. Today I

walked out of my office and promptly forgot where I was going. Roland caught me in the hallway looking perplexed. He's probably wondering what they've hired."

"Oh, he knows," Henry smiled. "From what Kris Ann told us you could have worked anywhere." He put on half-glasses, quickly scanned the returns, and signed them in a small, careful hand that was almost like script. "There," he said with an air of great accomplishment. "Let me fix you a drink."

"You're sure? I don't want to put off your and Mrs. Cantwell's dinner."

"Don't worry, Adam. Lydia's already eaten and gone to bed, so it's just me."

"I hope she's not sick."

He looked startled. "Oh no," he said quickly. "Sometimes she gets a bit tired and needs time to herself I'd be glad of a chance to talk."

"Then I would too," I smiled. "I'll have Bushmills on ice, if you have it."

He smiled back. "Irish whiskey. Of course."

He filled the glass carefully, measuring, stiffing, handing me the drink like a proffer of hospitality. When we had settled in our chairs, he asked, "How goes the job?"

"Pretty well, I guess. Like a lot of things, it takes getting used to."

"I'm sure. After all, you've changed your entire life in a very little time: first job, new marriage, moving here to Alabama. Some mornings you must wake up and wonder how it happened."

I had sat back, considering the room, its contents outlined in the evening light: an antique walking stick in one corner, a standing clock, an oil lamp. A blue Miro seemed not so much to hang as to be suspended. "Sometimes," I admitted. "I'll get this strange feeling—just at odd moments of the day—as though I've been exiled. I guess that passes when you've lived somewhere long enough to belong."

He nodded his understanding. "Your feeling's not so strange, Adam. The ancient Greeks considered exile the worst form of punishment. Socrates took hemlock instead." He smiled. "I expect you won't come to that. The South does take understanding, of course, and some of the people you'll meet may seem complex or even contradictory. But you'll grow to like it—very much, I think. Life here has great beauty, and a permanence most people never find."

"I'm beginning to see that," I agreed. "I'm not sure Krissy could have left."

Henry's glass stopped at his lips, his look curious and reflective. He put down the drink. "Perhaps not. But I've known Kris Ann since she was a child, and the one thing I'm certain of is that she needs affection from someone other than her father. Do try not to get so involved in meeting Roland's standards at the firm that she depends too much on him, or forgets that she married a different man. It's you she needs." He stopped, faintly embarrassed. "I apologize, Adam. I seem to be giving you too much advice, and all unasked."

The whiskey was feeling warm and sudden in me. I waved a deprecating hand. "It's appreciated, really. The firm isn't the greatest place for candid chats—about Roland or anything else."

He gave me a long sideways glance. "I suppose I'm a bit gun-shy, given our troubles with Jason. He's at an age where he resents suggestion."

His look and tone seemed strangely tentative, apologetic yet questioning. I decided he was in need of reassurance. "I was nineteen once, too," I smiled. "I'm not now."

"Then there's hope. He seems so angry."

"You'll be astonished," I said firmly.

His shy smile of relief was oddly touching. He reached suddenly to the shelf and took down *The Mind of the South*. "Let me give you a book. I think this might be good reading for a new southerner."

I hesitated. "You're sure?" I asked. "I worry about borrowing things."

"I'll trust you, Adam." He held out the book with both hands. "Please, take it. Perhaps we can talk again when you're through."

I suppose it was then I first sensed that he was a lonely man. "Thank you," I said. I took the volume from his hands....

I lit a cigarette. "Where were you last night?" Rayfield asked him now.

Henry seemed not to hear. He sat in the middle of a partitioned room with shuttered lights overhead and one window with Venetian blinds slicing sunlight into ribbons on a gray

31

tile floor. Cade and I flanked him, with Bast and Rayfield sitting on two desks in front of us. The stenographer, a young woman with straight black bangs, awaited his answer. I turned, trying to see him as Rayfield would. What I saw was a pallid man with skin almost papery, a ridged nose too large for his face, and crinkled lids that drooped to make triangles of his eyes. They were gray and wasted, and his face seemed drawn in upon itself, as if he had retracted an inch beneath the skin. His normal self showed only in ways that Rayfield might see as too fastidious but now were merely sad—small habits that, one by one, created order. His hair was combed, his suit pressed, and his shoes were shined. A white handkerchief pointed from his breast pocket.

"I was in Anniston," he said abruptly. He seemed removed from the words, as if recalling some small incident of childhood. "It was business, with loan customers. They wish to build an apartment complex. I visited the site and afterwards we went to a country club for drinks and dinner. By the time I left it was past ten o'clock, so I turned off at the Holiday Inn and got a room."

His speech had an eerie precision. Rayfield watched him coldly. "What happened then?"

"I awoke this morning and had breakfast in the dining room. I remember it was about nine-thirty when I finished. After that I decided to drive back to the apartment site to look at it alone." He paused, speaking the next four words distinctly. "Then I came home."

Rayfield's eyes became slits. "At the motel—was there someone with you?"

Henry blinked. "What do you mean?"

Rayfield reached for his pen, still watching Henry. "Can anyone confirm you were there?"

"No. No one."

"Did you call anyone from the motel?"

"No."

The questions came faster. "You didn't call your wife?"

"Well, yes—Lydia."

"When was that?"

"Not long after—I don't know exactly."

"Did she answer?"

Henry flinched. "Yes."

"What did you say?"

"I told her where I was. Sometimes, in Anniston, I would stop and drive home the next morning. I told her I might do that before I left."

"Did she say anything when you called?"

"No." Henry's voice weakened. "Not really."

"She didn't say someone was with her?"

"No, nothing like that."

"And you didn't ask?"

"No."

"What *did* you talk about?"

"Just that I was still in Anniston."

"How long did that take?"

"I don't know—I didn't notice."

"One minute? Two minutes?"

"I don't know. Perhaps two."

Rayfield switched tacks. "Who was the first person you saw this morning?"

Cade's deep-set eyes searched Henry. "The waitress," Henry answered in a chastened voice. "At breakfast."

Rayfield's cadence eased. "Anniston's not much more than an hour, Mr. Cantwell. Might could be easy for you to check into a motel, drive home, and then back again." He paused and asked coolly, "Is that what happened?"

"Is that an accusation?" Cade broke in.

"Are you instructing your client not to answer?"

"No." Henry had stiffened in his chair. His voice was a rasp. "I would never harm Lydia."

Rayfield said nothing. He began stroking his pen between thumb and forefinger, eyeing Henry narrowly. Bast turned to look at him, leaning slightly closer until I sensed him watching over Rayfield in some way I couldn't understand. Rayfield's voice was quieter still. "The coroner called a while back, Mr. Cantwell. He found semen traces in your wife." Henry's cheek twitched. Rayfield almost whispered. "Now how do you suppose that happened?"

"That's enough," I said sharply.

Rayfield's head twisted, eyes slowly moving from me to Henry and back again, almost contemptuous. Then he turned to Cade.

"You want to take Mr. Cantwell home?"

"Henry?" Cade asked.

Henry was staring up at Rayfield, his mouth

half-open, eyes glittering. The veins of his hands were purple welts. "Call it off," I urged Cade.

"No, Adam." Henry's voice was hoarse. "It's all right."

Quickly Rayfield asked, "Was there trouble with your wife?"

Henry shook his head and looked away.

Rayfield wiped his mouth with the back of his hand. The sun ribbons on the floor had faded. Outside, voices called back and forth—it was quitting time for someone, they would go to a party or watch television, they couldn't decide. "Y'all have servants?" Rayfield asked.

"Etta, our maid. Etta Parsons."

"How long you had Etta?"

"Over twenty years."

"When is she there?"

Rayfield's questions were again rapid. The stenographer shook her wrist and caught Henry's answer: "Weekdays. Saturdays if we entertain. She was off today."

"Any other servants?"

Henry leaned on his elbows, hands clasped in front of him. "We have a new yardman—a Negro." He sounded embarrassed. "I never spoke to him, don't know his name."

"Know anything about him?" Rayfield asked.

Henry shook his head.

"Know anyone who hated your wife?"

"No."

"Anyone who'd want to kill her, or molest her?"

"No. No."

"Or mutilate her picture?"

Henry's face was mottled. Without waiting for his answer, Rayfield asked, "You tell Jason what happened, Mr. Cantwell?"

Henry hesitated. "Yes."

"What did he say?"

"He yelled, about police." Henry's forehead bent to his hands. "We've had—"

"Trouble?"

Henry nodded almost undetectably. I moved between him and Rayfield. Cade touched Henry's shoulder and raised his free hand toward Rayfield in a restraining gesture. "Just two more questions," Rayfield said.

Cade looked at Henry, then Rayfield, nodded, and said tersely, "Two."

I turned angrily to Cade. Rayfield asked Henry, "You know your wife wanted to cut Jason off?"

"No." The answer came with seeming effort.

"Know why she would?"

"They fought—last week. I wasn't home."

"About what?"

"I don't know. She wouldn't say."

Rayfield stared at the pen. Musingly, he asked, "Would Jason do this, Mr. Cantwell—all of it?"

Henry's face collapsed in his hands and he began crying.

"That's it, Lieutenant." Cade's tone was final. "Ask the boy yourself."

I was certain they already had. But Rayfield merely shrugged. "There's more questions," he said. "We'll want Mr. Cantwell again."

Cade stood. "He came here voluntarily, sooner than was healthy. You've asked your questions and gotten your answers. Now get out and go to work, because if you want him again you'd better have a warrant."

Rayfield stared at Cade as if calibrating his power. "We're working on it," he said mildly. There was irony in his voice, and clear dislike.

Henry was slumped in his chair. I touched his elbow. "You okay?"

The stenographer left. Henry raised himself and mumbled, "Yes," his face ivory, expressionless.

"All right, Henry," Cade said. I helped Henry to his feet. Cade took his arm from me and steered him through the partition and toward the door.

"Get them an escort," Rayfield told Bast, who followed. Rayfield watched them leave. His hair was damp and flat on his head and one shirtsleeve had unrolled until it was longer than the other.

"You didn't need to tell him like that," I said.

Rayfield turned and looked me up and down with the same expression of curious contempt.

"Why did it bother you so much?"

"Because I've started wondering what you've got in for Henry Cantwell."

For an instant he looked surprised. Then, in exact, icy mockery of Cade, he said, "I take it we're through here," and left.

I walked from the partitioned room through

a larger surrounding one jammed with metal desks and plainclothesmen writing reports and answering telephones, then opened the door marked "Robbery and Homicide," which led to the corridor. It was jammed with reporters, their shouts echoing off tile floors and walls in a babel of sound. Two bulky police convoyed Cade and Henry amidst the whine of flashbulbs and newsmen jostling with TV cameras. Someone kicked my shin as I shoved to catch up. A voice barked, "You fucked up my picture." Near the glass doors in front I saw Henry's head bobbing in the crowd. I elbowed through until I reached the doors and got outside, trying to reach him.

Another crowd of reporters waited in the dusk. "Mr. Shaw," someone shouted. It was a green-eyed woman, standing at the top of the steps with a bearded man holding a TV camera that blocked my way. "What did they want to know?"

I stopped, trapped in the crush. Her voice was quick and intense. "Do they suspect Henry Cantwell?"

The cameras closed in, as they had when we buried my father, twenty years ago. A chill, misting rain had wet my neck. The grave smelled of dirt and wet grass. My mother's face was closed and harsh. She dropped the clump of dirt as Brian clutched at her. The priest chanted. Photographers moved among the black cars, taking pictures.

A flashbulb exploded in my face. "Will Mr. Cantwell be charged?" she was demanding.

"Why don't you rob some graves," I spat out. "Maybe take pictures."

She shrank from me. I grabbed her cameraman by the collar. "Get out of my way, you sonofabitch." His mouth fell open. I threw him to the cement and pushed down the steps through the parting crowd.

On the sidewalk police moved Henry toward Cade's blue Audi. They opened the passenger door as I reached his side. He turned to me, voice trembling. "Adam, you must believe I would never do this."

His eyes locked mine. Quietly, I said, "Don't ask again."

He nodded at the ground. Cade glared at me over the hood of the car. "If there's anything you need," I said quickly, "Krissy and I can move over there, whatever."

He put his hand on my shoulder. "It's all right. Roland's called my sister—"

"Let's go," Cade snapped. Henry Cantwell disappeared into the car and was driven away.

SIX

That night Kris Ann and I put on evening clothes and drove to the country club.

I'd come home to find all the lights on and the telephone off the hook, and no one waiting. No one answered when I called for Kris Ann. I went quickly up the stairs, nerves taut for a long half minute until I heard the shower. I called out, and in the moment of relief when Kris Ann answered knew how frightened I had been. I went downstairs to fix two drinks, and waited.

She didn't come. For a while I watched the ice melt in her drink, then drifted to the porch. It was dark and there were cricket sounds and the whir of a moth near the gaslight, but all I saw was Lydia Cantwell's murdered face, and Henry's as it fell into his hands.

"Are you all right?"

Kris Ann stood near the gaslight in a silk caftan, beautiful without makeup, the shock in her face now become something sadder.

"I was thinking about Henry."

She nodded. "Daddy said the police were such bastards."

"Only when he gave them an engraved invitation."

She watched me carefully, in silence. "So he called," I added.

"I called him, to see if I should stay with Henry. His sister's flying in. So I said I'd at least bring a casserole."

"I'll drive you."

"It's still baking." She walked to the end of the porch, staring out. I went to stand next to her.

"There's a drink on the coffee table."

"No. Thank you."

I hesitated, then asked, "Why is the phone off?"

"Reporters kept calling."

"I might have needed to reach you."

"It didn't matter. They kept wanting to know things..."

I touched her shoulder. She flinched, turning suddenly. "I want to go out," she said.

"Out? Where?"

She looked down. "The club."

"Jesus Christ—"

"Please." Her words rushed forth. "Just for an hour. It's a benefit Lydia put together for the symphony and what with it already planned they've decided she'd want it to go on. You know I'd rather be with Henry but here we are and they need money and dammit I don't want to sit in this empty house feeling sad and afraid instead of seeing friends and at least trying to cope—"

"Sounds perfect," I cut in. "Maybe Henry would like a ride."

She recoiled as though struck. I reached out. "I'm sorry...."

She backed away, gaze steady now. "I have to, Adam. Please. This afternoon, what we did—afterwards it made me cold."

My hands fell to my sides. "That wasn't meant."

She stood tense and quiet. I felt suddenly drained. "We'll go then," I said.

Kris Ann was still quiet on the way to Henry's. When we drove up, the house was dim and massive and Cade almost a shadow as he came to the window. He vanished when Kris Ann got out; then the front door opened and Kris Ann disappeared. I waited outside.

About ten minutes later Kris Ann emerged looking pale. "Henry?" I asked.

"He's sedated."

She lapsed into pensive silence as we drove off. "I'm sorry," she finally said. "You found Lydia, not me. I acted hysterical."

"No matter, Krissy. There's no good form for this."

"What I mean is that we can go home if you want. Really, it's been so horrible about Lydia, that I forgot your father—"

I took her hand. "It's okay. All that was a long time back."

She turned to me, questioning. I tried switching subjects. "I've been missing you all week. When did you get in last night?"

"Not until after midnight. I got the last Atlanta flight and didn't want to wake you. It all seems so long ago."

"But your cousin's okay."

"Fine."

"And the baby?"

She turned back to the window, her profile still. The stab of beam lights on the empty road ahead accented our solitude in the moving darkness. "He's precious," she finally said. "They're very lucky."

It was quiet as we both thought whatever we were thinking. "You're sure it doesn't matter?" she asked.

"About the club?" I tried smiling. "Not really. They can bore me, but they can't make me think."

We arrived at a staid building of English fieldstone set back from the road with the distance that money buys. There were two prowl cars at the end of the drive and a uniformed officer had replaced the doorman. Leaving the car with an attendant, we took an entrance hall, lined with pictures of dead founders, to the ballroom. It stretched across the blue hand-loomed rug to a large rectangular mirror on the far wall, two hundred feet from where we stood. Seven chandeliers swept toward it in a crystalline line to be abruptly reflected, the nearest the largest, like stations in society. Beneath a thin haze of smoke, men in tuxedos and women in evening dresses drank in small clusters from which the occasional one or two would drift toward the bar, then amble with a fresh drink in search of something new. Usually they would discuss vacations, children, their lake houses, the imbecility of the President and the next party where they would discuss all that again. But tonight there were police inside, and the talk was of Lydia Cantwell.

As we entered, couples turned to stare, their voices lowering. A flashbulb exploded from amidst a clutch of media people about three times too many and too badly dressed to be society editors. Kris Ann blinked, startled. Angrily, under her breath, she said, "Damn them."

I took her arm, kept moving as a hard-eyed tractor magnate stopped castigating Jason Cantwell to his willowy lawyer and their plump wives long enough to announce, "The little bastard should be executed," and look to me for an answer. He sounded as if Lydia's death were the ultimate thing that had gone wrong. For him and his friends too many things had gone wrong already—blacks, inflation, their children who couldn't stand them, that first burglary next door—until their pride of place had become mere twitches: harassing waiters, inspecting the greens, reviewing membership with a jeweler's eye as they slid gradually closer to that national nervous breakdown that produced angry shoppers, battered wives, charge-card deadbeats, and born-again Christians by the thousands. It was clear from their stares that my finding Lydia's body was common knowledge. "This is grotesque," I muttered.

"Adam, Kris Ann."

I turned to see Ardrey Carr tottering toward us, the fat of soured youth dulling his jawline, face florid to match his hair. Fifteen years ago Carr's forearm shiver had shattered the face of a Mississippi right end before a howling mob at Legion Field, where Alabama played, and brought him fame, a thriving insurance business, and the disgruntled look of a man who has passed his peak and can't remember where. "We're over there," he said, jerking his thumb toward a group we hadn't spotted. "Figured for sure you'd want to be with friends."

For once Carr watched me instead of Kris Ann, avid with curiosity. I wished fiercely I were somewhere else. But Kris Ann smiled with relief and went toward the circle of expectant faces.

"I'll get drinks," I told Carr.

The barman was a slight, smooth-faced black with a gray mustache and cautious eyes. "Evenin', Mr. Adam."

"How're you tonight, Carter?"

A dubious smile crossed his face like trouble. "Just fine, sir." He handed me the usual drinks and slipped quickly back into his profession, a small black man in a red jacket, polishing the clean wet glasses from the kitchen with a white towel, snapping the towel and polishing again, until they gleamed. Someone called for a drink. "Yessuh," he said.

From the end of the bar a pompous surgeon I knew just well enough to dislike was pushing toward me. Turning to escape, I nearly bumped the fortyish blonde they called West Lounge Winnie, sipping a fresh martini as her restless eyes searched over the rim for a man. For the five years since her husband had died she would arrive at parties in one-strap gowns and an intricate bouffant hairdo and then drink until gin had dulled her features and unwound her hair and psyche, so that by one o'clock she was talking about sex, to no one. Ardrey Carr thought she was very funny.

He was watching Kris Ann as the group talked back and forth. But then most men did. Even me.

★   ★   ★

It had first happened in a dingy apartment crammed with law students, beer cans, Salvation Army furniture, back copies of *Esquire*, and cigarette smoke that seeped through the screens of the open windows. A paunchy classmate was shouting with a Temptations album in a Mississippi accent, trying to sound black. It was hot and too close and the fall crispness of late afternoon kept looking better. I was about to slide out the door when I saw her.

She was watching the singer from a corner of the room, looking disdainful and a little amused as two first-year law students hovered near her, trying to think what to say. Even at a distance she had an energy of beauty like no one I'd ever seen. Above the chiseled nose and high, strong cheekbones her eyes were wide and black and lambent. Long black hair fell away straight on both sides of her face, and her mouth, full and regular, set off a clean, delicate chin. It was as though the strength in her face had been sculpted to the point of losing that for beauty, but not quite. I took in the cool, easy tilt of the beer to her lips until she ran through me. I went over without thinking.

For an instant her face clouded, as if I had frightened her. But when I introduced myself she mustered a lingering hint of amusement. She was Kris Ann Cade, she told me, a senior and just watching after that rotten game. "This is terrific anthropology. You've got

46

primitive mating rituals and what with two men to every woman, there's some absolutely vicious social Darwinism."

"Beats football," I agreed. "Vanderbilt may win some year but it'll take legislation."

The animal white smile came and went so fast it seemed almost a trick. She nodded toward the white soul singer. "God, he's awful, though." Her voice was at once smoky and metallic. "You know, I don't think I've seen you before. Are you a recluse?"

"Almost. I go to law school and work twenty hours a week, so nights and weekends I study."

She sounded mildly surprised. "Why do you do all that?"

"Because I'm here on scholarship," I smiled. "You've heard of those?"

Her gaze was cool and unembarrassed. "That was foolish, wasn't it? You must be hell-bent on being a lawyer."

"I guess I must be."

She inspected me with mock gravity. "I think the problem is that you don't look like one. More like Warren Beatty with a mean streak."

"*Now* you tell me, when I've got student loans to my eyeballs."

She smiled again, then wrinkled her nose and batted at a near curl of smoke. I stopped reaching for a cigarette. "Maybe we should find air someplace."

She raised an eyebrow. "You don't sing, do you?"

"I don't even hum," I grinned. "Plus I'm a virgin."

47

Her smile returned. "It's your schedule," she said, and allowed that I could walk her home.

We took the gravel path to Branscomb Quad, hands in our pockets, talking back and forth in the pale fall sunlight. Leaves crunched beneath our feet and there was the rich, damp odor of more leaves burning. Her father was a lawyer, she was telling me, which was where she got her notion of how they looked and acted. "Maybe you should be one," I remarked. "You don't look like Warren Beatty."

She shook her head. "I don't burn like that—whatever he's got that makes him a brilliant lawyer. I've never been sure I wanted to." She frowned. "He needed a son—someone to do what he does. The best I can do for him is *have* one."

"Is that the program, then? Kids?"

Her shoulders curled downward. "It's Daddy's. He's not always wild about the boys who come home but he wants a son from me."

I smiled. "Too bad he can't just start without you."

"Oh, I want one, too, someday. I think most women do"—she looked wryly across—"no matter what they tell you in the middle of the night."

I laughed. "Then you didn't believe me?"

She smiled back. "About being a virgin? You don't seem the type."

I shrugged, saying carelessly, "Easier not to be, these days."

"Easier to be a man, period." She became abruptly solemn. "Sometimes I wish Daddy had gotten what he wanted."

I was thinking she was funny, flip, and serious by turns, perhaps a little frightened under the cool. "If you were a man," I said easily, "I wouldn't have noticed you. And too many of them are lawyers already. After two years of this I can think of better things."

"I'm an English major now," she shrugged. "Shelley, Keats, and *Adam Bede*, and all functionally useless. But I paint a little."

The last sounded like more than a throwaway. "There are things you can do with art. Teach, maybe."

"Oh, I don't know if I could make it a job. It's more a release—painting to get rid of something until there it is on canvas."

I nodded. "I'd like to see what you've done."

She gave me a sideways look. "They're kind of private. Maybe sometime." We reached the dorm. "The thing is," she finished, "I've just been having fun, and I guess I've never wanted to face what comes next."

"I've had times like that. But something's always happened. It'll come."

"I guess so." She looked at me again, suddenly hesitant, as if waiting for something more. Then she shrugged and reached for the door. "Anyhow, thanks for the walk."

She turned in the doorway, poised to disappear, a tall, beautiful girl with a voice as stylish as gin and sports cars, eyes as deep and

49

tempting as the things I'd never had. All at once I had to say something, do something.

"About what's next," I tried. "Maybe you can start small. Like next Saturday."

She looked down. "What's next Saturday?" she asked innocently.

I hung there a moment. Then her eyes raised, and her grin cracked wide and sharp and clean, confirming her joke.

I smiled back. "There must be a party."

The party was louder now. The haze had lowered and people drank and smoked in the loose-jointed rhythm that comes with late evening, staring more openly as I moved across the room. Rayfield had materialized near a floral display, watching me. I looked past him. Through the sliding glass doors to the patio I could see only darkness, making the party seem self-contained, as if it were happening on a spaceship. I moved toward Kris Ann.

"Mr. Shaw."

It took me a moment to place the greenness of her eyes: the reporter who had questioned me. "Back from the cemetery so soon?" I asked.

She placed hands on hips. "I'd like to know what that was all about."

She spoke with a trace of Boston accent, its edge matching the knife keenness of her eyes and the quick, kinetic movements of someone who burned off calories just standing around. Her auburn hair was cut short and she had a pert face with no makeup and freckles on the bridge of her nose. Her jawline was square and her skin quite pale and clear. She could have been the girl I'd dated in high school, Mary Moore, who had closed her eyes when I touched her in the dark and had four children now.

"What the hell are you doing here?" I asked.

"This is an important charity event," she said crisply. "I'm covering it. What the hell are you doing here?"

"I married well." I began moving. "Excuse me."

"We're not through—"

I turned back. "What's your name?"

"Nora Culhane. Channel Seven."

"All right, Ms. Culhane. For openers, don't kid me. You're not that wounded and you already know what my problem is: you're scavenging a tragedy so the local voyeurs can get those goose bumps in the night, have their talk a little spicier, their sex a little sweeter. I don't like it."

A long-necked woman in sequins moved closer, head cocked. Culhane's speech was staccato. "Murder's news, Mr. Shaw. Henry Cantwell's money doesn't change that."

"No, it just makes them love it more, doesn't it, like with Patty Hearst—vicarious thrills for the mentally unemployed. We both know that if Lydia Cantwell had been a poor black woman no one would give a shit. But here you are, wearing the First Amendment like a Communion dress."

51

She flushed. "I suppose I should be covering the Pillsbury bake-off."

"Oh God," I said. "Not that, too. Look, you're not Bacall and I'm certainly not Bogart—I'm not having enough fun. So let's drop it."

"I've got something to ask you first. Tell me, when Rayfield asked Cantwell how long that last telephone call to Lydia was, what did he say?"

"You tell me."

"One or two minutes. But it wasn't. It was twelve. Rayfield's got the toll slip."

"Good for him. It's not hard for a man in shock to make that kind of mistake."

"Come on, Mr. Shaw. What were they talking about? It wouldn't take Henry Cantwell twelve minutes to tell Lydia where he was. He lied about the time, and he lied about what they said to each other. And if he lied about that, chances are he lied about other things."

I looked quickly around, speaking in a lower voice. "I'd be damned careful with your choice of words. If Henry wanted to lie, he wouldn't do it about the length of the call—it's too easy to check. He'd admit the length of the call and lie about its substance. Who would know? That he didn't makes my point."

She shrugged. "I'm using this on the eleven o'clock. I just thought you could tell me what they really talked about."

"I wouldn't know."

From a distance Rayfield watched us intently.

He seemed out of place, as if staring through a window. "And you've got no comment?" she was asking.

"Not a word. Just remember the law of libel. And say hello to Rayfield. It's nice of him to use this to tuck it to Henry Cantwell, and nice of you to help." I left her there.

Weaving through the crowd, I reached Kris Ann with her drink as she listened to Susie Threadgill talk avidly about Jason: "And after they threw him out of Phillips for beating some boy half to death, he came home and killed the neighbor's dog with a pistol, just from meanness. Henry had to beg them not to prosecute. He was so ashamed."

Clayton Kell edged over. "Adam, I'm sure sorry about this morning. You look ready to kill."

He said it straight out, not prying, the irony unintended. The usual Clayton, dry-witted and amiably lazy, saw both the world and his role in it as a little bit silly. It was probably a perspective worth having: Clayton puttered around Henry's bank like a large troll who had gone to prep school, getting by on charm. His secret was that, when it mattered, he was better than that. I relaxed for a moment. "Thanks, Clayt." I looked around. "Why all the cops and reporters?"

Clayton gave me a thin smile. "The police are here because some nervous people want protection from a madman they're afraid knows them already. The reporters are pretending to cover the party so they can snoop. I just hope they don't use Lydia's murder to dog Henry. He's been bad enough."

"How so?"

"You haven't noticed?"

"Not particularly. I haven't seen him that much. He's been lying kind of low."

"Well, you all are our counsel—you've seen how he usually is down there, kind of sleep-walking through business hours like his real life is happening somewhere else. But at least he's always pretty much the same. The last two months, though, he's been almost manic-depressive: hiding in his office with the door shut and then bursting out to insist on something foolish. There was one loan in particular, a high-risk deal with this white-shoe developer out of New Orleans where we ended up under-collateralized and in trouble with the Feds. I mean, Henry's no businessman, but he could usually spot quality."

"What do you make of it?"

He gave a shrug of vast helplessness. "You know Henry. Very private. But I figure it's the boy, poor bastard. Henry, that is." He sipped his drink, asking pointedly, "How goes it with Roland?"

"Same, same. He looks on me as the son he never had."

Clayton gave another thin smile, and the talk became general between the eight of us: Susie and Tom Threadgill, half-drunk and riding a kind of crazy animation; Clayton and Rennie Kell, gracious and looking oddly alike; Ardrey

Carr and his wife, Sandra, dark and thin, whose nerves had been ravaged by Ardrey and four children and now a murder, and who was looking at me strangely. At the last party, Tom Threadgill had asked brightly if everyone still masturbated and when he closed in on me, I'd said no I didn't have to, I was a hermaphrodite. Clayton had smiled, Tom looked disappointed, and Sandra had clearly been puzzled. From her expression now, she had looked it up.

"Goddamn Atlanta," Tom Threadgill burst out angrily to Clayton Kell. "Got stuck again in the screwed-up airport. I swear to God, flush a toilet south of Louisville and even the crap goes through Atlanta."

Clayton nodded politely as I half listened, wondering why either of us bothered. But with the exception of Ardrey Carr—and me—they had all been born with money and large houses to parents who were friends and then gone to prep school together and met during college vacations until they became part of a context, reminding each other of who they were and had always been. I thought perhaps to Kris Ann they were familiar things, like her mother's crystal or the pictures of Cade she kept. I forgot them and began wondering about Henry's last call to Lydia until I heard her name and picked up the thread again.

"Poor woman," Rennie Kell was saying.

"Nobody's safe." Sandra Carr's shrill voice seemed wired to her nerve ends. Next to her Ardrey tottered on his heels. She glanced at him, almost quivering. "You start out thinking you know how your life is going to be..."

Tom Threadgill had forgotten the airport. "Life plans are stupid," he pronounced. "It's all contingent. Lydia lives this decorous kind of life that's supposed to get you loving children and a party for your golden anniversary and instead she ends up murdered, like all along it's been this big fucking joke."

Clayton frowned. Sandra Carr turned angrily to her husband. "Let's go home, dammit. We should never have left the children with that girl."

"I don't know," Susie Threadgill was saying. "It's more like these other parts of you reach out so no matter how hard you try, they get you. I just wish Lydia had been more authentic—you know, more in touch with herself. Here she was always doing for other people and never anything but nice, and it makes you think inside maybe she was burning up and that somehow it all came out, and then—"

Ardrey Carr leaned forward, ignoring his wife. "They say she was bruised something awful," he said loudly. "Raped too."

I realized he was talking to me. The others seemed part of a frieze of rapt-faced people who squeezed their drinks in front of them. I took my time lighting a cigarette.

"They're right," I said.

Awareness that I'd snubbed him stained Carr's face with anger. Sandra Carr turned white. In the silence, Kris Ann turned to me holding out her glass. "I'm dry, Adam," she said quietly. "Could you get me another?"

She looked coolly to Carr until he stopped glaring and seemed almost to deflate. I waited him out, then took her glass. From a corner Rayfield ran a long appraising look from me to Kris Ann to me again as I went toward the bar.

It was crowded now. There was sweat on Carter's forehead as he worked among angry, competing voices, watching the party for signals from yet other drinkers, the privileged ones who'd slipped him a hundred dollars at Christmas. West Lounge Winnie watched him blankly, hairdo canted dangerously to one side. Next to her a towering woman who'd been flirting with someone else saw her husband moving toward them. "Here comes Donald," she drawled. "My God, I despise that man." Arriving, Donald looked at the pair with great, tragic eyes. "What will the symphony do without Lydia?" he asked, and began to weep. I took my cigarette to the veranda.

For a while I leaned on the railing. The swimming pool below was a turquoise rectangle that shimmered with submerged light. I hardly heard the footsteps.

Frenzied hands choked me by the collar. I wheeled with my fist in the air. The woman shrieked: "Doll lady, fucking doll lady," in a harsh, crazy voice, over and over.

"Shut up," I snapped. "What the hell is wrong with you?"

She stopped, staring at her shoes, abashed.

My arm dropped. In the dim light she was just a raddled blonde with overripe hips and the pigeon-toed stance of a drunk. "Find your husband," I said, more reasonably. "You're drunk."

"No blood." She nodded ponderously, as if that were very profound. "No blood."

She looked at me for approval. Through the window behind her, foolish mouths smiled and lips moved that made no sound. Then there was the sigh of a sliding glass door and a tall man stepped from the ballroom, glancing over his shoulder. "Joanne," he called in a low voice.

She stiffened, and as the man came out of darkness I placed them both. Dalton Mooring was the president of Maddox Coal and Steel. The woman was his wife.

He stopped short of her. They looked at each other in dim light from the pool, as if I were forgotten. In a strained, weary undertone, he said, "Again."

She looked pasty and about to vomit. "Better take her home," I told him.

Mooring spun, eyes angry and luminous, as if he were ready to strike. Subtly, quickly, he reconsidered. "I apologize for my wife," he said without feeling.

She began to cry with drunkenness and humiliation. He turned and steered her roughly toward the parking lot, avoiding the party. I went to the bar and got Kris Ann her drink.

Driving home, she said, "I'm ashamed I asked you to go."

"Don't worry, hon. It was a chance to think about things."

Kris Ann lay her head back against the car seat. "Like what?"

"Like that Tom Threadgill is the biggest waste of time since the Parcheesi board."

Kris Ann smiled slightly and was silent. I lit a cigarette. "Was there something wrong with her, Krissy?"

She rolled her head to see me. "Adam, you can't even be sure what Joanne Mooring was talking about."

I took a deep drag on the cigarette, its ash an orange circle in blackness. "Maybe. But Susie made sense for once. Something like this happens and you have to look differently at the woman it's happened to."

"*I* don't," she answered, "and don't want to. Lydia was our friend—my good friend."

For a moment I listened to the low snarl of the motor. "I had a friend once at Notre Dame—Eddie Halloran. Eddie was a skinny, sensitive guy with a nice smile. Everyone liked him. He was quick and funny, but when you needed to talk he had this special knack of listening, and somehow you knew that he could slip into your skin and feel exactly what you felt. When Eddie got beaten up one night in a tough neighborhood off campus I was as mad as anyone else. It never occurred to me to wonder why he'd been there.

"Eventually we all forgot it until about a year later, it happens. Same neighborhood, two guys with a knife take Eddie for a ride and kill him. It turned out he was trying to pick them up. You see, anyone could tell him their problems, but he didn't want us to know. So he played it too close to the line."

Kris Ann touched my arm. "You never told me—Adam, that's so sad."

"Sad, and to the point. What I'm wondering is why Lydia seemed so remote. If anyone knows besides Henry, it's you or Roland."

Kris Ann sat up in the car seat, staring out. "Whatever," she said tiredly, "I don't believe it was anything like I think you're asking. There's only one time I can ever remember her seeming less than perfect and I only understood it later, if I ever did. It was the summer I was twelve, I guess, and Daddy had a cocktail party on a Sunday afternoon. He would sort of let me be hostess and I was there in a blue silk dress he'd bought, feeling like a lady."

There was memory in her words. She paused as if to puzzle on it, then went on. "It was around the time that Martin Luther King was here. Claude Acton got drunk out on the patio and started carrying on about how he should be shot. Daddy and Henry and Lydia were there and then she just disappeared.

"A little later I went inside to look at my dress again in the mirror. When I started upstairs I heard someone crying in the first-floor bathroom. It sounded awful. I stopped there on the stairs, and then the door opened.

"It was Lydia. Her face was all tight and drawn so she didn't look herself. I just stared for a minute. Then I ran upstairs. I don't know if she saw me but I couldn't go back outside. The rest of the party I hid in my room—crying too, I'm not sure why. Maybe I was confused about adults." She shook her head. "I was confused about a lot of things, then. I remember being angry at King because people always fought over him and it had spoiled the party and my new dress.

"Later Daddy asked where I'd been and I told him about Lydia. He didn't say much, just that he thought Claude's talking like that upset her because of Grangeville and her father. I found out later that was about when the book came out saying those black men were innocent and that Lydia's father had fixed the trial so he could run for governor. I think maybe it just stayed with her all her life, like it was something she'd done or couldn't run from." She looked sadly ahead. "Maybe she never even decided who it was that had spoiled her party—she was young when it happened, and he was her father. But I never really knew."

Lydia's murder lent the story a horrible poignancy. I wondered at the doubleness that caused her to cry over Grangeville, yet hang her father's portrait on the mantel. Finally I asked, "Did she ever talk about it?"

"Not that I know of. She probably didn't want to. She must have known how some people felt about her father."

"Was there anyone she did talk to?"

"Besides Henry? I don't know, unless it was Etta, her maid."

"That seems odd."

"Not really. Etta would have been with her more than most. Why is that important?"

"I'm not sure. There's something wrong here—something more than Lydia being murdered. I can smell it even if I can't see it."

"What you smell is Jason Cantwell."

I turned to her. "Sperm and all?"

"Yes. He's twisted enough." Her voice tightened. "The only way a man like Jason can touch people is to hurt them. If you want one more reason for Lydia's sadness you can look to Jason. He's a bad seed, Adam."

Her intensity surprised me. More softly, I answered, "Even if that's true there's this man Rayfield. There's something off about the way he is with Henry, and how he's using that phone call, with Lydia not twenty-four hours dead. Roland made a mistake today letting him at Henry. He'll make others. He's set on handling this himself."

"And you?"

"I'm set on keeping Henry alive."

"So is Daddy." She looked at me closely. "For four years now there's been a kind of peace between you, or at least a distance. It's been easier for you both, for all three of us. We've made our adjustments. Please, don't upset that now."

I inhaled cigarette smoke, playing back what I heard in her voice. "Is that what you're afraid of? Or is it having to choose?"

She whirled to speak in anger, then bit her lip and looked away. In a low voice she said, "It's not just me who has to choose."

"What does that mean?"

She said nothing for a moment and when she spoke it was not to answer. "I love you and I love Daddy, and I know he's vulnerable right now. He's older, he's without a wife or son or grandchildren and now some of his investments have gone sour. He's worried and disappointed and maybe even a little frightened, and he's a proud man not used to that. It's not the time, Adam. Leave him be."

I shook my head. "Roland's not the point. It's Henry. This is the wrong case for your father to begin a new career in criminal law."

She faced me now, questioning. Quietly, almost tenderly, she said, "And your father?"

I stubbed the cigarette. "He's dead, Krissy."

She didn't answer. We were silent for the rest of the drive.

The house was as we had left it.

That night I couldn't sleep. Kris Ann-tossed beside me, restless and troubled. Her face in the darkness was Lydia's.

I smoked three cigarettes and decided to see the maid.

63

SEVEN

The light turned red and my car as it stopped spat gravel from the street. Two black girls watched me from the doorway of a dingy corner grocery. Near them, three youths on stripped-down bicycles leaned next to a rusted rain barrel, drinking RC from bottles and ignoring the heat and the girls. The tallest wore sunglasses and an Army jacket, the other two, pea hats, and they stared wistfully at the impossible red curves of the nude woman painted on the cinder-block walls of the "Night Time Café," across the street. Above the woman the block letters of a loan company billboard spelled out "Easy Street" below a row of green dollar signs. The air smelled of dirt and gasoline.

When the light changed I drove on toward Etta Parsons'. On my radio Linda Ronstadt gave way to a newsman reading in a tremor of spurious excitement: "Police continue to investigate the bizarre ritual murder of Birmingham socialite Lydia Cantwell. At a press conference this morning, Lieutenant Frank Rayfield outlined the investigation."

I found her address and pulled to the curb. Rayfield's radio voice was a monotone. "Since Mrs. Cantwell was found," he was saying, "we've reviewed evidence suggesting a possible psychopathic killer as well as questioned members of the family in hope of preventing any further incident. We now believe that the murderer was known to Mrs. Cantwell and that his motive was personal."

"They're already questioning relatives," Cade had told me a half hour before. "I don't know what you expect to add."

We sat drinking coffee in Cade's office amidst the Sunday quiet of a law firm on its day off. Manila folders for the Cantwell estate were spread on the desk in front of him. The dark hollows beneath his eyes became bruises as he leaned back to await my answer, tenting his fingers in an appraising gesture reminiscent of the three years as an associate I had spent in the same armless chair, responding on cue. The window behind him framed the cement tower of the Cantwells' bank, and from over his shoulder stared an iron-faced photograph of Henry Cantwell's father. On a mahogany bookshelf was the portrait of a dark young woman with melancholy gray eyes, Kris Ann's mother. Next to that Kris Ann smiled down at the traces on Cade's desk of his taste for money: a jade vase, a Wedgwood teacup, an antique paperweight of hand-blown glass. Beside that was a morning paper headlined SOCIALITE SLAIN above an old picture of Lydia and a bad one of Henry recoiling from the flashbulbs as he left the police station. "They talk to Jason?" I parried.

Cade scowled. "No one's seen him. I gather that when Henry called him yesterday he started screaming about 'being trapped.'

Henry thinks Jason meant that the police had gotten there before he'd broken the news. What I think is that Jason knew before anyone. I can't understand why you find that so difficult to grasp."

"The sperm test. By your theory, Jason would have had to rape his mother, then kill her. Or is it the other way around?"

Cade flushed. "I don't find incest that amusing."

"It's not that credible, either, and if Rayfield thought so he wouldn't be leaning on Henry. And that business of the telephone call makes Henry look bad."

"I take it you're suggesting I mishandled Rayfield."

"All that I'm suggesting is that we make a few careful inquiries on who Lydia might have seen lately."

"By stumbling around after the police, looking worried as hell? That's sheer foolishness."

"Look, when it comes to people like the Cantwells, Rayfield's on foreign ground. We're in better shape to ask questions and understand the answers."

Cade shook his head. "I would have thought that anyone who'd found Lydia like that would be damned glad there are police to handle it. And your Stafford Lumber trial is set for May. You should know by now that defending a five-million-dollar job-discrimination suit is full-time work."

"You mean especially when your client

thinks that manumission was contrary to God's law."

"Peyton Stafford's eccentricities are beside the point," Cade snapped. "You're a lawyer. Sometimes a lawyer's job is not to feel anything."

Cade raised his head in the prideful pose he shared with Kris Ann. Our eyes locked in a strange, distasteful intimacy, as though whatever we said didn't really matter, that what mattered was something else we never spoke but understood in the way of two animals circling each other in darkness. "Is it possible," I asked, "that Lydia Cantwell had a lover?"

Cade's stare turned hard. "It would contradict any notion people had of her. What's your basis for that?"

"The sperm. If it's not Jason, then it's rape or an affair, and we'd better start wondering which. And who."

"Good God," Cade burst out. "Try to appreciate what you're saying. Reputation is a fragile thing, lost in strange ways, often small ones and often unfairly. There will always be people now who think Lydia's murder reflects on Henry. You forget that this is basically a small town—society's small here, everyone's known, and no one ever forgets. It's not like the North. Slander Lydia with this kind of nonsense and you'll just add to the gossip."

I shrugged. "I'm not so sure that the Suzy Knickerbocker school of criminal defense will work here."

Cade eyed me carefully. Then he leaned forward, chin resting on his folded hands, as if musing. "You know, Adam, I begin to see it more clearly. A young man, a little bored with his work, perhaps disappointed with himself, and then suddenly a friend is in trouble and it's only the young man who's sensitive enough to understand the friend, and smart enough to save him. The police are on a witch hunt, and the friend's lawyer is only involved out of ego—he's an older man and the young man can see how others in their firm have indulged him until he's become like a spoiled child, blind to his own limitations." He paused to give me a look of infinite comprehension. "Isn't that how it is?"

His grasp of my view of him, the disparaging inversion of my motives until they were those I saw in him, left me off balance. I took a long swallow of coffee. "That's fascinating, Roland. Maybe you should try it out on Henry."

Cade's eyes flashed. His mouth opened, then closed. In a cold voice he said, "You'll do no good with this."

"You can't know that."

"It's enough that I *think* it. If you want to survive in this firm you'll do what I tell you and no more."

"Unless Henry overrules you."

"He's still in shock, for God's sake."

"That was my point yesterday. Unlike Rayfield I'm willing to wait until Henry knows what he's saying. We can talk to him tomorrow."

Cade looked astonished. "You'd do that,

wouldn't you? Even with what he's gone through."

I sipped some coffee. "If I have to."

Cade considered me a moment longer. Then he picked up a file with an air of infinite weariness. "Go ahead, then," he answered, suddenly bored. "I've got real work to do. But it goes no further than the Parsons woman. I want an end to this before you ruin Henry."

I stood, surprised but ready to leave. "I'll try not to get him arrested," I murmured, and closed the door carefully behind me.

I opened the door and got out, looking up and down the street. The ripe morning sun captured its neglect with merciless clarity. The place next to Etta's had boards for windows and a picket fence like a row of bad teeth. But her own house was whitewashed, with red roses growing behind the neat square of lawn and honeysuckle near the porch. I went there and knocked.

The door was opened by a light-skinned black woman with processed hair and obsidian eyes which seemed centuries old. A shadow crossed her face. "You're Mr. Shaw."

It was less question than an affirmation of surprise: I was out of place here, had ventured where I did not belong. "May I come in?"

She backed reluctantly into a living room whose formal couch and coffee table I recognized as having once been Lydia's. They mixed incongruously with faded brown walls and the faint smell of camphor, as if this were a halfway house between poverty and the Cantwells'. The blinds were drawn and the absence of sun lent the room the brooding sepia tinge of an old color photograph whose tints have blurred. On the coffee table was a miniature of Lydia Cantwell's mutilated portrait.

Etta pointed me to a cane-back chair, arranging herself on the couch with ankles crossed and hands folded in her lap. "How may I help you, Mr. Shaw?"

She had almost no trace of an accent.

The chill I felt was more than roses or a picture. It was her careful movements, the air of courteous interest to match a cool, inquiring voice, even the way she tilted her head like it was something fine. It had all belonged to Lydia Cantwell.

"I'm trying to help Mr. Cantwell," I said at last.

"Mr. Cantwell called here yesterday, crying." Her throat tightened. "I couldn't understand it any more than him. I'd been with her for twenty years."

I nodded. "Perhaps if we could talk about that."

Her look was sad yet prideful. "I don't know what good that will do."

"I know this is hard, Mrs. Parsons, but I'm trying to learn why anyone would kill her. You and she must have talked over the years."

"Some."

"About Jason?"

Her face set in the impassivity of an Aztec

mask. "I heard they fought last week," I prodded.

The small shrugging gesture she made was more a curling of shoulders. "They fought some—off and on."

Her tone was guarded. "She's dead now," I began, then realized that Rayfield had used those words to me. "What I mean is that she's got no confidences now as important as helping Mr. Cantwell."

She watched me without answering. "Do you know what they fought about?" I tried.

Her gaze moved to Lydia's picture. "They were in the library," she finally said. "I didn't hear much except that Mrs. Cantwell was upset."

"Exactly what did you hear?"

"Something about politics." Bitterness pulled at the corners of her mouth. "I can never make sense out of what Mr. Jason says, just a lot of craziness and screaming."

"What did Jason have to scream about?"

"Money, what she thought or did about things—it didn't matter between him and her. He loved her, and he hated her, too."

There were echoes in the words. "Enough to kill her?" I asked softly.

Her veiled glance swept the room, returning to the picture. It seemed to check her anger. She folded her arms. "I don't know."

I tried switching subjects. "Did Mrs. Cantwell have many visitors? I mean, during the day?"

She seemed relieved. "Surely," she nodded, "what with her committee work and things."

I hardened my voice. "Anyone special?"

Her eyes grew large with understanding. Reflexively she said, "What do you mean?"

I hesitated, suddenly wondering whether Rayfield had been there or was coming later, and then I saw what Cade had meant: "So Mr. Shaw came to see you, Mrs. Parsons?" "Yes, sir."

"And what did he want to know?" Leaning forward, I asked, "Have the police been here?"

She stiffened. The fetor of too much bad history came to me in the darkened room: a black woman, cornered; a white man wanting answers. I pushed all that aside. "Have they?" I demanded.

She shook her head. "No."

"They will, Mrs. Parsons, and when they do, they'll ask the same things and you'll tell them, because you have to. All I'm asking is that you do that much for Henry Cantwell."

She eyed the floor in confusion. For an instant I felt close to something. But when she looked up, her head was tilted in that haunting angle of repose. "I'll tell them she and Mr. Cantwell got on fine, if that's what you mean."

"It's partly what I mean."

"Mrs. Cantwell was a good woman," she said coldly. "It won't help Mr. Cantwell or anyone else to try to know everything about her."

She began smoothing her skirt.

I knew then it was useless. In her reactions—the crumbling poise retrieved by her symbiotic grasp of the dead woman's personality—was an unsettling glimpse of her own life. Over time, she had become half of someone else, until now she protected not just Lydia Cantwell. She protected herself.

I stayed long enough to ask the gardener's name.

EIGHT

I parked next to the L & N railroad yard and started up the street. On both sides were row shacks painted a flat green that peeled like dried bark. Except for cramped porches there was no shade and the street was pebbled with glass and gravel and lumps of tar and crowded with boys in cut-offs who pitched and batted a red rubber ball. Their parents—men in undershirts and women in cotton dresses—watched me from the porches.

On the third porch to my left a lone black man wearing Army fatigue pants hunched in a metal chair. At his feet were an old coffee can and a bottle of beer which sweated in the heat.

"I'm looking for Otis Lee," I told him.

The man spat tobacco in the coffee can, took a long, deliberate swallow of beer, and said, "What you want?"

The preternaturally deep voice seemed to go with the rest of him. He was thick shouldered, with thick wrists and forearms and callused hands. His face—deep black with large pores and a flat nose that looked broken—sat on a ringed, fleshy neck like some heavy object. But it was his eyes that set him apart. They were a bitter orange-yellow, the left pupil discolored by a white star. I stepped up on the porch, answering, "To talk about Lydia Cantwell."

His stare was red rimmed and implacable. "You the police?"

"Henry Cantwell's lawyer. I'm calling on people who knew Mrs. Cantwell."

"I heard she was dead." The words were devoid of feeling, as if it were a chance news item: a moon shot, the death of a stranger. "Workin' for folks, that don't mean you know them. I only worked there a month. Didn't know that lady at all."

And don't give a damn, his expression said. "Mind if I sit, Mr. Lee?"

He looked me over with stony dispassion and then nodded perfunctorily toward the metal chair next to his. Sitting, I could see only a sliver of his house through the screen door: a worn chair, a television, bare floors, bare walls—a transient's room. "Been in Birmingham long?" I asked.

He put down the beer and folded his hands, answering in a resentful grunt. "Maybe six weeks."

"You from around here?"

"I'm from nowhere. Been in the Army thirty years, bein' a drill sergeant. Just got out."

I placed his accent then: the low, emphatic chant of a noncom after years of order giving. "How'd you happen to pick Birmingham?"

"I was born in north Alabama," he shrugged. "Served at Fort McClellan. It's a place I knew, so I came here."

"How did you find the Cantwells?"

The porch was close and hot. A drop of perspiration ran down Lee's forehead to the bridge of his nose. "How's this gonna help you," he finally said, "botherin' me with these questions?"

"I don't know yet." I loosened my tie. "You have another beer?"

Lee's strange eyes widened in something like astonishment. "I'm fresh out. I didn't know you was plannin' on resting here."

"I thought maybe we could talk."

"Look here," he said impatiently. "I got out of the army with my children growed up, my wife gone off, nowhere to go, and nothin' to do. I got some retirement and I figure this city's as good a place as any to find work, maybe stay outdoors. So I get some temporary quarters and go around where the big houses are at to ask if they need a yardman. I figure I do that awhile, then get some nursery to hire me. I do Mrs. Cantwell's yard a couple of days a week and one or two other folks'." His voice turned thick and sarcastic. "Now, that satisfy you, or you figure I killed the lady?"

"That wasn't what I was asking."

Lee stroked his chin between thumb and forefinger. "Well, I figured you was fixin' to ask me that. I know how much white folks always worry about black men rapin' their women."

"Yeah, well, I thought I'd wait awhile and just sort of spring it on you."

75

He grunted, unamused, and turned toward the street. A bat thumped and a tall boy streaked after a fly ball, leaped twisting to hang in the air, and caught it. Lee watched him. "Mister," he said slowly, "the only people I ever killed was in Korea and Vietnam—and they was yellow, not white."

"Have any idea why someone would kill Mrs. Cantwell?"

"No way."

"Anyone ever visit while you were there?"

He sipped his beer. "You mean men?"

"If there were any."

"I wasn't the doorman. Just did the yard. It's the maid you want."

"I've done that. That's why I'm here."

He drank more beer, too casually. I imagined his calculations: what had Etta told me, how much did I expect him to know. He finished swallowing. "Only thing I noticed was a green Cadillac parked there two, three times. Don't know whose it was."

"What kind?"

"New model," he said grudgingly. "Dark green. One of the big ones."

"Would Mrs. Parsons know whose it was?"

"Prob'ly." It was said with contempt. "She was hangin' 'round Mrs. Cantwell all the time."

I leaned back. "Did Mrs. Parsons ever talk about Mrs. Cantwell's father or the Grangeville case?"

"Didn't talk to me about anything," he said harshly. "What the Grangeville case?"

"An old trial. They electrocuted two black

men for raping a white girl. I figured you'd heard of it."

Lee took a contemplative sip. "How long ago that happen?"

"Forty years or so."

"That makes me about eight years old, don't it? I wasn't readin' then and killin' black folks wasn't news."

There were cries from the street. The red ball bounced onto the porch, followed by a small boy with large, hungry eyes and a head too big for his body. Lee threw it back underhand and watched the boy run away, to his game. Without turning, he said, "You interrupted my peace. Go back where you belong."

I shrugged, standing. "Thanks for your time."

He didn't look up. "You gonna chase the cops over here?" he asked in a bored, accusing tone.

"Nope. I figure they can find you themselves."

I started to leave. "What you say your name was?" he demanded.

I turned. "Adam Shaw."

He plucked a wrinkled pouch of chewing tobacco from his pants pocket and stuffed some in his cheek, chewing with a grinding slowness as he looked me up and down. "Well, Mr. Shaw, you been askin' questions like you own this place and me' with it. How long you figure I'd last doin' that at white folks' houses?"

The hatred in his eyes was impersonal and years deep. "Not long," I answered, and walked back to the car.

I sat there thinking as Lee watched me from the porch. Then I drove toward Henry Cantwell's, stopping at the library for the book on Grangeville.

NINE

When I got there the Cantwell place had lost its magic. The roses looked tired and the house too large and gloomy. It was like revisiting a place you hadn't seen in years but remembered better than it was.

The thin woman who answered had coiffed and lacquered gray-blonde hair, thick glasses, and a bony face whose tension showed in the unnatural tightness of her mouth as she spoke. She was Mr. Cantwell's sister, she said tersely. What did I want?

"I'm Adam Shaw. Henry's lawyer."

Her mouth relaxed slightly, showing age lines on her upper lip. "I thought you were another reporter." Her tone was softer. "Your Kris Ann called just a while ago. She's been very kind—both her and Roland."

"We're all concerned about Henry. How is he?"

She didn't move from the doorway. Her glasses magnified eyes that even without them would have seemed large and nervous. "He's as you would expect."

"I didn't know how bad that might be.

Things got rough with the police yesterday."

Her shoulders drooped. "He just watches, and you don't know what he's thinking."

I nodded. She realized that I was still on the doorstep and motioned me inside. "I'm sorry," she said distractedly. "The last day has been very hard. I've been worried over Henry and afraid that whoever killed Lydia might come back. If it weren't for Roland..." She shook her head. "Even when I was small this house frightened me and now there's this business with the police."

"What business?"

"You haven't talked to Roland? I thought that's why you'd come. The police were here an hour ago."

I tensed. "Without telling us? Did they talk to Henry?"

"No, it was me they wanted. They called my home in Virginia and traced me here."

"What did they want?"

Her mouth tightened again. "What this Lieutenant Rayfield said he wanted was to ask about Lydia. But it all seemed to work around Henry, and finally I asked them to leave."

"What did he ask, exactly?"

She looked quickly behind her. Henry didn't seem to be downstairs. Our only company was the end table and an empty vase. "It was more what he implied. The lieutenant wanted to know how Lydia and Henry got on. I think what he meant was whether they were still intimate."

The old-fashioned word made it somehow

more disturbing. "Did you tell them any-thing?"

"Nothing. I didn't like the man. There was something cold about him."

"Did he let on what was behind all that?"

She was unbending now, and the anger showed. "He wouldn't tell me anything. But I think perhaps Jason. He has a very strange perspective."

"On what?"

She crossed her arms, hugging herself in a protective, virginal gesture. "They weren't demonstrative, that's all. There's such a thing as taste."

I nodded. "I always thought there was a nice courtliness between them."

"Explain that to this Lieutenant Rayfield. Or to someone like Jason. We—the family—were all surprised when they had that boy and now I wish they hadn't."

"Surprised? In what sense?"

"It was just, oh, I don't know exactly, per-haps a little after they were married, Henry told me they'd decided not to have children. Some-thing about Lydia. He wasn't specific."

"But you don't know what it was?"

"Not really, but Lydia was a tenser person than she seemed. You weren't born here, were you, and of course you wouldn't remember anyway."

"Remember what, exactly?"

She frowned. "The Grangeville business. It turned sour on Lydia's father. Some of the Birmingham papers even attacked him. Then he lost for governor and not too long after died of a heart attack when Lydia was only twelve or thirteen.

"We didn't know her then, of course, but when I met her mother after she and Henry were engaged, she told me it was hard on Lydia, that before the executions she'd been quite a happy little girl, very imaginative and a little spoiled by her father—not at all like Henry, whose father terrified him and asked too much. Apparently, she changed. I know there was some unhappy involvement with an older man in Grangeville before she married Henry. But the woman I knew always tried to be perfect. I suppose she thought she wouldn't be perfect as a parent." Her jaw worked. "Perhaps Jason proved she was right."

The last sentence lingered there. Her eyes froze as if shocked by its sound. "I'm sorry," she said in a chastened voice. "That was a terrible thing to say."

The apology wasn't for me. She held herself tighter, as if afraid of what was inside. I let it drop. "Henry—would it be possible to see him?"

Interrupted from guilt, she looked pensive. "I'd just like him to know I was here," I said.

She nodded slowly. "He's on the patio."

Henry Cantwell sat on a bench wearing a thin sweater, staring across the rear grounds at a secluded stand of pines. He was utterly still. His stillness bothered me; it mimed too well the sad, endless patience of those very old who have nothing more to expect. He looked like an old man on a park bench, who shuffled to his mailbox at the same time every day and combed the paper for coupons to clip, painstakingly, and take to cheap groceries to save a quarter on tea. I crossed the patio and stood next to him.

I couldn't tell if he had heard me. His face was ravaged, his eyes bleary and unspeakably tired.

" 'Lo, Henry," I said casually.

He moved over on the bench without answering. I sat down. We watched the grounds in silence. A squirrel rooted at the base of a pine tree, found something, and disappeared up the other side of the tree.

"It's unbelievable," he said. "She's here, then....no chance even to talk..."

I lit a cigarette. I took one deep drag and watched it burn in my hand. "It was Aeschylus who said, 'In our sleep, pain which cannot forget falls drop by drop upon the heart until, in our own despair, against our will, comes wisdom through the awful grace of God.' "

He turned to me. "Do you believe that, Adam?"

I shrugged. "I don't know. Perhaps it was something to say."

He seemed to ponder that. Then he shook his head, wonderingly. "Jason should be here, and instead it's you."

"I don't mind. I'm thirsty, though."

He marshaled himself with effort and stood to get me something. I let him.

He returned with a Bushmills on ice.

"Thanks."

He sat down again. "It's still peaceful back here," I said.

He nodded. "Twenty-eight years—my family's had it for seventy. Not many people last that long in one place."

"Maybe in the South."

He thought. "Maybe here. But it's changing."

I held the cool, icy glass in my hand. Sun fell through the pines on dark swatches of lawn.

"The funeral's tomorrow," he said.

"I know."

We watched together. The squirrel reappeared, scrambling down the tree onto the lawn. Henry's gaze seemed to follow it. "I've always wondered, Adam, why Roland never taught you to hunt."

I smoked the cigarette. "I suppose I was afraid I'd like it too much."

He nodded silently, seeming to lapse into thought. I didn't mention the green Cadillac or his last talk with Lydia. Finally I stood. "You know where to find me. If you need to talk, anything at all."

"Thank you." He still stared ahead. I started across the patio.

"Adam."

I glanced back. He had turned. "I'm pleased you read Aeschylus," he said.

I smiled. "You lent me that, remember?"

Henry gave a faint answering smile. "I remember." He turned back to the grounds.

I went home. Two reporters with a camera were filming Henry's drive.

TEN

At six o'clock Monday morning I acted out my fear of growing older: running four miles, doing push-ups and sit-ups and lifting weights, punching the heavy bag I'd hung in the basement, and generally battling what Kris Ann had smilingly identified on my thirtieth birthday, before leading me upstairs to forget it all, as the instinct we'd never be back in college. The instinct drove me harder than usual. Then I showered and dressed, kissing Kris Ann hastily as she uncurled from sleep. She awoke suddenly to say that the funeral was at two, as if recalling a bad dream. I checked the locks again on the way out.

The city was hot and drowsy. Bankers and businessmen in lightweight suits ambled toward new glass towers or older cement ones with dime stores, jewelers, and one-story diners squatting in between. I passed a newsstand, saw the headline, DISCREPANCY IN CANTWELL STATEMENT, and stuffed the dollar I'd reached for back in my pocket. In front of our building a wizened black man with no body below the hips lolled in a wagon, begging. I gave him the dollar, pushed through the revolving door, and caught an elevator.

The fifty-one lawyers of Cantwell, Brevard, Winfield, and Cade rented the top two floors of the brown bank building, which had housed them for sixty years. It was the partnership's pride that there was no need to move: as Cade had put it, over bourbon at the club, we were beyond showing off. Our reception area featured oak paneling with the firm name lettered in discreet gold script, a linen-suited receptionist, wing chairs for clients, and *Business Week* to read. Framed oils of the sacred dead—Messrs. Cantwell, Brevard, and Winfield—presided over the room like guarantors of probity. Coming off the elevator, I thought again that Cade had worked thirty years to be suitable for framing.

The receptionist looked up at me, vaguely flustered. She was a bony, middle-aged widow with a kind of fading elegance, a proprietary air, and a low, husky voice. I said good morning.

She gave a quick nod, like a hiccup. "It's horrible about Mrs. Cantwell," she managed.

"Yes, it is. She was here just last Friday, wasn't she?"

She glanced toward a wing chair. "Right over there, waiting for Mr. Cade. It's strange now to think about."

"Did she say anything to you?"

"Just hello. Usually we'd chat; she always remembered to ask after my son. But Friday she seemed upset."

"In what way?"

She looked back at the chair. "I can tell by watching people how they feel about their business here. Mrs. Cantwell sat quite straight in her chair, with her ankles crossed and her arms folded, looking at everything and nothing, if you know the look. Once she flipped a mag-

85

azine and put it down without reading it. She acted as women do when they're here on some upsetting problem."

"But she didn't tell you what, or why?"

"Oh, no." She shook her head sadly. "I didn't know until I read about the will. I suppose that *would* be upsetting. My son would never behave like that."

"Then you should count your blessings. By the way, I'm not taking calls from reporters. And tell them my wife isn't either. They can try Mr. Cade."

"Very well, Mr. Shaw."

I went toward my office.

The corridors droned with machines and work. In the library a table of shirt-sleeved associates read law books while another associate stood at a computer terminal that could spit out citations to any legal opinion in the last hundred years containing a phrase he wanted, like "sanctity of contract." The morning crew in the word-processing center typed on machines that recorded their work on a screen, corrected errors, and replayed the final copy at six hundred words a minute. Their new supervisor, a brisk young woman who went to college nights, waited by the telex for a wire from London or Brazil or wherever steel companies did business. Down the hall more computers were translating the daily time sheets for each lawyer and paralegal into monthly bills to be reviewed by a senior partner and sent to clients. As I passed, Johnny Bentham emerged holding a sheaf of time sheets. " 'Morning, Johnny," I said.

" 'Morning, Adam." He stopped, uncomfortable. "Damned awful weekend you had. Terrible about Lydia, just unbelievable."

"Unbelievable," I agreed.

He shifted awkwardly, a great shambling man with the owlish look of a tax partner, unsure of what to say. "That's a mess about Henry being gone," he ventured, "and now that phone call. The papers keep bringing that up."

"Of course they do."

He scratched his cowlick. "Yeah, this is all fun to them—the biggest thing to hit Birmingham since Martin Luther King, my wife says. I just hope we can keep the firm off the front page."

"Henry, too. But it's not easy with that will."

He looked at me sharply. "Well, you did what you thought best about that, I'm sure."

I guessed my handling of the will had been the subject of discussion. "I couldn't see getting Henry arrested."

"Sure," he persisted. "Still, when it's all said and done it's, going to turn out to be some psychopath. I mean, with the picture and all. Some real sickie, you'll see."

"We all will." I glanced at the time sheets in his hand, hoping for a change of subject. "Sending out six years of back bills?"

"Checking on the associates. I want to see who's putting in the hours." He decided to end on a hearty note. "I'm sure you'll be glad to get back into some normal work yourself."

"I'm sure," I said, and went to my office.

My secretary looked up blandly from her desk. "Mr. Taylor just left word about the Stafford case," she told me. "He said to call when it's convenient."

I stepped inside and dialed. "Hello, Nate."

"Adam." Nate Taylor's black-accented voice was roughly what Otis Lee's would have been after Harvard Law School and enough trial work to give him bleeding ulcers at thirty-three. "I told your secretary not to rush you to the phone. I figured you might not be in the mood."

"Consider yourself a diversion."

"All right. I've been sitting here reviewing the evidence of job discrimination by that fine gentleman of the old school, Peyton Stafford. I thought before I went to the trouble of proving at trial what you know to be true I'd see about talking settlement."

"I'm always glad to talk. Peyton's a little less flexible."

"You've got no defense, Adam. Tell him that."

"It's not quite true, though. Reread my deposition of your lead plaintiff. No jury's going to put some guy with four drunk citations in charge of a lumber mill."

"Clients lie to you all the time," he said matter-of-factly. "Even yours. My other plaintiffs are clean and your man has discriminated. Those are the facts."

"Okay. We'll sit down next week. I'm just

telling you, don't come expecting the sun, stars, and moon. You're not getting them." I said goodbye and hung up.

"Shit," I said aloud.

I looked down at the list. Most days I came to the office, drank one cup of black coffee, and went over the list of things to do I'd written the day before. Staring now at Friday's list—eight numbered items with the first three crossed off—I knew with a cold, clear certainty that I didn't give a damn.

I surveyed my office—a framed law license, two shelves of law books, and some comic prints of English barristers—until I came to my grandfather's dartboard on the far wall, pocked with contests between my father and me. I reached in my desk drawer for a dart.

It was wooden, with frayed feathers and weighted in front. I threw it. It struck the seven with a soft thud. I took another and began thinking. Lydia Cantwell's killer had a key, or she had let him in. He had raped her, or they had made love. And then he had strangled her with such intensity of hate that afterward he needed satisfaction from a picture. I threw again. It bounced off the metal ring of the bull's-eye and onto the floor.

I snatched a third dart from my desk drawer. There was a quick rap and the door opened. I looked up, surprised.

Nora Culhane's dark green eyes caught the dart in my hand with a sardonic glance. "Interrupting anything?"

"Any day now. What do you want?"

"I thought we might try having a civil conversation."

"Why? The last time we tried that you were setting up my client. Now your so-called 'discrepancy' is this morning's headline. You people are building pressure to indict Henry Cantwell whether the evidence is there or not." I threw the dart. "What the hell do you care—he gets indicted, you get a raise, and by the time he's acquitted, railroaded, or just plain broken you're Birmingham's first anchorwoman. You don't need me for that."

She hesitated, glancing downward. "Look, Mr. Shaw, we're both trying to find things out. Maybe if you'd quit being so emotional, we could help each other, okay?"

Her voice was cool enough. But her eyes were uncertain.

Maybe, I thought, she would know something useful.

Maybe, too, I'd sensed an ambivalence beneath the toughness, as if she were inhabiting a role she didn't yet believe. It didn't make me like her, exactly—I just liked myself less. But two hours later, when she asked why I'd agreed to lunch, all I said was, "Because I guessed you were Irish."

We were sitting in a flagstone courtyard bordered by bamboo plants, ferns, and trees in wooden planters. More trees grew from spaces in the flagstone to form a leafy arbor.

In the air was the lilting talk of women in silk and the clatter of plates. Black waitresses in print dresses dipped among the tables. "So you're an ethnologist," Culhane said dryly.

"It's just that you couldn't be anything else, even if the name weren't yours. Next time you're home—which I'd guess is Boston—look for women with china skin and bright green eyes or maybe freckles, and see that if their hair isn't reddish or black it's the kind of auburn you have. They'll be Irish."

"You're quite observant."

"No great trick if you're Irish, too. Frankly, though, I came to persuade you to lay off Henry Cantwell."

"He's too logical to ignore," she said bluntly. "And I've talked to anyone who'll stand still."

"Including Jason?"

"Jason slammed the door in my face."

"I wouldn't fool with him. His problem may be worse than bad manners."

She nodded. "He's pretty frightening. But Rayfield doesn't seem to be looking his way."

"So I gather. And you?"

She took a cigarette from her purse and snapped a lighter at it. "I think the Cantwells' problems were bigger than just Jason."

"Based on—?"

"Several things. To start, there's something I got from a friend of Mrs. Cantwell's who's just been divorced. They last spoke just two weeks ago. Lydia steered the conversation around to the divorce: how long it took, whether the woman had to appear in court, that kind of thing. Her friend recalls that she was very curious."

"From which you surmise what?"

Culhane raised an eyebrow. "I thought you'd tell me."

"I couldn't begin to." She gave me a look of cool disbelief. "Seriously," I added, "if Lydia Cantwell had wanted a divorce she'd have come to the firm."

"You're telling me she didn't?"

"I'd know if she had. Just who is this woman?"

New arrivals were drifting past us to be matched with namecards on empty tables. Next to us a plump-armed blonde squealed, "Marilyn, you look so *thin*," to a newcomer who didn't at all. Culhane shook her head. "I told her she'd be anonymous."

"Anonymous, or nonexistent?"

Her voice cooled. "What do you mean by that?"

"I mean maybe you fed me a line to see if we were handling a divorce."

"My source exists," she snapped. "You know, you must really hate news people."

"I prefer 'dislike,' or maybe 'distrust'. Whatever made you pick this business?"

"Whatever makes you care?"

"I was cleverly searching for a change of subject."

She stabbed her half-smoked cigarette into an ashtray. "Basically because I'd divorced my husband and needed work, if that's any of your business."

"What happened?"

She shrugged. "Charles was a heart surgeon I married in Boston when he was still a resident and liked playing his guitar. Then he got a position at the Med Center here and stopped liking anything but cutting chests. Eventually I got tired of begging for attention and asked him to move out. For a while I felt depressed and worthless and jogged five miles a day to keep it together. Finally one of my apartment neighbors who's a cameraman suggested I try news—after all, I was presentable and maybe even bright. By then I was sick of jogging and missing Boston. So I went to the station and asked for a job."

A thin, silent waitress in shocking blue tennis shoes interrupted with iced tea and a small blackboard with the fare scribbled in chalk. We stopped to order. It was hot even in the shade and our salt was stuck in its shaker. I asked for another one, and the waitress left, undelighted with me and her job.

"So what happened next?" I asked Culhane.

"The news director tried to screw me." Her voice held a note of warning. "He didn't, and I began to enjoy the work. It licenses my curiosity—asking questions, meeting people. I even like the hurry. The downside is hassling for airtime and never finishing a story; a thirty-second spot is for shit, you tell nothing. So when you get a story you can stay with, like this, you jump on it."

"One man's tragedy—"

"Is my opportunity. Look, I didn't kill Lydia Cantwell, I'm just covering the story."

Her role as tough newslady interested me. I was getting an impression of where she stood: a late-blooming new woman, throwing out the makeup with her husband, paying the bills and liking it, but still not quite sure where she fit. "How long have you done this?"

"News?" She sipped some tea, her gaze growing distant. "Around two years, I guess."

I guessed she'd counted back to the divorce and been pulled into the vortex of memory, wondering how it had all happened and who she'd been before. I quoted a line of poetry. " 'I see my life go drifting like a river from change to change...' "

She looked up as if troubled. "You're good at divining mood," she said. "Who wrote that?"

"Yeats."

She smiled fractionally. "You're quite Irish yourself. Except that 'Adam' sounds very Old Testament."

"My father's idea. My middle name is Francis."

"Your father had a point. Have you ever been there—Ireland?"

"Once. It was green and beautiful and very poor, and it rained too much and was cold. It felt like I'd been there before."

Culhane nodded. "I felt that, too."

Our waitress brought two crab casseroles that smelled and tasted good. Culhane ate with small, thoughtful bites. As we were finishing she said, "The next thing is that Henry Cantwell's strange."

"Is he now?"

"Of course." She sounded impatient. "I've talked to the people who should know him best. They start by saying he's a fine gentleman, mention the family—down here they still like to know where you're from and who 'your people' are. It gives them a handle on you. But they all end up saying they don't know him very well and that he seems off somewhere, almost secretive."

"You do understand what that's about?"

She shook her head.

"Mother of God, Nora, his wife's just been murdered. They're all preparing for Henry to have sinister secrets. At least try to distinguish between reticence and guilt."

She was plainly galled. "We're talking about strangeness, not reticence. People at his bank will tell you the past couple of months he'd be listless, then become totally irrational. Two months ago he threatened to resign if they didn't approve a loan for some shaky project in New Orleans that made no sense, got the bank in a mess, and then he retreated to his office and was hardly seen for days."

"I've heard all about that. Look, Henry's big problem is being born with money and a bank when he should have been an English professor. I agree with anyone who says he's out of place negotiating loans with some slab-handed wheeler-dealer whose life's dream is to finance trips to Las Vegas and season tickets on the fifty through some real-estate scam. But that's no crime, just a sad incongruity."

She sloshed the tea in her glass, as if examining it for something important. "What about affairs?"

I was getting annoyed. "Henry's never shown the slightest interest in any woman but Lydia, except perhaps the ones in books. You're not dealing with Richard Burton, just a slightly dreamy middle-aged gentleman who likes to read. Nothing strange about him. If you want strangeness, try Rayfield."

"Why him?"

"Because he's got the look of a classic obsessive-compulsive personality. He began acting like Henry was one of his obsessions before he'd even met him."

She shrugged. "Maybe he's afraid Cantwell will do it again."

"That's droll."

"I'm serious. There are a lot of scared people out there."

"And Rayfield's helping to scare them."

The waitress came with key-lime pie. Culhane took a bite before saying, "Rayfield *is* sort of a Jesuit: no other interests, no family or friends outside the police and not many of those, no women anyone's heard of. All he wants is to track down sin—you know, 'man the hunter.' He even told one of our people once that the relationship between him and a suspect is a personal thing, like he' almost breathes with the guy. It's a little obsessive, sure. But I don't think he's off about Cantwell. Put together what bits I know: in the last two months Henry begins acting irrational, Lydia shows an interest in divorce and is killed, and then Henry forgets to tell Rayfield about what obviously was a twelve-minute quarrel. You don't have to be brilliant to guess that one of them was having an affair."

"Just irresponsible. Do yourself and Channel Seven a favor. Watch what you say."

She looked at me seriously. "We've got lawyers, too. I'm just telling you not to invest too much in this." She took another bite. "Incidentally, what does your client say about his little lapse on the telephone call? I'll be happy to report it."

"I haven't asked him."

She shot me an incredulous glance. "I'm glad I don't have your driving lack of curiosity."

"Yeah, well, I thought I'd wait until after the funeral. I've lived in the South for a while and developed some manners."

She reddened. "All right," she said curtly, then checked her watch. "I'm late for work. Better eat your pie."

The check arrived as we finished. We split the bill and hurried silently to the car. She looked wryly across from the passenger seat, as if trying to ease the strain. "No Holy Mother on the dashboard?"

"I've given all that up."

"Have you really?" she asked, more serious.

"Haven't you?"

"Yes and no. I still remember things like my first confession: the priest chewed peppermint

Lifesavers, I could smell them through the screen. I was too terrified to laugh."

I started the car. "You got the whole dose, then."

"Lord, yes. Mother says the Rosary every day. I remember when a Russian family moved in behind us, poor people. One morning I caught Mother sprinkling holy water in their backyard. She was saving them from communism."

"Back then you couldn't be too careful," I smiled. "Even Ike had it. Anyhow, we all have our mothers."

"Do we not. Where is your family?"

"Cleveland. My mother, anyhow. My father's dead."

"What does she do?"

"Works for the clerk of courts. Files things, mostly."

I turned from the parking lot toward downtown. Culhane's hair rippled in the breeze. "So how did you get to Birmingham?" she was asking.

"My wife's from here."

"Is she the tall, dark-haired woman?"

"Uh-huh."

"I saw her at the party. She's absolutely beautiful."

"She is that." We were near downtown. "Tell me where to drop you."

She pointed to a parking garage. I pulled over and stopped. "One thing," I asked. "How'd you get past our receptionist?"

"I said I was late for our appointment."

She got out and gave me a fleeting smile. "Thanks for the time."

"Sure."

She walked to her car. I drove off to take Kris Ann to the funeral.

ELEVEN

By the time we reached downtown the dance of bad memory was like tocsins in the brain. "I know you hate these," Kris Ann said finally.

I shrugged. "It's just that Protestant, funerals are such dismal affairs. There's no catharsis, just one more dutiful rite of forbearance. No one will cry—not even Henry—and then we'll all go home."

But then that was all I'd done when they'd buried my father.

The Episcopal church was a large gothic structure, its stone walls blackened by time and weather and a thickening overcast, Inside it was dark and vast, with a high vaulted ceiling. Along both walls intricate stained-glass windows portrayed the life of Jesus in bright, jagged sections. A blood-red carpet declined between pews overflowing with mourners to a marble altar with an ornate silver cross. Toward the right front, my partners grouped in white shirts and gray suits, trying hard to look what they were. We joined them.

Muffled sounds came from the rear of the

church. Five relatives and Cade bore Lydia's casket, covered by a white pall and resting on a low metal platform with wheels. A blonde acolyte with the processional cross and two clergy with prayer books preceded it. At the rear, Henry Cantwell stood with his sister.

We all rose. The pallbearers began rolling the casket noiselessly toward the altar. A grim-faced Cade held one handle. I couldn't find Jason. The clergy read in hollow voices:

" 'I am the resurrection and the life, saith the Lord: he that believeth in me, though he were dead, yet shall he live...' "

I saw Rayfield standing by the rear door. The voices moved nearer:

" 'I know that my redeemer liveth, and that he shall stand at the latter day upon the earth: and though this body be destroyed, yet shall I see God....' "

Henry's eyes fixed emptily on the acolyte's cross. He passed Etta Parsons, face rigid as if fighting tears, then Dalton Mooring, head averted, his blonde wife next to him looking wretchedly hungover. The clergy continued:

" 'We brought nothing into this world, and it is certain we can carry nothing out. The Lord gave, and the Lord hath taken away...' "

—"Deserter," my mother had shrieked until they pulled her from the coffin and dragged her upstairs.

My father lay in the front hall. "A fine-looking man, Kieron Shaw," they kept saying, and him dead and waxy and looking like someone else.

Brian babbled the Rosary by the head of the coffin—

The foot of Lydia's casket was placed toward the altar. One of the clergy read over her: " 'For I am a stranger with thee, and a sojourner, as all my fathers were. O spare me a little, that I may recover my strength, before I go hence, and be no more seen. Glory be to the Father, and to the Son, and to the Holy Ghost...' "

—"In nomine Patri, et Filii et Spiritu Sancti..." The old priest chanted over my father amidst the smell of incense. Three candles had lined each side of the closed black coffin. My mother wore black, the priest black vestments. Brian, nine years old, watched him—"

I watched the clergyman now as he read: " 'Jesus said, let not your heart be troubled: ye believe in God, believe also in me. In my Father's house are many mansions: if it were not so, I would have told you.' "

He looked shrunken in his vestments, his gaze through wire-rimmed glasses touched with uncertainty. I sensed his isolation: a middle-aged man repeating an inherited ritual in a reedy voice and doubting his own efficacy.

—Brian wore the priest's collar I could never quite believe. "Good God, man," he said, "you send Mother money instead of visiting, can't bear to see the old neighborhood or anyone in it, and live outside the Church, beholden to a man you despise. For all your beautiful Kris Ann and fine house you've at last no sense of who you are."

"Will no one rid me of this meddlesome priest," I jibed.

"Don't spar with me, Adam. You can make a sadness of your own life, but our mother deserves better."

"I'm here now."

"For our uncle's funeral. That's quite a gesture."

"Dammit, Bri, since I was twelve all I got from her was 'don't be like your father, don't look up to what he did' and all the time knowing she hated him for being killed. Hell, she'd say I looked like him and it was like a curse. So I did as she wanted, and if that's taken me other places, so be it."

Brian raised a finger to his lips, glancing toward the stairwell. Upstairs my mother had said the Rosary and slept alone, as she had for the twenty years since my father was shot and killed and buried in a spring drizzle like the one that spattered the windows, reminding me of the smell of wet earth. Instead, drinking wine with Brian in the living room, I smelled the same trapped mustiness. A small lamp lit the familiar things of my mother: a Belleek china cup, lace on the couch, the tortured Jesus, the cameo of my father, wolf-faced, with cold blue eyes. I sat in his chair. Brian faced me, a brown-haired replica of the pale sleeping woman. "I know you paid the price for Da's dying," he said.

I shrugged. "At least it didn't make me a celibate."

He nodded in wry acknowledgment. "No

doubt I found comfort in the Church, if only the sense that someone was looking after me. Who's to say that's a bad thing?"

"Well, what I remember is our dried-out priest mouthing all that cold business of God's will, and me knowing all the time that we were losers in an arbitrary and very nasty lottery. I've not become so weak-minded as to cherish that."

Brian flushed, "It's worse than weak-minded to hate your past and neglect your mother," he came back. "You've been at war with God twenty years now, and it's left you empty. You're a cynical man, Adam, there's no purpose to your life—"

And no purpose in rehashing it, I thought now. It was just that I hated funerals.

I found myself staring at Lydia's casket, ashamed to wonder, yet wondering if my stricken friend in the first pew was a sad, bewildered cuckold with a wife he'd never understood, and shouldn't now. Perhaps better to let it be, and hope that Cade was right, that no one else would come to harm and Henry would go free.

"Unto God's gracious mercy and protection we commit you," read the clergyman. A little late, I answered silently. "Amen," he finished.

We rose again. The pallbearers shuffled to the casket and inched it back up the aisle. Henry trailed, eyes bleak with cold comfort. They rolled the casket to the door of the church and were gone.

Kris Ann took my hand. Mourners edged from their pews looking up or down like strangers in an elevator. We moved in the halting file of reticent bodies, out the door.

Rayfield stood watching in the stone archway. I passed him without speaking. In the street below it was raining and almost dusk. There were newsmen on the other side. Nora Culhane was next to her cameraman, shooting footage for the evening news. Then I saw Etta Parsons.

She stood with her back to me, staring from the top of the steps toward the sidewalk. Joanne Mooring waited there alone. Then a dark green Cadillac glided from the street to stop in front of her. As he pushed open the door Dalton Mooring's face appeared. His wife got inside. Etta Parsons watched the car drive silently away.

I left Kris Ann and walked behind her. "Mooring?" I said softly.

The single stare she gave me was hard as sculpture. Then she turned and walked away, into the rain.

TWELVE

The next morning I called on Jason Cantwell.

The night of the funeral I had found Kris Ann in our bedroom, loading a black revolver.

"What's that?" I blurted stupidly.

She gazed at me across the bed, gripping the revolver. It was blunt and smooth and oiled. "Daddy gave it to me this morning, after you left. To protect myself."

"From what?"

"Jason Cantwell." She looked away. "I'm afraid of him."

"Why, exactly?"

"Because of Lydia. Isn't that enough?"

She stood framed in the blackness of our window, shoulders curled as if cold. "I don't like guns," I said quietly. "Roland knows that. You know it, too."

Her face burned. "I just need one until this is over."

"Krissy, I want you to take it back."

"Please—"

"I'm here, dammit. Isn't *that* enough?"

Her look across the bed was level and silent. Then she repeated simply, "I need it, Adam."

Her eyes held mine without wavering. Softly, I asked, "Do you know how to use that?"

"I haven't in years. But Henry taught me when I was younger, for target practice. His father was a crack pistol shot." She paused, then added, "He taught Jason, too."

For a long time I stared at the gun. "Put the safety on," I finally said, "and stick it in a drawer."

She silently placed the gun in the drawer of her nightstand and closed it. I lit a cigarette.

"I'm sorry, Adam."

She turned out the lights and got in bed. There was nothing more said, or done.

In the morning we sat in the sunroom as we usually did, with coffee and the paper. The headline read, CANTWELL FAMILY CENTER OF PROBE. We said little about that or anything else, and nothing about the gun. Riffling the back pages I found Kris Ann's picture above the caption "Mrs. Kris Ann Shaw, Chairman of the Junior League Volunteers for Retarded Children." In the picture she smiled as she had the day I'd watched her kneeling in a circle of the children she taught, seemingly oblivious to dirty hair or tantrums or runny noses as she helped them shape clay into whatever they imagined. At the circle's edge a small girl with taffy hair and guileless clear eyes had hung back watching her, unnoticed in the clamor of children thrusting lumps of clay toward Kris Ann for the smile she gave. Then the girl had put down her clay and walked to Kris Ann, touching her hair. Kris Ann had looked up, and then her smile had faded and she pulled the girl close, her eyes shut.

"I'm glad you still work with those children," I told her now. "You're good with them."

She took a sip of coffee, her face abstracted. "Art's something they need, that's all. There are no wrong answers." She rose, touching my shoulder, and went upstairs.

I stared out the window. Above me Kris Ann started running her shower. I got up abruptly, called the university for Jason Cantwell's address, and left.

In the aftermath of rain, the morning was lush and bright and fresh as Creation. The campus—tan brick buildings with no trees around them—looked scrubbed clean. I found Jason's apartment at its edge, a worn brick building stuck between an orthodontist and a marriage counselor. I parked, climbed one flight to the end of a dark hallway, and knocked.

The door was opened by an olive-skinned man with full black beard, flat cheekbones like hammered bronze, and black liquid eyes. His chest strained the dark T-shirt, and his arms were ridged and heavy.

"What do you want?" he demanded, surprised and ready to be hostile.

"I'm Adam Shaw. You remember. I represent your father now."

"He send you?"

"No. This is my idea."

The volatile eyes seemed to change like some unstable element. I was recalling more about him than I had thought: a nineteen-year-old boy at our engagement party who seemed somehow uninvited, a stray yet the center of a chemistry that kept Lydia glancing toward him, Kris Ann a careful distance she maintained wherever Jason moved. He had made an impression then, and after that—when I had seen nothing of him and heard nothing good—almost none. But the man who stood now in the doorway had the primal force of a prophet or a Mansonite. "You've got five minutes," he said at last, and moved grudgingly aside.

His apartment was cramped—a small living

room with a kitchen nook off that and one bedroom—and its contents a riot of confusion. On the far wall a poster of Ho Chi Minh watched from above the color television. A half-finished macramé lay on the couch to the left, there was a cocaine spoon on the coffee table, and I stood on a costly looking Persian rug. A bookshelf of bricks and boards held a revisionist history by Eugene Genovese, some Herbert Marcuse, and a gothic romance, in paperback. In the kitchen, a blue-jeaned girl with long brown hair washed dishes by a spice rack and copper teapot. I figured those, and the paperback, were hers.

"Hello," I said.

She turned, eyes turquoise and unsure. She was tall and pretty, with tawny skin and small delicate features. Her body stretched with a young girl's leanness to sudden full breasts, and there were tints of honey in her curly hair. "Hi," she said in a near whisper and turned quickly back to her dishes.

I felt Jason's eyes warning me off, as clear as speech. He stood in the center of the living room, thumb stroking one side of his beard. "I hear you found the old lady." His voice was slow and guttural and half-curious. "The cops said her neck had these purple welts."

He could have been discussing a dead hamster. But I couldn't make him out. His neck was bent to the side, his body rigid, and each word seemed molten and heavy. There was something old about him, and terribly young. I nodded. "That's right."

Jason stared at his feet. "Yeah, well, that's how I found out, you know—from the cops. By the time old Henry called, the pigs had been all over me. He must have thought they'd trap me first."

I caught the edge of hostile pride. "That's my doing," I told him. "They were on the way before Henry got home. I had the will with me when I found her. You did know about the will?"

"No." The pulse throbbed in his temple. "The old lady made noises but she never said she'd done it."

"Well, she had, and that's why the cops came after you. I thought maybe now you could tell me who else might have killed her."

He gave me a sharp look. "I don't see how it much matters."

"Yeah, I noticed you missed the funeral."

The girl had left the kitchen and moved to the corner of the couch, watching Jason. His eyes turned bright and violent. "So what? I'm sure you being there was enough for Henry."

I shrugged. "Another man might have come, for his father's sake."

Jason's chest rose. "You feel real sentimental about him, don't you, Shaw?"

"We've spent some pleasant evenings. He's a sensitive, intelligent man. People could have worse fathers and generally do."

"Well, I'm just fucking thrilled you've gotten so much out of him. Let me tell you, man, I used to get a handshake when they sent me off to prep school. Old Henry, the walking secret."

"None of which explains who killed your mother."

"I already told that pig lieutenant I was right here with Terry." He wheeled on her for confirmation. She nodded and Jason turned back with dark satisfaction, as if he'd scored some point about the girl. "But the pigs wanted to push me around. They asked how I liked Lydia, looked for pieces of her skin under my fingernails—" His throat began working.

"They were horrible," the girl broke in.

Her words seemed to draw out his poison. Jason's face relaxed and his breathing eased. "Maybe they'd heard you'd quarreled," I said.

"I just reminded her," he said in a succinct voice, "that her family were corrupt fascists who got rich exploiting miners. That her father murdered two black men for racist votes. That her little civic works were one pathetic daisy on the family pile of shit."

It was clear that Jason Cantwell was a wounded man. But he made it hard to care. "Perhaps your mother was trying, in her own way."

"Yeah, by taking a busload of black kids to the symphony. Poor Lydia, she had the soul of a fucking Barbie doll—'Give the niggers presents, make them feel better.' She didn't like me saying that. I told her whites covered the brown man like thin scum on the surface of the world. You could see her get scared. Hell, she was so paranoid about blacks that the last time I saw her she was all uptight that the fucking yardman was watching her. I said, 'Sure, in your dreams.' She got pissed and said she'd cut me off, she always did." Jason kept saying more than he needed, as if he cared more than he wished. He caught himself. "I didn't do it. I didn't need money or anything else. From her or Henry."

There was a faint aroma from the kitchen, something boiling I couldn't quite place. "You tell Rayfield about the yardman?"

"I forgot." His one-sided smile was no smile at all. "You're worried about old Henry, aren't you? Well, it wasn't Henry, not that he gives a damn for anything that breathes. Henry likes poetry and vases. He doesn't have the guts for killing."

"Not to mention that he loved your mother."

He repeated the same unpleasant smile. "Who you been talking to, Shaw? Henry? He never even touched her. Hell, they had separate bedrooms. I could never see how they got it up to have me."

"They probably knew what they could look forward to."

It was as if I'd struck a match. Jason stepped forward, fists clenched, eyes full of prep school fights and murdered dogs and all the people who had called him a curse to his parents.

"Jason," the girl said sharply.

He blinked, stopping in his tracks. I went on as if nothing had happened. "Maybe she had someone else. Was your mother friends with any men?"

"No." His voice was low and murderous.

"Ever see her with Dalton Mooring?"

His body strained. "Did you?" I prodded.

The girl perched on the edge of the sofa, watching Jason. The room seemed like a cage. Jason stared at his fingernails. "He was there the second last time I went, sitting next to her on the couch. They were having tea." His voice rasped. "Lydia always liked to have tea."

"What happened?"

"Nothing. They looked surprised, then Mooring started asking about school, how I was doing, bullshit like that—like it was really a big deal to him. He acted strange, kind of embarrassed. She was sitting close to him with her eyes all bright and funny, smiling at me like she didn't know what to do. I got sick of them both and left."

"Think he and your mother were having an affair?"

His voice lashed out in sudden pain. "Look, I don't give a shit what Lydia did."

The smell from the kitchen was tea.

Jason's face was contorted in a torment of hate, instability, and thwarted love. "Okay," I said flatly. "Thanks for the talk."

"Hang on, Shaw." Jason's stare brightened with sudden, malevolent curiosity. "I want to hear how you're making out with Kris Ann Cade."

His gaze was keen and oddly excited. The

girl looked fragile, her eyes deep blue and scared. "Fine," I answered.

"I was just wondering. I remember old man Cade was all bent out of shape, you being Catholic and all."

"That was a while ago."

The soft answer drew him on. He looked eagerly at the girl, then to me. His voice seeped adolescent taunting, getting back his own. "Yeah, I guess you kissed that off to go fuck Kris Ann and live off her old man's money. She must be good. You've really got it made now, don't you?"

The girl turned to me, lips parted in mute appeal. "As running dogs go," I answered mildly. "Of course nothing's perfect. You never come to our parties."

He moved closer. "I wouldn't come near you or your cunt wife. You're just a fucking leech."

All at once I'd had enough. "Look at you," I said, "dancing on your mother's grave and spouting drivel while your girlfriend does the dishes. Christ, you haven't the moral sense or compassion God gave a maggot. Your father's worth ten of you."

His fist smashed into my forehead.

I wobbled, staggering against the wall. His second punch cracked against my cheekbone. My knees buckled. I ducked by instinct as his next swing crashed into the wall above me.

He yelped, losing a split second. As he grabbed for my throat I spun, still crouching, and hit him in the stomach with a left hook. He grunted, air gasping from his mouth. I hit him in the ribs with a right cross, then sent a left to the stomach that doubled him over and drove him back. The girl screamed. I pivoted and sent a right to his jaw with all the force I had.

Pain shot through my arm as the punch stood him up. He dropped to the floor. The girl sprang from the couch and bent over him.

My face and throat ached and blood was rushing in my head. "I'm sorry," I told her, and was. But she didn't answer or even look up. As I left, the sound of Jason's moans came through the hallway like keening.

I made it to the stairs and then down to the car, one step at a time, leaning against the wheel until my head cleared. But I had decided to find Mooring by the time I drove away.

THIRTEEN

Dalton Mooring's home was fake antebellum, opulent but without the grace of time. The white brick and pillars were too new, the grounds too crammed with shrubs, the interior, with its porcelain and restored antiques, too clearly decorated. The effect was striking and a little desperate.

I waited in the foyer while the maid went for Mooring. The living room had the glossy heartlessness of new money and no children:

silk flowers, deep blue rug, some wire sculpture, a bright abstract painting in a chrome frame. Above the mantel a smoked-glass mirror inverted the room. Here and elsewhere were small signs of drunkenness: a burn hole in the rug, scratches on a doorknob, rings marring the coffee table.

My head and throat ached and my right hand had swollen. I was feeling it for breaks when Mooring appeared, dressed for golf and looking annoyed. Without preliminaries he asked, "What do you want?"

"Ten minutes or so."

He gave his watch an irritated glance. "I'm due in twenty."

I hesitated, still shaken, doubtful now that I had come this far. But Mooring's executive crispness seemed less real than calculated. "Your golf can wait," I told him. "This can't."

He looked me over, taking his time. Then he nodded curtly and led me through the kitchen. His wife sat behind a butcher-block counter sipping a daiquiri. She had circles beneath her eyes and too much lipstick. Her gaze was wary and unsurprised, as if she knew me but had forgotten how.

"Hello," she breathed, emitting a ragged nimbus of cigarette smoke.

I said hello. Mooring steered me quickly past her, through the family room and down four oak stairs into something unexpected: a greenhouse in the shape of an A-frame, refracting trapped sunlight that made me squint. The room was hot and steamy, its greenery—rubber trees, a ten-foot corn plant, some snake cactus that looked ready to strike—an oppressive jungle of exotica, completed by the babble of a rococo fountain.

Mooring said, "You could have come to my office," in a low, flat drawl.

I couldn't square him with the house. He stood by the corn plant about ten feet away, his back to the sun, hands placed on his hips in a pose of impatience. He was trim, though as with slim men in their forties he carried himself carefully around the middle and there was a subtle hardness in the face, a closeness of skin to bone. He had gray eyes set over broad cheekbones, an aquiline nose, and a cleft jaw beneath an angry slash of a mouth whose stamp of drive and temper warred with the vaguely feline look of a cynical diplomat. His overall presence, shrewd and carefully governed, clashed with his surroundings. I guessed there were reasons besides his wife that he didn't want me here: the place embarrassed him. "You were out," I answered. "So I came here."

"Then tell me what's so important."

The fountain splashed in an unnerving rhythm. Quietly I said, "Your relationship to Lydia Cantwell."

His mouth thinned. "If you're referring to that scene with my wife, I'll ask you to be gentleman enough to forget it. When she's not"—he searched for the word—"responsible, she imagines things."

I realized that Mooring was unsure of what

she'd said. "Then why doesn't she imagine something else?"

His voice lowered and became almost confiding. "Because she's a jealous woman. Frankly, we started with almost nothing and she feels inadequate next to women like Lydia. It's an old story, one I'm sure you've heard before."

I paused, wondering when Mooring had begun to speak so well. He had none of the southerner's studied lapses—the "ain'ts" and "might coulds"—and his diction was clearly acquired. I guessed that he'd outgrown his wife and her decorator long ago. The house had begun to seem like a prison, with the woman its Mrs. Rochester. "I don't think your wife's insane," I said finally. I have it from other people that you and Mrs. Cantwell were close. If I can put that together, so can the police."

He folded his arms, frowning as if puzzled. But in his stillness I sensed a subcutaneous tension. The conversation had begun oddly enough without my feeling that there was a wordless second conversation stranger than the first: that something he expected me to know kept him from inviting me out. "I'm a little unclear," he probed, "as to what your interest is in this."

"Roland Cade and I represent Henry Cantwell."

Mooring's face closed against me. "What are you after?" he said coldly. "A boyfriend?"

For a moment it threw me off. But his challenge seemed hollow and too late. "If you think I should be."

"I don't think anything. My 'relationship' to Lydia, as you put it, was confined to work we did jointly for the symphony. Jason saw us drinking tea. Whatever else he saw exists only in the mind of a confused and unhappy young man."

"Yeah, I was curious about how that happened—the symphony work, I mean."

"Lydia asked me." His voice turned almost bored. "She was our largest stockholder. I've known her almost since I began at Maddox."

"When was that?"

"About nineteen fifty-two." He looked straight at me. "Please understand, Shaw, I'm sick about what happened. But I'm in no position to help you or the police."

His voice had thickened. I kept sensing a split in him, a choked undercurrent of real feeling channeled as artifice. "You can't be sure," I answered. "For example, when was the last time you saw her?"

His eyes flickered toward the kitchen. "What makes that of interest?"

"Several things. Time of death, for instance. The police will be looking for anyone who saw Lydia so much as breathe after three P.M. on Friday."

His stare turned frank and hard. "I'd better ask you something first. Does Cade know you're here?"

"Not specifically."

He placed his hands on his waist. "If I'd known that, I wouldn't have let you impose like this. How do you think your questions would affect my wife?"

"I don't know," I shrugged. "Maybe I should ask her."

A second persona leapt abruptly from the first, angry and physical. He moved toward me. "Now hear me well, Shaw, because I'll say this just once: if you make these insinuations anywhere else—anywhere at all—I'll sue you for slander and take your law license in the bargain."

My hand was throbbing. "Go ahead. Then you can tell me in open court where you were the night Lydia Cantwell was murdered."

"I don't have to tell you anything."

"Not now. But you keep forgetting the police. You do know they found semen traces on Lydia's body?"

"So?"

"So when the lab men take semen smears, they comb the woman's pubic hair. The man leaves his own hair, you see. After that they just keep clipping hairs off suspects until they get a match. And there's not a damn thing you can do about it except wait for them to clip some of yours."

Mooring straightened as if struggling for control. Then he inhaled, glanced at his watch, and said, "Get out, Shaw. I'm late."

His tone was again even. For a moment we stood facing each other. Then I turned and left.

On the way out I passed Joanne Mooring, hunched over the counter with a blender full of daiquiris. She didn't look up. I walked to the car and drove home with one hand.

FOURTEEN

I was sitting at the kitchen counter with my hand in a bucket of ice water when Kris Ann arrived from teaching. She smoothed back a damp tendril of hair, glancing quickly around, and saw me.

She started. "Adam, what happened?"

I raised the swollen hand. "I fought with Jason Cantwell."

She turned white. "Here?"

"No. I went to his apartment."

She stared at me in silence. Then she took my hand, turning it gently from side to side. "I think you'd better see a doctor."

"I'm going to."

She rested my hand on the counter. "How did it happen?"

I told her, beginning with Jason's girl and finishing with the fight. She listened without speaking or moving. Then she went to the kitchen table and sat staring out the window, quite still. In an undertone, she asked, "What else did Jason say to you?"

"That's all, Krissy. It was enough."

She turned to me, questioning. Finally, she said, "You should never have gone there," and lapsed into quiet, unapproachable.

It was strange. Alone at the counter, I began missing her, even though she was four feet away—missing some better times we'd had: staying up in school to smoke dope and smile at old movies, perhaps sitting outdoors at a

Paris café inventing lives for passersby, or talking in the beach house late at night with the windows open and heavy gulf air smelling of salt.

The images were freeze frames perfectly captured and imprinted on my mind. Like her eyes the first time we made love. Silver light through my apartment window had crossed her face. Her hair, soft and thick and clean smelling, fell back on the pillow. Just before it happened, she stiffened and then touched my face, eyes large with questions. Slowly, her arms closed tight around me.

It was sweet and intense.

Afterward we lay damp against each other, content to say nothing. Suddenly she grinned. She couldn't stop. I buried my face in her hair and we began laughing together out of pure crazy happiness.

When we had stopped, she said, "You're beautiful."

"And you." I was serious now.

She drew some strands of hair over her lip in an absurd mustache. "And if I weren't?"

I brushed it away. "Then you'd have to make your own clothes."

She smiled, knowing how I felt. The newness of things imposed its own wisdom. We didn't talk about it.

Later she was looking around the apartment, not shy. Her walk was lithe and gliding, and I thought then that she carried the South inside her, and in her eyes and the brownness of her skin.

"What are you doing?" she asked.

I was reaching in the closet for a shirt. "Laying out clothes for tomorrow."

She looked intrigued. "Can't you just get up and dress?"

"You're spoiled," I grinned. "In the morning you can stumble out to hunt through that mess in your closet for something to wear, and cut English Lit if you can't find it. But my job starts at seven and nine's my first class."

"Prrretty compulsive."

"Gets me an extra fifteen minutes sleep." I turned to see her leaning over my bureau. "You okay?"

"Uh-huh. Just taking out my contacts."

She finished and began walking toward me in the semidarkness with short, myopic steps. I smiled and reached toward her. "Don't you have glasses?"

"A naked lady in glasses? That's obscene." Our hands clasped. "Besides, they're thick."

I laughed, pulling her to me. "I think I can live with it."

I felt her smile against my shoulder. "I'm not scared now," she murmured. "It was good for me, Adam. Gentle. I needed it gentle."

"I know."

We went together to the bed, and lay down again....

The phone rang. Kris Ann rose from the kitchen table to get it.

"Hello, Daddy. Yes, he's here." She listened, taut, then asked, "Can you stay for dinner?"

She paused, answered, "It's fine, really. See you then," and hung up.

She turned to me. "He sounds upset."

"So I gather. Nice you invited him to beard me in our own home."

"Which he bought us."

"I'd forgotten that." I glanced at my hand. It was various shades of purple. "I'd better have this checked. Your father knows where the bourbon is. Just lock the doors until he gets here, okay?"

Her brow knit. "Don't make a scene with him. Please."

"I don't think that's up to me."

Her look at me was long and thoughtful. Then she turned away as if speaking to herself. "Why are you doing this, Adam? Why are you doing this now?"

Her question lingered in the silence. I left for the doctor's.

When I got there an officious nurse gave me a form to fill out. I did that, still remembering how Kris Ann and I had begun to learn each other, after that first night.

We were together often, doing everything and nothing. I would tease about her debutante party, watching amused as she accepted service at the cheap diner I could pay for with the ease of manner that suggested we had just come in from riding, when more likely we were fresh from making love. Lovemaking left her shamelessly hungry, and she would stalk from our bed to the refrigerator, ripping through my leftovers with noises of mock disappointment until we had to go out. "This isn't a refrigerator," she said one evening, "it's an aluminum mine," and after that she had stocked the kitchen with food and spices and begun cooking fine dinners of pasta, served by candlelight at my kitchen table, with red wine. She'd learned pasta from a book, she told me, because it wasn't southern, and she was full of questions about the way I'd lived: about my home and father and how I'd made it since, about the steel mill I'd worked in and the ore boat with the drunken captain that I'd served on one summer, running ore from Minnesota to the docks in Cleveland. My job now was our dishes, but sometimes we would look at each other and leave them. One night, afterward, she lay on my shoulder, absorbed in her own thoughts. "It's funny," she finally said.

"What's funny?"

"I don't know. It's just that sometimes I think that life is this giant maze, very dark, with people wandering through it bumping into each other and going on, groping for that thing or person that will make the difference—you know, get them to the end—and it's all so much chance. Look at us. We start at different places, you in Cleveland, me in Alabama, from people who are nothing alike, and then enter the maze to go through all the things that make us the way we are now and deliver us by sheer coincidence to a bad party in the middle of twelve thousand people, and by the time we've met maybe these same experiences mean that we're people

124

who can't help each other, that at some point we'll have to go on alone, bumping into more people and things. I mean, it's hard to know when you've gotten to the end, isn't it?"

I looked up at the ceiling. "For some people, I suppose."

She rolled over, head propped on her elbow. "Adam, did any of what I just said make sense to you?"

I grinned. "Infinite sense."

"Then how can you sound so *blasé*?"

"Because I know."

"Know what?"

I turned to see her face. Her eyes were deep and dark and serious. I reached out, touching the nape of her neck, and said softly, "Because I know the maze ends here."

For a long time she looked at me, seeming hardly to breathe. Then as if on impulse she stretched to pull me out of bed. "Come on."

"Where?"

"You'll see." She tugged harder. "Hurry up."

I began laughing. "Okay, okay. I'll go quietly."

We dressed and went down to campus with the key to the stark, unfurnished room that held her paintings, where she had never taken me. Beneath one bare lightbulb was an easel covered with white muslin. She went to it, removed the muslin, and turned.

Beside her was an oil of my face, each feature carefully drawn from memory. It was so much like my father I felt a kind of *frisson*.

Kris Ann studied me closely. "Do you like it?"

"It's incredible."

I couldn't move my eyes from the painting. Then she stepped in front of it. Slowly, without speaking, she unbuttoned her blouse until it lay on the floor beside her. "Make love to me, Adam. Please. Right here."

We did that. I held her for a long time after.

That Saturday we packed my car with her dishes and dresses on hangers. In the country we found a spool bed and mattress, and for Cade's sake ordered his and hers telephones to go on either side.

The next week Cade called her, to invite us down....

When I came back from the doctor's she met me at the front door. "Daddy's here."

"I can hardly wait. Incidentally, it's not broken."

"What isn't?"

"My hand. Where is he?"

"In the sunroom."

She looked tense and wooden, the look I remembered from when I'd come to Cade's that first time, every southern gentleman's notion of the perfect son-in-law, an Irish Catholic northerner, and broke at that. The pinstripe I'd worn on the flight down was my only suit and I was somehow sure that Cade would know that. He rose from the living-room couch to shake my hand, conveying ease and power in a cardigan sweater. I began feeling like a dress-up doll with sweat glands. Kris Ann stood to one side, watchful and unnaturally quiet.

"That's a long trip," Cade had smiled. "Would you like a drink?"

"Yes, thanks. Any kind of whiskey."

"Good." He brought two bourbons. We sat at opposite corners of a couch set in front of a Chinese wall hanging and surrounded by antiques I admired for a moment. When I glanced back to the room Kris Ann had disappeared.

"It's good to finally meet you," Cade was saying.

"And you, too, sir." I flinched inwardly at the sound of "sir," waiting for him to wave it away. He didn't.

"You've done quite well in law school. I'm impressed."

"Krissy's biased."

Cade scowled as if he didn't like the sound of "Krissy." "I happen to know she's right. You're fifth in your class and on law review." He saw my puzzlement. "The Dean's an old classmate," he explained. "I hope you don't mind." He sounded quite sure I wouldn't, or wouldn't say so.

I shrugged. "I guess I'd mind more if I were bottom quarter."

"A good answer. With those grades you can write your own ticket. It all depends on what you want."

Late sunlight through his window warmed the rich colors of the rug and suffused Cade's bookshelves with a kind of glow. It seemed a good room to discuss good futures. "The justice department has an honors program, in its antitrust division." Whiskey warmed me to the subject. "Antitrust is a growing field, and the government gives you more responsibility, earlier. I think I've got a pretty fair shot."

Cade balanced his glass in both hands. "Justice is a useful connection," he said judiciously. "But I've seen government ruin young lawyers through lack of training." He paused, then said abruptly, "Adam, I'd like you to visit our firm. I can set up appointments tomorrow, if you'd like."

The warmth turned sluggish in me. Cade raised a mollifying hand. "I gather Kris Ann hasn't mentioned this, but you'd be doing me a favor to consider it, and not just because you're seeing my daughter. You've got brains and ambition and those are things no large firm can afford to overlook." His voice turned easy and comfortable. "Besides, any interview is good practice."

"It's just that I never thought to live here."

Cade nodded as if that were natural and reached for my glass. "Let me get you a second drink."

He limped off while I tried to construct an answer. I was still puzzling when he returned with the fresh drink. He paused to look out the window, then jerked the drapes closed with sudden violence, like a man hanging a cat. He handed me the drink, asking, "How does it stand between you and Kris Ann?"

I hesitated. "Fairly serious, I think. At least I am."

Cade settled back in the corner and took one

sip, tasting it on his lips and eyeing me thoughtfully. Then he spread his arms in an avuncular, confiding gesture. "You're adults, of course. I only ask because Kris Ann's always lived here. The South is home to her, and of course she's been spoiled—perhaps more so because her mother died and I've tried to make up for that. But I wonder whether you'd be handicapping yourself were you to ask her to move to a strange place and leave what she's had."

I was feeling uneasy. "I guess that's up to her."

Cade seemed not to hear. "After all," he went on, "there are other differences."

"Such as?"

He glanced carelessly around the room. "Just that the two of you are used to different things. And of course there's the Catholic business."

"The Catholic business?"

He gave me a probing glance. "You don't think being of different faiths is a problem?"

I wondered why responding was so hard: I only went to Mass at home, and was home rarely. I paused, then said, "I've sort of let that lapse.

"I see." He was cheerful again. "I don't mean to pry, you understand, but I do worry. Perhaps someday you'll be a father, too."

"I hope so."

"Then you'll consider my offer?"

I looked past him at the books and antiques. "I'll talk to Krissy," I finally said.

"Fair enough." He broke into the wide-as-the-plains smile I would later see him flash on clients like a sudden gift. "Let's have another drink, Adam."

"Let's do this on the porch," I told him now.

Cade sat drinking in our sunroom, under an antique brass fan Kris Ann had salvaged from an old hotel. He rose with a long upward glare and followed me outside.

Cade took the wicker couch facing the house and set his glass on a low marble table as I sat opposite. Kris Ann's plants hung from the canopy behind him, and beyond that our front grounds sloped gently to the street.

"Dalton Mooring called me." Cade's voice was soft with anger.

"Did he now?"

Cade leaned slowly forward. The skin near his eyes seemed tight with the effort of self-control. "Mooring threatened to sue us for slander. What you've done is the single most stupid and irresponsible act ever committed by a member of this firm."

"Mooring won't sue, Roland, and you know it."

A vein pulsed in Cade's forehead. "You can guarantee that."

"I can. First, because I haven't slandered anyone. Second, because a slander suit only spreads the slander. Third, because to the extent I suggested that he was Lydia's lover it's probably not slander at all."

"Jesus Christ." Cade slammed his fist on the

130

table and the drink slopped over. "Just how do you figure that?"

"It's easy enough. The police found semen on Lydia, Henry was out of town, and Jason's her son, for God's sake. There's no sign of a break-in, which probably means a lover. The Cantwells' yardman saw a car like Mooring's several times in the past month, and Jason found Mooring there alone with Lydia. Mooring's known her for twenty-five years, he's got a wife that drinks and was jealous of her, and, if you believe Jason, Lydia and Henry weren't sleeping together. Yesterday I heard that two weeks before she died Lydia was quizzing a friend on how to get a divorce. Plus, the one civic thing Mooring seems to do gave him an excuse to see her. Which he used."

"You call that evidence?"

"I call that funny. And when I tried it out on Mooring he did everything but act normal."

A slight breeze blew the cocktail napkin from Cade's lap. He snatched it back. "Your theory's a disaster."

"How so?"

"Because it leads the police right back to Henry, as Mooring was kind enough to point out. You've taken a client with no alibi and found him a motive to go with it: a potential lover."

"It also gives us at least one more potential killer. We could use one. The police and media have ganged up on Henry, and Jason has an alibi."

Cade glanced at my hand. "Yes," he said

coolly. "You'd better tell me what happened with Jason. And don't leave anything out."

I described our talk. Cade listened, intent and nearly motionless. When I got to the fight, Cade cut in. "And that's all he said?"

"That's right."

"Jesus," Cade exploded. "And for that you picked a fight with a madman. We don't in this firm go around brawling, or insulting people like Dalton Mooring. We couldn't survive. After seven years you still have no mature concept of your responsibilities. I helped build this firm, dammit, and I won't let you tear it down just because you had the good luck to marry my daughter."

A retort came to my tongue and died there. "The point is," I finally said, "that without Jason as a suspect, Henry's in trouble."

"My God, you're fresh from fighting with Jason and you still think he couldn't kill?"

I shrugged. "I suppose it's possible. He's violent, his feelings about Lydia are a tangle of pathology, and the girl's his only alibi. That has a strange look to it: she's mother, lover, and cheerleader all rolled into one. But incest is hard to accept."

"I've known Jason since he was a child," Cade said coldly, "and I assure you that he could kill his mother and the rest of it, too. All it would take is something to make him feel that Lydia had abandoned him. Like that will."

"That's wading pretty deep in the Freudian slime."

"Christ." Cade gave me a slow, disgusted look. "Did you see Lydia's picture?"

I rested the cold drink on my hand. "Is that why you gave Kris Ann the revolver?" I asked. "Or to make some other point?"

"She should be able to protect herself." His voice was contemptuous. "With you out stiffing up Jason and God knows who else, I'm damned glad I did. He's insane and now you've gone out of your way to draw his attention. Someone has to protect my daughter from your own carelessness."

I flushed. "I'll let her keep it, for now. But the next time you want to introduce guns into my house, ask first. Ask *me*."

Without answering, Cade took a long sip of his drink, watching me over the rim until he put it down. In a tone of polite inquiry, as if continuing another conversation, he said, "Nothing's worse than being poor, is it?"

I looked at him, surprised. "I don't know. There are a lot of things I haven't tried."

"Nothing's worse," he repeated. "That's why you came here."

"I came here for Krissy."

"But you've stayed, Adam. You didn't like being poor any more than I did." Cade got up and began pacing stiffly. "You know how I felt when my daddy lost everything? Like I'd been weeded out. The sad truth is that if you make it, most people don't care how, but if you're poor, well now, they just pity you and shake their heads." His voice took on a rolling, angry cadence. "Hell, with money you can even get away with being liberal. But if you're poor and liberal, people just think you're peculiar. Oh, they'll never be sure whether you're a liberal because you're poor or poor because you're a liberal, but they're damn sure it's one or the other.

"Now you wonder why I tell you this." Cade stopped to glower at me with a strange, transcendent rage. "It's because I don't ever intend to see my daughter beholden. I love her more than you could ever understand. I have no wife, no son to call my own, but by God I have Kris Ann. And I've always planned that she not need anything.

"But life has a way of surprising you. You can't plan for everything. Lately some of my investments have gone a little sour. So I might need your help now." His voice turned sarcastic. "You might even have to be a little bit of a success. That's why I can't let you ruin Henry Cantwell. Because if you turn up something that gets Henry indicted you'll not only destroy my friend but your own reputation. And then you couldn't find work as a bootblack."

"Henry's not your ward, Roland. And neither is Kris Ann, like it or not."

Cade reddened. "I'm taking you off the Cantwell case. Tomorrow you're going to march to your office, close the door, and start preparing for that Stafford trial."

"All for Kris Ann and Henry."

"For them, and for the firm."

I shook my head. "No, Roland, it's mostly

for you. I've heard that speech about loving Kris Ann one too many times, when you've done your damnedest to leave her without any sense of herself outside of your world. That's not love and never has been. It's ownership."

Cade was very still, as if holding back. Then, with a thin smile, he said softly, "But you didn't take her north, did you, Adam?"

I stood. "You miserable sonofabitch—"

Kris Ann opened the front door to announce dinner, saw our faces, and stopped in mid-sentence. Cade murmured, "We'll finish this at the firm," and then looked to Kris Ann and said in a different voice, "We're coming, honey."

Dinner was better than the conversation. I ate in silence while Cade asked Kris Ann about her tennis and her cousin's baby. Watching her was painful. Her gestures were sharp and nervous and her smile came late and left nothing behind. When Cade purred, "The next few weeks Adam's to be quite busy on our Stafford case," she lapsed into silence, as if at some unspoken punishment for her choice of a husband.

Finally I cleared the dishes, something I did when the maid wasn't there. Kris Ann liked cooking, but hated to clean. When we'd first been married she would throw things in the dishwasher still dirty, so that they'd come out with traces of last night's dinner baked on, like the evidence of some geologic period. When I'd joke that the progress of her cooking would be preserved in layers, for posterity, she'd grinned back and said dirty dishes weren't her *metier*. So I'd taken them on again, while she drank coffee and offered me solemn advice. It had all been very droll, once.

I was alone in the kitchen when the phone rang.

"Adam," the familiar voice said. "Can you come by?"

FIFTEEN

I left right after Cade, locking the doors behind me. Kris Ann watched me go in silence.

The Cantwell place was almost black. When I knocked, Etta Parsons answered and led me to the library with an air of cool unrecognition. "Mr. Cantwell will be down momentarily," she said, and left.

For a while I paced the sitting room. It was the same, yet eerily different. Someone had replaced Lydia's picture with one that was older and smaller. The effect was uncannily that of a fading presence. Two sliding oak doors sealed the dining room.

I went back to the library.

The evening paper was folded by Henry's chair. I began riffling the sports section for box scores, as my father had taught me.

"Hello, Adam."

Henry Cantwell had appeared with two

snifters of cognac. I put down the box scores to take one.

"How are you?" I asked.

"Better."

I wondered. Henry had lost the pallor of the day before, but the hesitance of his movements, a slight dreaminess in the eyes, were like those of a man after his first stroke. There was a rim of loose skin beneath his eyes and the start of slackness in his jawline I hadn't noticed before. The haircut for Lydia's funeral made his ears too large. "I've been wondering how to help," I told him. "Sometimes I think people hover when what they're really doing is relieving their own grief, not a kindness at all."

Henry gave a thin smile, and his expression turned curious and kind. "Your father was murdered, too, wasn't he?"

"Yes. He was."

I glanced around, unsettled by the familiar surface of things: the cognac and quiet, a space in the bookshelf, something being reread in another part of the house. Henry followed my glance to the space. "I'm leafing through *Lady Chatterley* again," he said calmly. "Lawrence treats the emotions so well, don't you think?"

I flushed, managing to nod. Henry swirled the cognac in his glass, seemingly lost in Lawrence's impotent husband and restless wife. Then he said, "Jason called this evening." His eyes rose from the glass. "He was raving.

But he managed to get across that you were asking about Dalton Mooring."

"I was," I said flatly. "Roland called me off. He says it hurts you. I'm afraid I've hurt you already."

He shook his head. "Don't be. I've already faced what my life has come to." He looked slowly around the room. "When my grandfather built this house, he'd already founded your firm and married my grandmother, whose father owned the bank. He left this house, the firm, and," he smiled wryly, "a bank for leftover Cantwells. The way most people see it I was fanned out in my twenties. I've hated that bank ever since, and done badly. Caring for other people's money was a responsibility I never wanted, and now—" He stopped to look straight at me. "I failed there, and failed even here. You see, Adam, our marriage was a charade."

I could think of nothing to say. The light on Henry's face was yellow and pitiless. "Lydia and I hadn't been truly married for a very long time. Something in the chemistry, I suppose..." His voice fell off. "It's so odd—last night I was trying to remember first being with Lydia and all that came back to me was that her shoes always matched her dress. Imagine remembering Kris Ann for something like that." He shook his head. "The void showed up in Jason: love is learned and Jason had little to learn from watching us. I withdrew and Lydia smothered him as if he were her hope in life. It was a problem for the boy. He fought to be free of her, but she was his obsession."

Henry paused to stare out the window next to him, black and flat and skyless. "You could see that in his politics and even in his girlfriends. It wasn't enough for Jason to sleep with someone. His mother had to know, poor boy." He turned back to me, voice quiet with embarrassment. "I failed them both miserably. So there's little now that can hurt me no matter what you find, unless Jason had some part in it. And that I can never accept."

"You may have to. Roland thinks he killed her."

Henry's expression was tragic. "That would be too horrible." He almost whispered. "You see, Jason's birth was the only reason Lydia and I stayed married. For it to end like this..."

I sipped some cognac. "He does have an alibi, you know. His girlfriend."

He nodded. "What kind of girl is she, Adam?"

"I don't know. She seems quiet and not quite formed. Perhaps I'm getting older. But she clearly cares for him."

"That's all Jason wanted," Henry said sadly. "It doesn't seem much, does it?"

"It doesn't necessarily seem easy, either."

"He said you fought. How did it happen?"

"He said something. I lost my head."

"He has an instinct for hurt. It's ruined sensitivity, I'm afraid."

I shrugged. "I pushed him too far. I shouldn't have."

"You're all right, I hope. You look bruised."

"I'm okay. I boxed some at the CYO when I was a kid and it kind of came back."

"Stay away from him," Henry said seriously. "I mean that. He's an unstable man, full of jealousies you don't know anything about."

"He managed to get some of that across."

"So it seems." Henry's voice was tentative. "Adam, why did you ask about Dalton Mooring?"

I hesitated. "Nothing hard. Just little things, times they were together. Is it possible, Henry?"

He rocked back and forth in his chair. "It's possible," he finally said. "It never struck me particularly, but at the club they would always dance." He closed his eyes, as if to see them dancing. "He's known her for a long time," he murmured. His eyes opened. "Adam, I want you to check this out."

I shook my head. "Roland absolutely forbids it."

"But I have to know." He pointed at the newspaper. "You've seen the headlines, I'm sure. All day reporters have called or just pounded on the door. I can't keep on living under this shadow."

"Rayfield's got toll slips, you know. They prove your call to Lydia was twelve minutes, not two."

He looked chagrined. "I suppose I was foolish. We'd fought, you see. Sitting there, I just couldn't talk about it."

"You shouldn't have been there at all. But now you'd better tell me what was said."

"Nothing, really. Just"—his mouth twisted—"accumulated disappointments. Personal things. Nothing about the will."

"You're sure."

"Yes."

"And after that you just stayed there."

He nodded. "Yes. Please, Adam, I need your help on this."

I hesitated. But Henry's voice had a desperate edge. "You're the client," I finally said. "It's your job to tell Roland what you want, and who."

"I will," he said flatly. Finishing the cognac, he dabbed his lips with a cloth napkin. "Is that any better—you and Roland?"

"Worse. We had a blow-up tonight. I've committed heresy by thought, word, and deed."

"That's a problem with Kris Ann, isn't it?"

"It can be."

Henry's face hardened. "What Roland did to Kris Ann was a terrible thing. It was unnatural—I don't mean literally, but psychologically. I remember talking to her after her mother died. She was maybe seven or eight, wide-eyed and a little sad, and beautiful even then. She was talking about Margaret's death like a child does, not quite understanding, and then she said Roland had told her that she could take her mother's place and then they'd never need anyone else. She seemed excited and a little disturbed. God knows it disturbed me.

"Later it disturbed me more. Roland never showed interest in remarrying. Instead he devoted himself to becoming a local power and running Kris Ann's life. He sent her to private schools and all those lessons—piano, dance, everything but art—as if he wanted to starve the thing she really cared about. And more and more he began to substitute her for her mother, using her as hostess, taking her to dinner, making her the central figure in his life, as he was in hers. Love or ego, whatever it was, he was too central. The result was rather sad: at times, Kris Ann would seem self-confident and even precocious, and then she'd shrink in his presence, as if he could turn all that off like a switch. I wouldn't be surprised if on some level she resents him terribly."

"If she does, I wouldn't know it."

"But then you're very close to it, and you don't know the background. Kris Ann grew up always comparing young men to her father, who intimidated them. Gradually the local boys learned to shy away. That had to be very difficult for her. One thing Lydia and I agreed on was that we were glad you came along. We thought perhaps you were strong enough to give Kris Ann a chance. I still think that."

I shook my head. "It may be too late. I should never have moved here."

"Roland takes over lives. I wanted to tell you that he needed you close because you were the one he couldn't get rid of. But I didn't know you then."

"God, Henry, I wish you had." I fumbled for a cigarette. "What was her mother like? Krissy hardly mentions her."

He leaned back, empty snifter cupped in his

hands. "Margaret was very much a lady, pretty in a delicate way and rather passive. That's not an unusual choice in domineering men. She treated Roland like he hung the moon, which is what he wants. As for intellect or vitality, I'm afraid Kris Ann owes those to Roland. In any event, Margaret became ill with cancer and just withered away. And that left Kris Ann with Roland."

The last was said with clear distaste. "I've always wondered," I said, "how it is that you and he are friends."

His mouth was a bitter line. "I suppose we're playing out something that began when we were young. I admired his sureness then. Perhaps I was even flattered that he seemed to cultivate me. After a time he came here so often he was like family. My father was quite taken with, him. Eventually Roland became my father's protégé at the firm, and I was eased out to the bank. I think now that Roland had always had that in mind: he wanted money and power very badly. But he was charming, worked like the devil for his clients, and more and more my father came to rely on him." Henry sounded almost bemused. "I still saw him, of course, though not so often. But by the time my father died he'd been handling our family's affairs for several years and it just went on from there. As I said, Roland takes over lives..."

The sentence died off. Carefully, Henry added, "I may ask too much, pitting you against Roland with Kris Ann in between. He'll do anything to keep the upper hand."

"You should worry about yourself. Roland says I'll end up getting you indicted as a jealous husband."

"I'll take that chance. It's your career that concerns me, and your marriage."

I lit the cigarette. "Our marriage is what we've made it. As for my career, what good has that ever done anyone? We sit down there filling up time sheets so that every month we can send bills to the x-many corporations who pay for big houses we don't really need. Hell, you're one of the few clients I like or even think about."

He smiled wispily. "What else would you do?"

I shrugged. "I used to know, when I was a kid. I don't anymore."

His smile vanished. "Permit me, Adam. I've done badly with Jason, I know, but please, don't live one of those lives of 'quiet desperation.' Find out what it is you want."

"Right now I want to help you. There'll be time for the rest."

He gave me a complex look of gratitude, worry, and relief. "You're certain?"

"Of course. There is one thing, though. About Rayfield, do you know of any reason for him to have feelings about you one way or the other? Run-ins with Jason, even?"

He paused. Then he shook his head and answered tonelessly, "It makes no sense to me, Adam."

His voice was tired. I decided he'd had enough. "I should be getting back to Kris Ann."

"You should. Especially now."

I stood, began to leave, then stopped. "About you and Lydia—"

"Yes?"

"It's just that I'd never have guessed."

His smile was wan. "Then I suppose we succeeded—on one level."

"I'm sorry it wasn't more, Henry."

"That was never meant," he said gently. "Here, let me see you out."

We walked through the silent house, past the dining room. Opening the door, he said, "I hope you know, Adam, how much I appreciate this."

I placed a hand on his shoulder. "No need. God knows how many reasons I have to help."

The cool clear look he gave me said he understood perfectly. "Don't worry about Roland," he said. "I'll tell him myself." We left it there.

I drove off, absorbing what I'd seen and heard. There was something inconsolable about Henry Cantwell that seemed to reach beyond Lydia to the core of his life and steep him in a terrible calm. I figured he had faced the worst, and told me everything.

I began thinking of Henry and Lydia and Jason until, suddenly, I wanted to talk with Kris Ann—of my own parents, of Cade and her, and how the flaws of one generation could run through the next like a bad inheritance, if you let them. But I found her sleeping amidst a black tangle of hair almost phosphorescent in the moonlight, the revolver lying next to her. I put it in the drawer, and gently closed it.

Downstairs, restless, I roamed the house until I saw the book I had borrowed, *Grangeville: A Southern Tragedy*, next to a chair in the sunroom. I picked it up and began turning its pages.

After a moment I sat. Four hours passed in smoking and reading by one dim lamp. I hardly noticed.

It was beautifully written. The author drew me into the warp and woof of the past: Grangeville in the thirties, a courthouse and some red brick buildings in north Alabama, its people embittered by the Depression and the loss of a railroad yard, scratching crops from red clay mostly rock and sand. The town's eccentric Republican past, back through the Civil War. The irony that few blacks had ever lived there, just a handful.

One sweltering summer day in 1937, an old farmer with a shotgun had found one of them in his barn, mounting a white girl with her dress pulled up. A second black was there: the blacksmith, the first man's brother. A man with a wife and son.

They were prodded with shotguns to the small jail, the first man saying he'd paid her three dollars and that his brother, the blacksmith, had come to warn that sleeping with a white girl was no good. The blacksmith swore to that, and it was known that other men had paid her. But the girl said she was raped. A mob gathered in front of the jail shouting for the blacks.

Her white customers stopped talking, joining the frenzy of a town whose real enemies could not be punished.

Within two weeks the men were on trial for rape before Lydia Cantwell's father and an all-white jury. Judge Hargrave ruled out evidence of prostitution. Three days later the blacks were found guilty and sentenced to death. In a riptide of publicity, against all reason except politics, clemency was denied. In January 1939, appeals exhausted, both men were electrocuted.

I finished too wrung out to look back at the pictures. But, two cigarettes later, I did.

The trial had been well covered. Judge, jurors, spectators, and accused had been amply photographed, and the writer had chosen with care. White spectators in bow ties or overalls stared from history's fever swamp, dim eyes seeing nothing of how time would view them. Lydia's father presided from his hand-carved bench, mouth a dutiful line. Northern newsmen in hats were there for another glimpse of the Sahara of the Bozart. The two black men leaned away from their white lawyer. Outside the spired courthouse the family of the blacksmith, Moses McCarroll, waited. A wife and a small boy.

I stopped there. There was something wrong with the picture. Something else.

I went to the kitchen and pulled a glassine bag of marijuana from the cabinet. Then I got a bowl and strainer and set them with the bag on the kitchen table. I sat down, opening the bag to put some of the brown, dirt-smelling dope in the strainer. I rubbed it back and forth until only seeds were left and the dope was fine powder in the bowl. Then I went to a drawer for the roller, put in powder and paper, licked the paper, and rolled a joint the size of a Lucky Strike. I did that twice. Then I pushed the excess powder from the bowl to the bag, and put away bag, roller, and paper. The two joints went with me to the porch.

There was nothing outside but crickets and a moon and wet, dank air. I lit a joint, lay back on the wicker couch, and smoked and slipped away into the second joint, and then the crickets were all around me...

I was trapped. The pictures roared around dark corners in an express train of white streaks and flashes. The back of my eyes and neck hurt like too much whiskey but the pictures wouldn't stop.

Lydia Cantwell's blue shoes matched her dress, but her tongue came from a rictus smile. Then a black man twisted with orange lightning while a small boy watched and I stood back. The man kept on shaking until my father threw me the baseball, beneath the elms in back.

It was all right, I remembered that. I could even feel the stitches as I threw it back to him, though he was quite pale. "You'll be a pitcher, then," he said.

But I knew now. "No sir, I want to be a policeman. Like you."

My father looked concerned and held the ball. "But why, Adam?"

"Because I want to know the truth."

Before he could answer, the police were at the door and my mother screamed that he was murdered. It was funny. It was happening again and still I couldn't cry. Then Cade said I could have the dark-haired woman if I did as my mother said. The champagne turned bitter in my mouth.

It was cold now and there was noise from the gnarled bushes next door. I had to kill the noises, but couldn't move. My vertebrae had snapped. Footsteps stamped the leaves and branches. Henry Cantwell with no eyes quivered with orange lightning that lifted him out of sight as someone laughed. I knew the laugh but couldn't place it. The fish swam away. The black boy followed alone.

The noise came closer. They would kill me now. There was nowhere to go and I had to tell my father I was sorry.

I awoke just before morning when the night is like thin smoke. The sweat had dried cold on my face. There was no one in the bushes.

I got the bag of dope and threw it out.

Kris Ann was still asleep. I laid out some clean clothes on a chair and went for a run. The morning was bright and clear and filled with nothing but facts.

I came home, showered, and drank coffee with Kris Ann without speaking of Henry, or us. Then I crossed the backyard to the car.

I was behind the wheel before I saw the scrap of paper crumpled beneath the rubber blade of my windshield wiper. I got out and lifted the blade to unfold it.

It was Kris Ann's picture, from the newspaper. A pencil had etched harsh age lines by her eyes, nose, and mouth until she was a wrinkled old woman. There were holes where her pupils had been.

SIXTEEN

Kris Ann was in the attic, old shirt half-unbuttoned, staring at her easel in shafts of sunlight that came through the window behind her. Resting one hand on her shoulder I glanced dully at the painting, a nightmare of blues and purples surrounding the orange stick-figure of a woman. Then I held the scrap in front of her. "I found this on my windshield," I said.

As if by instinct she brushed her fingertips across the surface of her face. Her voice was flat. "Is that how Lydia's picture was?"

"The eyes. It's probably just meant to scare us."

"Why?"

"I don't know." I put the scrap in my pocket and pulled her up to me. "Krissy, I want you to go to your cousin's for a while. Just until this is over."

Her lips parted. "We should call the police."

"We will. I want you safe. But I'm still not

sure you would be. Last night Henry asked if I'd stay on the case."

I felt her stiffen. "And you told him you would," she said tonelessly. "In spite of Daddy."

I nodded. "That's why you've got to leave."

"But if we've gone to the police—"

"It's not that simple. I'm caught in a vise. I know things that might make Henry look different than he is. Rayfield's going to sense that. Protecting my wife won't be his first priority. You'll be safer out of state."

She leaned back from me, searching my face. Then she shook her head in a long, slow arc. "I'm staying, Adam."

I grasped her shoulders. "Please, listen. This won't end well, not with you here. Even without this threat you'll be trapped between Roland and me in a case where Henry's over-ridden him. Those cards are going to be played out this time. You don't want to be a part of that."

Her stare was long and probing. "But I am now," she said quietly. "Aren't I?"

My palms were damp. "Think, Krissy. Last night you were so afraid of Jason Cantwell I found you sleeping with a gun. This morning I'm at least that scared. It's not just Henry now. This thing has become part of our lives. Don't make it any worse than it is."

"And running away would help? How do I know *you* won't be killed?"

I tried smiling. "I'm too young."

"You're thirty-two," she said levelly. "So

151

was your father. Isn't that beginning to bother you?"

"Why should it?"

"Because of the way you're pushing—"

"Look, I need to find out who's doing this. I don't want you to be hurt before I do. It's that simple."

She shook her head with finality. "No, Adam. You've made your decision. Now I'm making mine."

"But it's senseless—"

"To you." She stepped back, eyes burning with a low, angry, smoky intensity. "Look at me, dammit. I'm twenty-nine and it feels like I've spent my whole life waiting for you and Daddy to decide how I'll spend the rest of it. I can't stand by anymore. I can't go cover my eyes while the two of you fight this out."

Her face had set in a remote determination hauntingly like Cade's. The attic seemed filled with trapped heat and the smell of paint. We faced each other, waiting. "I'll go see Rayfield," I said in a low voice. "Call Rennie Kell. I'll drop you there."

She watched me another moment, then silently began cleaning up her paints. I went through the house checking doors and windows while she finished and called the Kells. When I dropped her there she turned, said slowly and seriously, "I don't want you hurt, Adam," and got out of the car without looking back. I watched until she was inside.

I found Rayfield arranging a deskful of ragged papers ripped from his notebooks, as if trying to make sense of a senseless world. Surprised in thought, he seemed for a moment both old and innocent. Then his face went tough.

"What do you want?"

I tossed the scrap in front of him. "That used to be a picture of my wife. Someone did the artwork and left it on my windshield."

He looked at it carefully, turning it once to check the back for marks. "Know who, or why?"

"Not who. The obvious why is the Cantwell case. I want protection for Kris Ann."

"And what will you do for us?"

"My job. I'm asking that you do yours."

He looked at me shrewdly. "Then tell me who drives the green Cadillac Otis Lee saw at the Cantwells'."

I paused, glancing at my fingernails, then back to Rayfield. "I don't know."

His eyes narrowed. Coldly he said, "Tell your wife to take a vacation."

"She won't go without me, and I can't."

"Yeah." His face was hard. "You so busy and all. If you wanted to be your father, Shaw, you should have just been a cop."

I flushed. "You've been wasting time."

"We check backgrounds. After I found you'd been poking around Otis Lee and the Parsons woman I checked yours." He sounded as though information were power. "I turned up the usual things. At St. Ignatius you were all-city quarterback but got an academic scholarship for Notre Dame and another to Vanderbilt Law. When you married Cade's daughter you were flat broke."

"Brilliant work, Lieutenant."

"And then," he went smoothly on, "I dug some more and discovered that of all things your father was a cop. I'm sorry about what happened, Shaw."

I looked around at the dim hanging lights, gray tile, gray desks with gray faces behind them. "It's like you said about Grangeville," I answered. "That was a long time ago."

"It's strange, though, how your family has a history of violence. Like your grandfather leaving Ireland because he'd killed a British soldier."

I shrugged. "He needed work, unemployment being what it was. Maybe when you quit toying with me we can get back to my wife."

A telephone rang across the room. Rayfield watched it until someone answered. "Who else have you been talking to?"

I guessed that he was still looking for a driver to go with Lee's description of the car. A sad, stray thought of Kris Ann went through me as I said, "No one."

"Quit playing games," he snapped. "You want protection for your wife and you won't tell me shit. You'll end up getting her killed."

"Is that a threat?" I asked angrily.

"It's an observation." His face turned curious, analytic. "It seems you're more interested in protecting Henry Cantwell than your own wife."

"That's an odd remark."

He kept staring. "Is it?"

"Look, Lieutenant, Kris Ann needs protection. I'm not asking for me or Cade or Cantwell, but for her who's got no part in any of this."

Dislike for me warred on his face with whatever kept him a cop. Finally he scribbled some numbers on a pad of paper. His voice was flat. "The top one's the police emergency number. The other two are where she can get me or Bast if we're not here. Days I'll have a patrolman look in and if she calls someone will be there. You'll be home nights, I hope."

"I should."

He looked down at Kris Ann's photo. "Tell me, Shaw, how do you know Cantwell didn't do this?"

"That's ridiculous. Henry's known my wife since she was small."

He paused. "Thing is, we've never let out what had been done to the eyes. You tell anyone?"

"Just Kris Ann."

"Then the only other person who knows for sure is the one who killed Mrs. Cantwell. I'd think about that. You in particular should think about that."

"I already have."

"Think harder," he said harshly. "Because I'm going to get him even if it's Henry Cantwell. You don't want to be in the way."

We stared at each other. At length, I said, "Thanks for your help."

He shrugged. "They told me your father was

a good cop. Except maybe the last." He looked down at the scraps of paper and began working again.

I shut the office door behind me and slumped in my chair, thinking. Then I picked up the telephone and dialed the main number at Auburn University. Five minutes and four transfers later a deep voice answered, "Ransom."

"This is Adam Shaw, Professor, a lawyer, in Birmingham. I've just read your book on Grangeville."

"Yes?"

"I'd like to ask about your research. It's for a case I'm working."

There was a pause. "Grangeville was forty years ago, sir. I don't see what it could relate to."

"I'm not sure, exactly, but it's about Judge Hargrave's daughter, Mrs. Cantwell. She's been murdered."

"Yes, I saw that." Ransom's voice—rheumy, ancient, and bourbonous—lent the odd sensation of speaking to history. "Whom do you represent?" he asked.

"The husband. Henry Cantwell."

"The papers made it sound like he killed her."

"Forty years ago, Professor, some of the papers made it sound like two black men raped a vestal virgin."

"True enough. What do you want?"

"The blacksmith, Moses McCarroll had a small boy. Do you know where he is?"

"Nooo," he said thoughtfully, "never found

him. It was 'fifty-seven when I started my research. You can guess how popular it was back then, especially after Little Rock when Eisenhower sent the troops in. People weren't always helpful. Anyhow, Moses McCarroll's wife had died in nineteen thirty-nine, and the boy just disappeared. Never found any relatives who would talk about it."

"Know who I might try?"

"Most everyone's dead, Mr. Shaw. Except Luther Channing."

"The assistant prosecutor?"

"That's right. Channing's retired now, but still alive. One of my students tried to interview him not too long ago and got thrown off the porch. He's a steely bastard. Wouldn't talk to me, either."

"I'll try him anyhow. Thanks, Professor."

"No thanks needed. Mrs. Cantwell was one I always felt sorry for. Tried talking to her once at her house. When I said what I wanted, she began shaking her head. Could hardly talk. Finally she said she was sorry and shut the door. Two weeks later I got a note apologizing. I remember it: small, ladylike writing—I've still got it somewhere. Said she understood my reasons, but she couldn't speak of it and hoped I understood. I never published it, felt too badly for her. She was just a child back then, too."

"Yes, sir. She was."

There was a long silence. "Mr. Shaw," he said slowly, "that boy, if he's still alive, is over fifty now."

"I know."

"If I follow your reasoning, that would be a terrible circle, wouldn't it?"

"Yes, it would. But then people's lives seem to be full of them."

"Well, let me know if you find him." He spoke heavily, as if feeling the weight of the past. "Though I almost hope you don't."

I said I could understand that, and hung up.

I called the Kells to give Kris Ann the telephone numbers and ask her to stay. Just a few more hours, I promised. Then I went to the car and drove north toward Grangeville.

SEVENTEEN

Yellow stripes split the two-lane blacktop in a blur racing backward toward Birmingham. Ahead the road ran through fields of crops and rock and harsh red clay, hacked from pine forests and marked by stunted oaks. Amidst a sprawling cornfield the sun-blackened figure of a farmer hoed patiently. Now and then I passed desultory civilization: junkyards, stores, trailers, roadhouses, Baptist churches and cemeteries—the small towns whose people lived, died, hunted, prayed, made love and whiskey, and were carelessly killed in a sun so hot it took the stomach from you at midday. Vaporous heat rising thinly from the road lent the landscapes a cruel, shimmering beauty. Birmingham had ceased to exist.

After an hour or so I passed a blue sweep of lakes nestled in low piny hills and speckled with rowboats and a few shirtless men standing hip-deep with flyrods. Then bait shops began, then gas stations, a small sign marking the turn for Grangeville, two miles of bare asphalt, and I was there.

Past a few stores and a Church of Christ whose sign promised that "Blessed Are the Optimists," the road stopped at the town square. It was surrounded by quaint stores and packed with shoppers strolling among sidewalk stands. At its center was a green rolling lawn shaded by oak trees. From their midst the bell tower of the county courthouse rose to a painted gold spire, gleaming in the sun as it had when the black woman and small boy had stood outside, waiting.

I parked and began walking toward a corner phone booth at the end of the crowded sidewalk, weaving among stands and people there from long tradition: Grangeville Trading Day, held for eighty years the first Thursday of the month. Parents and children ambled among handmade quilts and factory-made junk while vendors watched with studied indifference. A sidewalk fiddler in wire-rimmed glasses sawed vigorously and on the grass boys chased a small black dog past shade trees where men sat whittling with keen-edged knives. Their seamed faces spoke of lives spent in harsh sun and the older ones were strikingly the same: sharp chins and noses, spectral eyes, flat cheekbones with cheeks so gaunt they were like grooves. They talked and whittled with utter lassitude, like the fallout from a hundred years of inbreeding.

I got to the phone booth and went through the directory. Then I approached one of the old men, whittling in overalls, wood shavings curled at his feet. "Help me find something?" I asked.

He spat a brown stream of tobacco juice and looked up with a surprising smile that lacked several teeth. "Might could." The words were guttural and half-swallowed. "What you looking for?"

"Montgomery Street. Luther Channing's place."

His smile inverted. "That'd be the old Hargrave place," he said flatly.

"How do I get there?"

He looked me up and down, then pointed. "Take Main and turn left at the third street. Big, shadowy white house on the right. Only one like it."

"Thanks."

He spat and looked away. I went to the car.

Montgomery Street was lined by maples and haphazard small-town architecture, mainly tan brick houses built close to the street. Two blocks down the right side was a lawn several acres deep with a straight drive running between a quarter mile of parallel oaks. I turned, driving across their shadows until I spotted the white frame house at the end, concealed by more oaks. When I finally parked, I saw that the house was three antebellum stories. Its wide, shady porch had stairs at both ends, and in one corner two empty gliders hung facing each other. Five whitewashed steps rose to it between lilacs a soft mauve color. The grounds were still save for a single orange butterfly jittering among the lilacs. I went to the front door and knocked.

After a moment there were footsteps on the other side of the door. It was opened by an old man with eyes a shocking, opalescent gray.

"Yes?" he demanded.

"Mr. Channing?" He nodded. "I'm Adam Shaw, a lawyer from Birmingham. If it's all right, I'd like a moment, of your time."

"Without calling? What about?"

"The Grangeville case, partly."

His eyes glinted. "I've talked about that once in forty years, and not to a stranger." He poised to slam the door.

"Also about Lydia Cantwell," I added quickly. "You saw she was murdered?"

His hand stopped. "Go on."

"Just that it may have something to do with your case."

"What's your interest in Lydia?"

"I represent Henry Cantwell. The husband."

I looked past him as he scrutinized me. Through the hallway was a dark living room: two chairs, a lamp, and a standing clock, all antiques, as neatly arranged as if no one lived there. There was something deadly about it: Channing lived in a museum. The clock ticked behind him.

"I'll listen," he said at last and stepped onto the porch, slamming the door. "Out here."

He pointed toward the two gliders, moving toward the far one. He was a tall man and his walk, straight and gliding, held the last vestige of youthful grace. But his vulpine face was ravaged. Two red scrapes on his cheek looked like skin cancer, with a white mark beneath them where more had been removed. Lank, white-yellow hair hung lifelessly over his forehead and to his collar in back. In his linen suit, he looked like a well-bred version of the whittling men, in worse health. I wondered who the suit was for.

"Speak up," he said harshly.

"I'm sorry. I was wondering if Mrs. Cantwell used to live here."

His eyes riveted me, as though he knew of their effect and used it. "She did," he said finally. "When she was Lydia Hargrave. I bought the place after her mother died. She didn't want it."

I could see why, though, looking at the shady grounds and flowers in orderly plots, its air of perfect unreality seemed to match Lydia's. "You've kept it up nicely," I said.

"Someone had to. Is that what you came to say?"

"No. I wanted to ask about one of the defendants. Moses McCarroll."

His voice, rough and old and hollow, held a note of malice. "What about him?"

"I wanted to know about the trial, and what happened to his family afterwards."

"Don't know much about the last." He crossed one leg in a seeming act of will. "You find that strange?"

"I'm trying to imagine myself in your position."

"Understand something, then." He coughed, phlegm rattling in his throat. "The two nigras weren't the issue."

"I suppose that depends on your point of view."

He held a handkerchief close to his mouth and spat into it. "Where you from?"

"Cleveland."

"And raised very right-minded, I'm sure. The one thing more certain than that you didn't know any southerners is that you didn't know any blacks."

"I'm not arguing. I came to ask you things, not tell you."

"All right." He looked at me sharply. "Driving through here, did you look around?"

"Some."

"Look very wealthy to you?"

"Just this place."

He ignored that. "Forty-odd years ago it was worse. The soil had gone from bad to farmed-out. When the Depression hit, Grangeville was so poor that for a while you hardly noticed. Then the L & N shut down the railroad yard. Three hundred men lost their jobs. Stores shut, just flat closed. People starved. They'd sweated and prayed and had nothing to show for it except rain that washed away the topsoil. One farmer hanged himself in his barn. Lucy Vines—the one with those two nigras—turned whore because of it.

"I'd been at law school and came back young and full of ambition, looking to lawyer awhile and then run for state senate. What I found was a town full of angry people and half the legal work in foreclosures where people hated your guts. So I got on at the prosecutor's and started going to meetings, just listening and being seen. And what I heard was anger.

"I hadn't been prosecuting six months—a couple of chicken thieves and a farmer who shot his wife for fornicating and admitted it—and then Roy Cobb found that nigra in his barn, rutting on Lucy Vines. Roy was a man of settled opinions, and right then and there he fetched his shotgun and ran all three of them into the courthouse: Lucy, the nigra, and his brother. It was blazing hot, nothing but fat, lazy flies coming through the windows and the usual bunch sitting on the steps that there'd been since the yard shut down. When, they saw Roy prodding the two blacks and Lucy she began screaming rape. News got out fast. Pretty soon a whole crowd of those blank-eyed morons were on the front steps howling for the nigras and some rope, all crazy and excited. Might have done it, too. The nigras were something they could reach out and touch."

He spoke with dispassionate savagery: the McCarrolls seemed hardly to exist and his compassion for the townspeople was mingled with contempt. "What stopped them?" I asked.

He didn't answer, suddenly absorbed in a black fly that had landed on the glider. It crept nearer his hand. Two inches, then one. The fly stopped. Seconds passed. Channing was perfectly still. The fly turned and began marching back across the cushion. Channing watched narrowly. Two inches, three inches, four... I felt a foolish relief. With a sudden snap Channing's palm smacked down and closed. Then, slowly, he brought his fist to chest level and opened it. The smashed fly dropped on the porch. Channing's eyes were like clear ice.

"We've talked enough," he rasped.

I stared at the fly. "You haven't told me anything."

"Why should I? What are you to me?"

"I'm nothing to you. I'm just here."

He turned toward the grounds. Afternoon shadows were moving toward the house and sluggish winds wafted the scent of lilac. Channing's long fingers rubbed silently together. There was no sound except the glider creaking under his weight. "George Naylor was the prosecutor," he said abruptly. "He sat there, sweat dripping down his three chins, mumbling, 'We never had no nigra problem,' which wasn't surprising since we'd never had any nigras except the McCarrolls. By then the lawn was covered with townsfolk and farmers in overalls making that low, ugly mob sound that's not like anything else. Our moon-faced sheriff, Bohannon, is pacing in front of George's desk whining that he can't hold back the crowd. 'I know these folks,' he keeps saying. 'They're my friends.' George stares at him without answering. Finally he sucks himself up and steps out on the porch. The sound gets even lower, like some animal. George has this high-pitched voice; I can barely hear him trying to ask the mob for trust. 'Just give us the rope,' a voice yells back. 'Before you do that,' George pleads, 'stop and think if being part of a mob isn't the lowest thing a man can do. If you men let the law just handle this we'll try these nigras in two weeks.' I remember thinking two weeks was pretty fast. But after George promised that, they just milled around without rushing the jail. Finally he came back in, sat down sort of heavy, and said, 'We've got work to do, Luther.' 'Then you'd better find out what your case is,' I answered."

Channing still looked away, voice edged with disdain.

"We went down the hall and had the sheriff bring in Lucy Vines. She sat on a stool, slack-mouthed and not looking up, saying the McCarrolls had raped her—the boy, anyhow. George asked about six different ways if that were true. Lucy wouldn't budge. When she'd left, George just shook his head and mumbled, 'Jesus Christ.' "

"I guess Lucy couldn't have said anything else."

Channing turned to stare at me. "Well," he said coldly, "she could have confessed to whoring with nigras."

He spoke with contempt, I thought for me. "What about the McCarrolls?" I asked.

"George and I went to look them over. The one that'd had the girl—Lucius—was shaking. Moses stood with both hands on the bars asking in this deep nigra voice to see his woman and boy. 'Don't be a fool,' I told him. 'You want them lynched, too?' Big tears came rolling down his face, and he said, 'But I didn't do nothing.' 'Then you're better off here,' I answered, and after that he shut up."

My stomach felt tight. "How did he get convicted?"

Channing folded his arms. "What's that have to do with Lydia Cantwell?"

"I think she may have been killed because of how her father dealt with the McCarrolls. That's what I'm trying to learn about."

For once someone didn't say that Grangeville was a long time back. "John Hargrave was an idiot," he said flatly. "Handsome in an empty way but vain as a peacock. Even of Lydia: when she was only seven or eight he'd parade her around the courthouse in braids and ribbons just to see you smile. She was pretty, too, even then. But that was Hargrave. He looked at you as if your face was a mirror, like he didn't really see you except to wonder how he should feel about himself that day. Hadn't been a judge but one month when he hangs a painting of himself in the courthouse. Let it out he was going to be governor. Three years later he was gone and so was the painting. Only thing he's remembered for is this.

"Morning after they brought the nigras in, Hargrave came to George looking very serious, especially about himself. He sat in front of George's desk and told him in his pompous way that if he and George wanted to stand tall in Monroe County they'd better give this nigra case their best. He didn't have to explain his meaning. George just stares at him, sweating. He'd already turned on the ceiling fan and it had blown half the papers off his desk, but George kept wiping his forehead. Finally he answered, 'I understand, Judge.' Hargrave gets this peculiar look in his eye, kind of far off. Doesn't say a word more. Just nods and smiles.

"When he's gone, George just sits there with the fan blowing his silly flowered tie in all directions. After a long time he mutters, 'Biggest case since the monkey trial,' sticks on his hat, and goes home.

"He didn't show until the next afternoon, with purple hollows under his eyes and hair hanging down his forehead. For two weeks he didn't say anything that wasn't business, even about Lucy. She came in to prepare her testimony eating an ice cream cone. George snapped at her to throw it away, not like him at all. Then he drills her on her story and after she's got it down and he's told her how to dress, he throws her out and starts fussing over the next detail. It was the most overprepared rape case in human history. None of that helped. Come the trial, George was a sight.

"The thing was won from when Hargrave appointed C. W. Baxter to defend, who'd been drunk ten years and just wanted to get back to the barn without losing friends. But the court was jammed with townsfolk and Yankee reporters who'd come down by train, and all that plus the heat started making George a little sick.

"Except for Hargrave we were all in suspenders. It was so hot that even with the windows open my shirt stuck to me, and after a spell the crowd settled down to breathing and fanning themselves with this kind of low whoosh. First day they pick a jury of impartial white men and then George puts on Lucy, wearing pigtails and a dress buttoned to her Adam's apple. She swore she'd been raped, real firm like she'd been practicing with George, looking everywhere but at the nigras. On cross Baxter hardly touched her.

"It was going like George planned, except I noticed he was looking worse and worse—almost pasty. They got to where Baxter called Moses to say he didn't do it. Hargrave starts watching real close. The whole trial he'd been playing judge, fresh black robes every day and hair pomaded just so, but he hadn't had much to do. The nigra begins telling his story right along, looking straight at the jury, about how he went looking for his brother and found him with Lucy. Then he gets to the part about Lucy being a whore. Hargrave frowns at George, waiting for him to object. George doesn't say a word. The nigra's still talking when Hargrave bangs his gavel. 'Miss Vines is not on trial here,' he says, very stem. Baxter starts arguing sort of feebly that the testimony goes to whether there was rape at all. Hargrave orders him to sit down. So he does. All this time the nigra is just watching."

Channing paused in a seeming trance from the rhythm of his own recall. I loosened my tie. Between Channing and the pictures I'd studied I could see the courtroom. Behind the railing sat twelve white jurors in shirtsleeves. One fanned himself with a long flyswatter. A table full of reporters took notes behind the bank of typewriters they banged at recess. From his hand-carved bench Judge Hargrave peered sternly down at Baxter, half-drunk already, his courage used up. "What happened then?" I asked.

Channing rasped scornfully. "After that, cross examination should have been easy. But George can't do it. He whispers to me, 'Think you can take cross, Luther?' His eyes are yellow at the rim. You can hear a pin drop. I freeze. They're all waiting. Then someone coughs. Before I know it I'm on my feet walking over to the nigra. 'You were there,' I say, 'weren't you, Moses. There, with your brother on top of Lucy Vines.'

"He was so black he looked almost purple. 'Well, sir,' he begins, 'I was just tryin'—'

To rape a white girl?' 'No, sir.'

170

'But you didn't stop it.' 'No, sir, but—'

'Didn't try to pull him off.' He blinks. 'I just got there.'

"And you were just watching, weren't you, Moses?' His mouth falls open. Almost whispering, I say, 'Watching—and waiting.'

"He stares at me. Before he can answer I turn my back and say, 'That's all, Judge,' sort of floating it over my shoulder while I look at the jury.

"But they're all looking past me. Behind, the nigra's stood up and starts shouting, 'I been here all my life and never had no trouble. You all know me—got a wife and boy. What I want with that girl? You listen to me, Lawyer Channing.' "

Channing paled as though transported. "I turn and he's pointing at me. Right quick Hargrave shouts for the sheriff. Two deputies slap cuffs on the nigras and take them off while the newsmen and photographers are scurrying and taking pictures and scribbling notes. All at once half the folks in town are up slapping me on the back." Channing's words were bitter. "But that didn't last."

"How do you mean?"

His eyes turned sharp with malice. "Oh, it lasted for the trial. George pulls himself together to sum up. Hargrave did the rest. He instructs the jury that if Moses had been there and not stopped it they should find him guilty. They took one hour. Then the sheriff brings the two nigras in handcuffs back in front of Hargrave. He looks past them at the crowd, making a speech on how the law protects the purity of southern women, every posturing inch a judge. Then he asks if the defendants have anything to say.

"Moses sort of gathers himself, standing up slow but straight. 'We didn't rape that girl, Judge. You know that.' He talks real deep and quiet, so each word drops like a stone. 'If you punish us who are innocent, if you take me from my wife and boy, then in his own good time, and his own way, the Lord will punish you and yours.' Hargrave turned white. Then he sentenced both nigras to death.

"It didn't go bad until afterwards. George and I are on the courthouse steps in a crowd of reporters when someone asks him what he thinks about both nigras getting the electric chair. For a minute George looks fishfaced. Then he gives this sick grin and says, 'Maybe we'll get special rates.' It got real quiet, and the smile died on George's face like he'd heard himself. It was stupid, George blustering to cover how he felt. He had no dignity, never did. The Birmingham papers crucified him. And some of it slopped onto me."

"In what sense?"

Channing fixed me with an angry glare. "It was over before I knew it. Every time I wanted the senate nomination they had someone else. 'It's not your time yet,' they'd say at the meetings. Took me a while to see it never would be my time. They were *ashamed*, damn them. I was just there when it needed doing and afterwards the bastards shunned me for it. Oh, they never said right out what it was, but you could feel it—they'd never warm to you. George left office and died. Hargrave was almost comical. He thought he'd be a hero, but when he tried to get backing for governor the party laughed in his face. It near to broke him; the vain stupid fool wouldn't look you in the eyes. He even stopped bringing Lydia downtown, so for a while I hardly saw her. Funny thing is it was all for nothing: everyone but him could see being governor was never in the cards. Two years later he died on the bench probating some farmer's estate. They passed me right over, didn't even ask if I wanted it. Just hung those two nigras like a millstone 'round my neck and walked away.

"Hargrave was dead and so I got stuck here paying for what they'd wanted and he'd wanted to give them: to hang those nigras." He jabbed a finger at me, voice rising to an angry blast. "For a hundred years we were all about nigras—hell, we choked on 'em. Got stuck with the tub-thumping trash while quality men like Richard Russell couldn't be President, all because of the nigra. My God, the sheer waste of that—it took someone like Nixon to make Sam Ervin respectable. Now we've got civil rights and air-conditioning and all the sudden we're a fit place for Yankees to live in. That's the biggest joke of all—not long before this goddamned trial a mob of white men in Detroit lynched a nigra for sticking a toe on their beach. And now there's riots in Boston and Yankee companies flocking here like lemmings to get away from snow and nigras. But that's fine: now we've got *civil rights*. And a hundred years of our best men paid for their hypocrisy."

Channing glowered with dammed hatred. In one terrible moment, I understood: his Grangeville was a white man's tragedy, with Channing its Richard Russell. "What about the McCarrolls?" I asked quietly.

"They were executed."

"I meant the wife and boy."

"Don't know," he snapped. "Never saw them again."

"You mean you saw them during the trial?"

"Outside, maybe."

"Ever look at them close?"

His stare lit on the glider next to me. "What does it matter?"

"I was wondering if there was something unusual about the little boy—a discoloration in one of his eyes."

Channing's face was momentarily thoughtful. "I think there was." Brusquely, he added, "I didn't really notice. You want to know about the boy, check down at the courthouse."

"I'll do that." I rose to leave. "Thanks for your time."

Sitting, Channing seemed suddenly brittle and disrepaired. "Wait." His upward look was furtive, almost shy. "You were talking about Lydia Hargrave. What's the boy to do with that?"

"I think perhaps he knows about Lydia Cantwell's murder."

The coldness in his eyes had vanished. "You found her, Mr. Shaw, didn't you?"

"Yes, sir. I did."

"What—what was she like?"

"She was strangled."

There was a long silence. Channing looked away to where I'd sat on the glider. In the shadows his face was almost yellow. "She was beautiful then," he said softly. "I tried to tell her, right on this porch—explain how it was. She didn't understand. Said she was leaving to marry someone else. 'Please', I begged her. 'Don't go. Is it that I'm too old?' "Channing's voice fell. "She turned her face. 'You're dead inside,' she answered. I tried to stop her. She pushed me away and ran out into the darkness."

I left him there.

The courthouse square was still crowded. I angled through mothers and children and vendors selling belts and lamps and old beer bottles, passing a bookstall. A lean young black with cornrows stood thumbing a worn copy of *Soul on Ice*, oblivious to the aching past where Luther Channing lived suspended in bitter memory, like a fly in amber. Three white girls with Cokes and lemonades slid chattering around him. The old men still whittled. I wondered which of them might have milled outside the courthouse forty years before. But it hardly mattered now; the ones touched by it were dead. Except for Channing and perhaps one black man, bound by Grangeville and a murdered woman.

I crossed the lawn, went up the courthouse steps and through its white pillars inside. The corridors were dim and sleepy. On the way to the clerk's office I passed the double doors of the courtroom. I hesitated, then stepped inside. The jury box was there, and Hargrave's bench. But the room was dark and empty, the way only a stage or courtroom can be empty. It looked like nothing had ever happened there, or ever would. I backed out.

The clerk's office had brown walls and a varnished counter with one swinging door. Behind that were a baldish man with three missing fingers and a strawberry blonde in her twenties. I spoke to the girl. "I'm Adam Shaw, out of Birmingham. I wonder if you can help me."

She smiled all the way to her round blue eyes. "We can try."

"I need some birth records from the early thirties."

"Inheritance case?"

"In a sense. The family's named McCarroll."

"Don't know them." Her brows knit. "Family still here?"

"I don't think so, no."

"White folks?"

"Black."

"Ummm." Her mouth made a little bow. "Let me check in the back room. But don't get your hopes up. Sometimes the records weren't that good."

"I know."

She went through a door behind her and closed it. The man frowned at me. I smoked three cigarettes, waiting.

I was stubbing the third when the girl came out, gingerly holding a single worn document. She laid it on the counter, turned toward me so I could read it.

It was a yellowed birth certificate. On May 4, 1930, it said, Moses and Jane McCarroll, Negroes, had a son. Otis Lee McCarroll.

"Is this what you were looking for?" she asked.

"I'm afraid so."

Outside, I called Kris Ann to say I'd be a few more hours. A van full of teenagers waving beer cans careened around the corner, soul music trailing from their radio. I got in the car and drove south again.

EIGHTEEN

Perhaps Kris Ann's picture had made it personal. Perhaps I felt the lives of others becoming part of mine. I drove to Lee's shack without calling Rayfield.

Lee wasn't there. His neighbors—women, children, or sullen idle men—didn't know him or where he was. I felt almost relieved. Then the last old woman said sometimes she'd seen him in the park by the county courthouse.

Maybe he liked it there, she said. It was quiet and there was all that shade.

The park was a wooded square surrounded by the public buildings of the city and split into quadrants of oak and lawn by narrow stone walks that issued from a central reflecting pool like spokes. I parked and entered, looking to both sides as I walked toward the pool. At its center a gold-painted Statue of Liberty gazed toward the police station, her face in shadows. Old men on benches, wearing hats in the shade, waited for nothing to happen. One got slowly up to study his reflection. He stood over the brackish water, bent and patient and puzzled. I stared down in silent imitation. Beneath me was a dim, dark-haired figure, faceless from a low wind blowing ripples through it. I looked up.

Otis Lee watched from a bench beneath a grove of trees on the far side of the pool. We stared across the water in mute acknowledgment. He didn't run, or move. I circled the pool until I stood over him.

"Did she make it up to you?" I asked.

His gaze upward held a cold curiosity. "How you find me?"

"A neighbor. Or do you mean how I knew?"

"That."

"By digging, like the police are now. It would be better to turn yourself in."

His eyes filled with smoldering bitter resignation. "I didn't kill that woman."

"You tracked down Lydia Hargrave and

got a job at her house. You had only one reason to do that."

"You know about Grangeville," he said flatly.

I nodded. "They killed your father and uncle. You were about eight then. So was Mrs. Cantwell."

"Always something to keep it fresh." His voice had an awesome literal quality, as if the forty years since had happened overnight. "Daddy's in his shop, sayin', 'Yes, sir,' to white folks so he can come home evenings to hunt for me out back, laughing, 'Otis, gonna find you, Otis,' in his deep voice because he's pretending not to know where I hide—and then he's gone. My stupid uncle buys the same piece of white ass been peddled all over town and just like that they've locked them both up and Hargrave's walking past us staring straight ahead like the judgment of God. Every week he'd parade that girl by our shop, noddin' and smilin' at us, and now he's killing Daddy by inches. And he knows."

"Hargrave's dead," I answered. "The ones who killed your father are dead or so old and bitter, strangling them would be a mercy. Instead you murdered an innocent woman."

"I didn't kill no one," he repeated.

"Then go to the police."

"You don't know nothing." He spoke with granite authority. "The first thing a black man learns is that he's got no *control*, that you can't *decide* things for yourself and make it stick

179

because someone or something can come from nowhere and just wipe you out. A black man can't go asking the police to fix things for him. They taught me that by killing Daddy."

"That was forty years ago."

Lee stared through me until I felt the weight of his obsession. "It was yesterday," he said tonelessly, "and so hot Mama brung a jug of water and a rag to cool my face. We're waiting on that goddamned lawn. All around us there's white folks staring but the only one talks to us is Daddy's red-faced lawyer, whining, 'It's a hard case,' like it's something that's happened to him. He breathes liquor; every time he talks, Mama's eyes go dead. I don't understand nothing except that Daddy's in trouble and time's passing so slow I can feel it in my stomach.

"It's the morning of the third day and Mama's holding my hand like if she holds it tight enough he'll be saved. Every hour it gets hotter. Mama starts praying out loud. All at once there's hollers from the courthouse. Mama stops, and then she looks way off, and I can see her shrink. Then there's more shouting and people are running up and down the steps and that fat bag of guts Naylor and the snake-eyed sonofabitch that was with him are gettin' slapped on the back and some man in a straw hat's reached his hand through a car window to blast his horn like he's driving back from a football game. They're bringing my daddy and uncle through the crowd in handcuffs. Daddy's staring straight ahead. He don't want to look at us, don't want to break down. I try running to him. Mama pulls me back. I'm fighting but she won't let go. I just watch them drag him off until I can see him no more.

"I start cryin' in front of all those white folks. Courthouse is just a blur, but I don't wipe 'em. Don't want to see nothing. Then through the blur there's Hargrave comin' down the steps. A big redneck farmer shouts, 'Praise God, Judge.' The blur clears and I see Hargrave turn to the, farmer. What's he gonna say, I wonder, this man who's killing Daddy. But he don't say nothing. Just nods and smiles, like he was strollin' past our shop with that girl of his. By the time he slammed his car door and drove off I told myself I'd grow up to kill him."

Near us an old man in an outsized coat shuffled through lengthening shadows. Lee stared ahead, oblivious. "Next day Mama takes me to the jail. It's dark. Daddy's in a corner watching the floor. When he sees us he comes to the bars reaching his hand through saying, 'Come here, Otis,' and bending down. I come, but I can't say nothin'. He takes hold of my hand. I just hold it, thinkin' how rough it is and how my hand almost disappears. He says, 'You watch over your mama, Otis,' looking so sad it's hardly like him. Then he lets go my hand and calls Mama over to the side. 'Don't bring him again,' I hear him say. 'Can't stand him seeing me like this.' Mama's eyes turn wet and she puts her arm around me and sort of shepherds me out. Daddy stands with his back turned until we're gone. That's the last thing I ever saw—his back.

"For two years Mama turns to bone and leather while some white lawyers from New York try saving him from the electric chair. 'Just want him alive,' she keeps saying. 'Just want to know he's breathing somewhere.' And after they strapped him in a chair and shot him full of electricity and the lawyers come by to say how sorry they were and went home, she died." He raised his head, the white star on his pupil like a brand, and finished savagely, "So now you say let them do to me like they did to my daddy. But I *remember*. They needed a nigger to make themselves feel better and now they'll be needing me."

The sunlight had faded and the old men gone. Lee and I were alone. "You followed her here," I told him. "No one made you. Twenty years ago a man killed my father. He's in prison now, or dead—I don't know which. It doesn't matter. I won't waste my life on him. You did that with Hargrave and then Lydia Cantwell, who'd done nothing. Don't make this out a lynching. You put yourself in the way."

Lee's eyes shone with a terrible intensity. "You talk like things *end*," he said. "Like I had no reason to come here. But for all my life Daddy kept coming back to me with a due bill in his hand, asking what I'd done; and I'd done nothing. I knew what he'd told Hargrave, standing up in court like a man. But when Mama died I got moved away to a farm with

182

my aunt and uncle. Hargrave was a judge and I was a ten-year-old black boy with no way to reach him. But I knew I'd grow up to kill him—told my uncle I would. 'When you're a man, Otis,' my uncle said. I thought about that all the time I watched myself get big. Used to measure myself against an oak tree with a slash I'd cut to mark how tall my daddy was. When I got closer to sixteen, I stopped measuring for a while. On my sixteenth birthday I stepped out back and walked to the tree. The slash was level with my eyes. It was time." Lee smiled bitterly.

"And then I went inside and my uncle told me Hargrave was four years dead.

"My uncle's face went dark in front of me. I grabbed his throat with my fist raised. His lips started quivering. 'Goddamn you to hell,' I said, and let him go. That night I run away.

"For a while I scrounged and did odd jobs. When I run out of food, I went down to an army depot in Nashville and went in." His voice was sardonic. "Nothing else to do but serve my country. Met a woman first stretch at Polk and before I knew it there's a girl and then a boy who looked like Daddy. So I told myself training men was something I could do to take care of my family, even though I hardly saw them. For twenty years I keep Daddy in a corner of my mind I save just for that while I'm drilling and training, training and drilling, over and over until it was like I been asleep.

"I woke up one day in Vietnam with my kids gone and my wife run off, fighting a white man's war in a yellow man's country with a platoon that's half black and all poor, and it come to me: I was helping white men murder niggers they'd needed to do some dying for them, like they'd needed Daddy. We was easy to send there and yellow men was easy to kill—niggers fighting niggers and nobody cares until they started taking white boys after college." His stare challenged me. "Wasn't hard to see why they don't come themselves: the jungle's hot and wet and filled with the V.C. cutting up my men and sendin' them back in bags or missing something or maybe just paralyzed from the waist. Month after month we ship out body bags and cripples and they ship more blacks and poor whites to replace them. All I want is to ship some back alive; keep them from getting killed over something foolish or because they're so bored and scared they've turned zombie on the same stuff college boys smoke for fun.

"About two weeks after I learn my wife run off I'm standing with Curtis, my scout. We're near this jungle full of bugs and punji traps with bamboo stakes in them that the slopes rub with their own shit for poison. Curtis is this quick, rabbity kid with sharp eyes good for scouting, and we're trying to figure where the Cong are. All the time he's slipping out there nights to find them and then smelling and groping his way back through the bush. He's got guts, but he gets more scared every time he goes out, so now even when he's back he thinks about it all the time, and never smiles. He's got two months left. I've started makin' deals in my head: if Curtis makes it, don't matter what happens to me. Just want him out alive.

"We're talking. He stops to puff a cigarette kind of nervous like he does, not really pulling the smoke down, and still watching the bush. He's gotten old around the eyes. Scouting's hard, and he's got two months of hard waiting. I try getting him off it. 'What you gonna do back in the world?' I ask. He puffs and thinks. 'Gonna move things,' he says. 'Get me a truck and move the man's shit all over the country.' He's almost smiling. Then his face just disappears. Don't even hear the whine."

Lee's fingers gripped the wooden bench until veins raised in the back of his hands. "I brought the rest of him back and put him in a green bag. He was nothin' but a lump of canvas. I lit one of his cigarettes and sat next to it. Looking at the bag I didn't see Curtis no more. I see my daddy, hammering at the forge. 'You gonna grow up strong as me,' he says. 'Better start workin' now.' Then he gives me a hammer he's made, just like his only smaller. I take it in my hand. And then Hargrave walks that dark-haired girl by our door like she was a princess, nodding and smiling.

"I remember what my daddy promised Hargrave and then I understood, sitting there next to Curtis. It didn't matter who killed Daddy. Daddy hadn't raped that girl; they'd killed him for being black. Like Curtis. The V.C. didn't kill him, they just finished him off.

It was the white man put him there—for being poor and black. When I'd finished his cigarette I knew I was going to find that woman and kill her like I'd known about Hargrave. For bein' his daughter, and for bein' white."

I flashed on Lee squatted by the body bag, a blasted-out life staring at a trail of devastation and wasted time. He spoke with an inexorable, pounding anger. "I thought about it, long and hard until I got out. After that it took time to find where she was. But when I walked up that long driveway, I thought, Isn't this fine. Forty years no one paid for my daddy and she's been living here like it never happened. I knock on the door and that stuck-up maid answers and looks at me like I was trash. I had to beg and shuffle on the front steps to get the white lady even come to the door.

"Finally she steps out, closing the door behind her so I can't look in. She's older but it's Hargrave's girl all right, and dressed real nice; you can see the money in the way she stands, straight and lookin' at you like you better speak up. 'Well, ma'am,' I say, 'I'm going around to some houses hopin' for yardwork. I don't drink and I pack my own lunch so the maid don't have to make me a sandwich. Maybe one, two times a week you might need me, and I'd sure appreciate it.'

"The whole time I'm looking her over. She's tight, not like that girl at all, and she don't say nothin', just stares. It's sure she don't need no help with the yard and I figure she's gonna tell me that. Finally, she says, 'I don't know your name.' I say, 'Otis Lee.' She keeps staring like she don't hear. Then she says, 'You can come Tuesday and Friday, in the afternoon.' Don't ask me what I charge or nothing. Just backs through the door and closes it.

"When I come back next Tuesday she answers the door herself. There's shadows under her eyes like she hasn't been sleeping and I notice white hairs at the side of her head. 'You're here,' she says. 'Yes, ma'am.' She just nods. Finally she asks me to prune her roses and slams the door shut. I go to the rose bed, wondering how I'll know when the time comes. Then I see her come to the window, to watch.

"It goes on like that, every Tuesday and Friday. I knock on the door. She answers—quick, like she's been waiting. She gives me money and orders and shuts the door again. Then there she'd be, staring at me through the window—five, ten, fifteen minutes without moving. Pretty soon I can sense when she'll come out. She always does that, the same every time. She waits until I'm away from the front door. Then she'll open it and walk to some far corner of the yard, pretending to garden while she watches me. Sometimes I can feel her staring before I ever know she's there. It's just the two of us then, and quiet. Anytime I could have walked over and wrung her neck like a chicken. But I just waited. I liked *deciding* about her. Every Tuesday and Friday, I decided for that day.

"She never went out the whole time I'm there and nobody comes except the gray-haired man with the Cadillac. Only time I seen her smile was one time he drove up. Before the car has even stopped she's opened the door, smiling with her head held up. But not with me. She just keeps staring. She's looking tired now. But every time I'm there she comes outside to watch, until it's like being near a flame.

"The time it happened I was digging out the rose bed. It was cool and cloudy and I wasn't thinking about her for once but about Germany and how the sky was there when it rained, flat and gray and different from anywhere else. I hear the front door open. She's standing in the doorway. Then she walks out toward the roses until she's stopped right near me. It's time, I think, like it's taken me by surprise. I watch her out the corner of my eye. She starts pruning the roses. I hear the clippers snapping next to me. Then they stop. She gives a little cry. I look over and she's staring at a fingertip she's pricked on a thorn. On the end there's a round drop of blood. She keeps staring at it. Then she looks up at me and her eyes get real big. She don't say nothing. Just stands there with her mouth half-open. I stare back. Without saying a word she turns and walks back to the house, slow and sort of broken-like. Don't even close the door.

"That's when it came to me. She *knew*— maybe knew inside the first time she saw me. She hadn't forgotten.

"I didn't go through that door. Just stood in the yard, waiting. Nothing happened. I went home and for three days and nights I waited. The police never came. She never did nothing about it.

"Friday I went back and knocked on the door. When she opened it, all I saw was this scared, skinny white woman with dyed hair, holding my money in one hand and not able to talk. I took the money and went to the rose bed without saying a word.

"It was finished. I didn't want to kill her anymore. It was enough I could decide.

"End of the day I knocked to say I'm quitting. She nods with her head down. 'Do you want anything?' she asks. Her voice is shaking. 'No,' I says. 'I don't want nothing.' Her face gets real funny. 'Thank you,' she says. I just turn my back on her and start walking down the driveway. When I get to the end, the green Cadillac passes me going the other way. I don't even look back.

"I was sitting around the next day wondering what to do when it come on the radio she'd been murdered. It was crazy. Whole time I was workin' there I wondered how it'd be when I'd killed her and the police came. I never decided—imagined it all kind of ways. Then she was dead and I hadn't killed her, and I thought, 'They're comin' like they came for Daddy. And now I'm not ready.'"

For a moment I could almost imagine it: Lydia's death as fate's last trick, turning what redemption had passed between them into a tragic joke. I stopped myself "What about the picture of my wife?"

189

He looked up, as if surprised I had spoken. "Mister," he said indifferently, "I don't know what you're talkin' about."

"The person who killed Mrs. Cantwell threatened my wife."

Lee's eyes grew careful. "You're going to the police, then."

I nodded. "There's too much on one side. Mrs. Cantwell. My wife. My friend and client. And what's to balance that? Your word, and white man's guilt."

"Then why'd you come here?"

"I'm not sure. Maybe I've come too far to not look you in the face."

I sensed his weight shifting from his haunches to the heel of his boots. His eyes took me in, measuring, judging the distance. "That was stupid," he said softly. "All this talk, all this *tellin'* you how things was, and now I may have to kill you."

"I wonder if you want that."

Lee shrugged. "Won't bother me none. Already done that to a V.C. with the knife I got in my back pocket. Come up behind him on the balls of my feet and hook his neck. For a second we're so close I feel the pulse in his throat. Then I draw the knife across it. He don't even scream. Just flops back quivering against my chest until I let him slip down me into the bush. Never thought their eyes could get that big. He was already dead." He stood. "I killed that yellow man just because he was in the same stinking patch of jungle. But I got reason to kill you."

"Then you'd better decide about *me*. Now."

For a long moment we faced each other. Neither of us moved. Then I turned and began walking toward the police station.

It was near dusk and the park was silent. Between me and the police station was fifty yards of lawn, some steps down, and the street. The fastest route was to cut straight across the grass. Instead I took the walkway where I might hear Lee's footsteps. My strides lengthened. Forty yards to the steps, then thirty. I listened. In one swift movement Lee's imagined knife-edge crossed my throat. Shock as warm blood spurted down my neck, quick, searing pain, then blackness. I loped from the park, across the street and up the steps to the glass doors. By the time I got inside I was breathing hard. There was no one behind me.

"What's wrong with you?" Rayfield asked.

I leaned on his desk with both palms. "Moses McCarroll's son is across the street. The gardener."

Rayfield moved quickly from behind his desk, calling, "He's in the park," to Bast. Bast slammed down his telephone.

"How did you know?" I asked.

"Army records," Rayfield said curtly over his shoulder and rushed out the door behind Bast.

By the time I reached the steps they were across the street running into the park. I followed them to its edge. Perhaps part of me hoped he was gone. But he wasn't. He sat like

191

a carving as they trotted up with drawn revolvers.

I turned and walked slowly to my car.

NINETEEN

That night I refused calls from reporters until Kris Ann left the phone off the hook. I had several drinks and no dinner. I felt drained. When I called him, Henry sounded the same. "Do you really believe it's the black man?" he asked.

"It has a certain demented symmetry. But right now all you should think of is that you're free."

"I suppose I am." For a free man he sounded oddly dispirited. "You sound tired, Adam."

"I'm okay. We'll both be better when it hits this is over."

"Over." The word fell emptily. "Yes, I suppose so. I should thank you."

"Just get some sleep. I'll call you in the morning."

"In the morning. Surely."

I said goodnight and put the phone back on the kitchen table.

Kris Ann was stretched out on the couch in blue jeans, staring up. I sat on the floor with another drink. She said, "It's this man Lee that's bothering you, isn't it?"

I nodded. "He could have killed me, Krissy.

Why lie about Lydia's murder and then just watch me go to the police?"

"I don't know." She propped on her elbow to look at me. "I don't know why you were there at all.

"I was afraid for you."

"The police could have found him." She sat up, her gaze long and penetrating. "What you did was almost suicidal, like you have a death wish or something to prove—and I'm not even sure to whom. It scares me."

I slid next to the couch. "I'm here now."

"You don't understand." She looked away. "I'm scared of you."

I reached out. She whirled in sudden anger. "Who are you, Adam? Are you a lawyer, a policeman, my husband, what? This afternoon I could have lost you to something I don't understand. I look at you now and I don't know you. What do you want for us? Can you tell me that? Can you even tell me what you want for yourself?"

My hand froze in midair. "I want you."

"Oh God, Adam, that's not an answer. That's just something you say."

"But it's the only answer I've got. I can't sit here and tell you 'What I Want from Life' like it's some sophomore exercise. I don't know anymore and even if I did it might not be true five years or even five days from now. All I know is that I want you. That's true no matter what."

"But *why* do you want me?" She held up her hand as if to prevent an answer. Then she ran it across her face, murmuring, "I need time to think things out."

She rose and walked to the stairwell, paused, and turned to watch me, head angled and still. "What happened to Lee is terrible, Adam. But once you found him there wasn't any choice. You can't feel guilty now."

I glanced down at my drink. "Guilt's out, anyhow. Now they're selling books like *Kicking Ass for Number One* and *How to Be a Shit to Your Friends and Like It*. It's just that sometimes I think that guilt is the only thing that keeps us human."

She shook her head. "That's conscience, Adam. Guilt just keeps you looking back." She hesitated, then added softly, "But I'm grateful he let you go," and went up the stairs.

I stared after her. Then I finished my drink and turned on the eleven o'clock news.

The screen crackled and then the white dot at its center widened to become Nora Culhane, standing in front of the police station. "It's quiet here now," she was saying, "and police spokesmen have not yet released the information leading to Lee's arrest. But it follows by less than twenty-four hours an apparent threat against Kris Ann Shaw, wife of attorney Adam Shaw, who discovered Mrs. Cantwell's body five days ago. There is no word yet on whether Lee has confessed to the murder. But this first break means that the intense police efforts to find the killer, may be drawing to a close. For TV Seven, this is—"

"Nora Culhane, girl reporter," I said aloud, and switched her off.

I went to the kitchen for the fifth of Bushmills and stayed up killing it. It was like going through a wall. The last three drinks didn't touch me. I walked into the kitchen and tossed the bottle in the garbage with a heavy thud.

I leaned against the kitchen door and smoked two cigarettes. Then I picked up the telephone.

"Hello?" It had taken Culhane five rings to answer and she sounded sleepy.

"Laid it on pretty thick tonight, I thought."

"Who is this?"

"Adam Shaw."

"Adam. God, I tried to reach you all night."

"I had the phone off the hook. Listen, I think you missed something. They should have run a test. Clipped some of Lee's pubic hairs to match with those they found on Lydia Cantwell."

"I didn't miss it." She sounded annoyed. "They just didn't have results by airtime. There's a problem with that. The hair they found on Mrs. Cantwell isn't Lee's. He may have strangled her but he didn't rape her."

All at once I felt drunk. "Oh, Christ," I blurted and hung up.

At seven-thirty the next morning, five minutes after I put the phone on its hook again, Culhane called back. "Were you really that surprised?" she asked.

"Just tired." I leaned against the kitchen wall, rubbing my eyes. "When I'm tired 1 like things to make sense."

"And this doesn't."

"Maybe it will when I've thought awhile. It's just that rape-murder was logical. Anyhow, Rayfield owns the problem now."

"Unless you turned in an innocent man."

"In which case it's still his problem. That's what cops are for, and juries."

"You're very tough this morning," she said tartly. "When it was Henry Cantwell's ass Rayfield couldn't be trusted."

"Henry's my client. Lee isn't."

"That's the trouble, isn't it? You thought you'd wrapped this up and now it still might be Cantwell."

"It's not Henry. Lee still looks good."

"So does whoever raped Lydia Cantwell."

I stared out the window. It was sunny and the world had a mean, clear-edged, hungover brightness. "Last night I celebrated," I told her. "This morning I haven't shaved yet and even my hair hurts. Catch me later at the office. I'll be charming. I'll tell you everything. I'll even have brushed my teeth."

"Two-thirty, then. And quit smoking. It makes the morning worse." This time it was she who hung up.

I took three aspirin and arranged some orange juice and black coffee on the kitchen table in front of me, downing the coffee in stiff gulps. Then I got up and called Rayfield.

"I want to talk to you," he said. "Lee keeps saying he didn't kill Mrs. Cantwell."

"What can I do about that?"

"Give me a statement: say how you found him, what he said to you." His voice turned edgy and aggressive. "You might even figure out who Lee's gray-haired man is—the one he says visited her. That man's gone important on him since he landed in jail."

"Then you're not sure Lee's the one who killed her."

"For sure not the one who had her. Tell Cantwell not to go on vacation."

"Why? You going to, charge him with rape?"

Rayfield laughed for the first time I could remember. It was short and unpleasant. "Maybe he sent someone." I didn't understand that, and didn't answer. "Maybe the black man killed her," he went on, "and then maybe Cantwell didn't want to lose her money."

"He has enough to live on."

"She had more. Rich people have strange ideas of enough."

"Some do. Henry doesn't."

"We're wasting time. I want you to come down."

"In the afternoon," I parried. "I need time to think on your question, try and come up with a name. And I still want Kris Ann looked after until you're sure that Lee killed Mrs. Cantwell, or find someone better."

I heard him inhale. Finally he said, "We'll do that—for now. You'd just damned well better be here at four. And think about that man."

"Fair enough. There's one thing more, though. When you arrested Lee, was he carrying a knife?"

"Big one. Why?"

"Just that he could have used it on me."

"Could have," Rayfield said, and rang off.

I leaned back against the wall. Then I called Nate Taylor and told him about Lee. "I don't know if he's got a lawyer," I finished, "but you might want to ask."

"Thanks. I'll go down there."

I said goodbye without telling him Mooring's name.

My coffee was cold. The cigarette I took one puff of tasted bad and smelled worse stubbed in the ashtray. I poured fresh coffee, letting its aroma rise to my nostrils as I rubbed the back of my neck.

When the phone rang I let Kris Ann answer in the bedroom. After two or three minutes she called down the stairs. "Pick up the phone, Adam. It's Daddy."

I went to the stairs. She was in a silk peignoir, long hair falling over her shoulders. "I'll see him at the office," I said.

"He's upset and worried about me. Please talk to him."

I went reluctantly to the kitchen phone. "What the hell are you doing?" Cade demanded.

My ears rang. "Talking to you."

"With my daughter, damn you."

"Trying to keep her safe. Trying to find

the man who killed Lydia. Trying to handle the police. Trying to get off the fucking telephone, frankly, and get some time to think."

"As if you were capable. I'm through with you, Adam."

"Not through with me. Stuck with me. We're stuck with each other."

"Only as long as Kris Ann wants."

I paused. "No, Roland. Only as long as you live."

There was a long silence. Almost whispering, he said, "By the time I die, Adam, you'll be past fifty and your balls the size of raisins. I promise you that."

I lit another cigarette. "You called. There must be a reason."

"All right. I want it clear that you're no longer on the Cantwell case. Your sole job is to protect Kris Ann."

"I mean to. And Henry. I assume he's talked to you."

"That changes nothing. I won't be undercut by a junior partner, particularly you. If Henry doesn't wish my advice the firm will drop him as a client."

"But he's your oldest and dearest friend, remember? Besides, the partners won't let even you do that. The Cantwells pay those whopping fees that line our various pockets. The trips to Europe, the beachhouses, the new Mercedes—"

"Don't talk to me of greed." He bit off the words. "Not you. Not ever."

There was a click, like someone hanging up.

Cade said, "I'm coming over." His phone slammed down.

I went to the stairs. Kris Ann stood above me on the landing, face streaked with tears.

"Why did you do that?" I asked.

She didn't answer. I stood looking up. It seemed a long way. "He's coming," I said finally. "At least there'll be someone here. I have to go."

"Where?" She said it absently, indifferently.

I shook my head. "He'll ask you, sure. Better to keep out of it."

"You're so selfless." Her voice was drained of feeling. "From moving here, to this—all for me. I never have to ask."

I climbed the stairs to grasp her shoulders. "What he said, Krissy—that's not right. You know it isn't."

She turned her face, squirmed free, and ran to the bedroom. I started after her, then stopped myself. There was no way to reach her, now. I had to finish it. I went slowly to the kitchen and stood over the phone, thinking. Then I dialed.

A singsong voice answered, "Maddox Coal and Steel."

"Mr. Mooring, please."

"I'm sorry, sir. Mr. Mooring is on another call now. Can you hold?"

I was already heading out the alley for Mooring's place when Cade's dark-blue Audi turned in from the street. His mouth opened to shout. I passed him without stopping.

200

TWENTY

It was only nine-fifteen when I got there. But when Joanne Mooring answered the door I knew it didn't matter.

Leaning on the doorframe, she was half-drunk already. For a moment we shared a kind of recognition. Perhaps I looked as bad as she did. "Yes?" she said thickly,

"I'm Adam Shaw. Remember me?"

"Doesn't matter." Her voice, tinged with empty gaiety, seemed dragged up from the floor. "You're welcome, anyhow."

I followed her inside. She motioned me carelessly toward the kitchen. It was done in instant French country, with new copper pans hanging on the near brick wall next to some butcher knives and assorted utensils that I guessed had never been used. She sat behind a butcher-block counter with an ashtray and the same blender full of daiquiris, patting the barstool next to hers. "Sit," she commanded.

I sat, surveying the damage. With the blue beneath her eyes not quite purple, the veins of her nose not quite burst, she was a wreck-in-process, not quite finished. She tapped some ash off a cigarette that lay burning in the ashtray—the ladylike gesture of some thinner, more fastidious person trapped within the sagging body—and peered at me. "Want a drink?"

I nodded reluctantly. "Sure."

She pointed toward the cupboard. I took the smallest tumbler and half filled it, sitting back down beside her. She watched my drink until I took a sip. It tasted sicksweet. Her smile was bemused, as if summoned by distant laughter. "I've always hated the taste," she said. "You hate it too, don't you?"

"When it makes me feel like less."

She nodded solemnly. "You mean the waves. You have to keep drinking 'til the tide comes back in."

"It always goes back out though, doesn't it."

"Yes, dammit." She stared at the blender. "Why did you come?"

"To talk."

"What's there to talk about?"

I turned to her. "You."

The smile she managed seemed stolen from time, the almost flirtatious smile of a pretty girl with a present behind her back. Thirty years ago the smoke of early womanhood would have shown in her hazel eyes, and the delicate nose and chin would have made her pretty. But now harsh sunlight through the window exposed bleached hair and the puffiness of drink, and her smile was the last relic of a widowed sexuality, sad as a stained-glass window in a slum. "More daiquiris?" she asked.

"Sure. I was wondering why you drink so much alone."

"Or drink so much, period." She filled my glass. "It's not by choice."

I raised my drink. I would have hated myself

even without the hangover. "What were we talking about?" she asked.

"Your husband."

Her smile faded. "It wasn't always like this. Not at the start."

"Then you've been married a long time."

She nodded. "Twenty-nine years-thirty next June thirteenth. We were both eighteen and ran away just out of high school. I put him through school at Alabama." She looked joylessly around their overdone kitchen. "It's funny. The hardest times are the best. He was so straight and serious and handsome then, and we were together."

"That's too bad—that it changed, I mean."

"*He* changed."

I tried for a note of mystified empathy. "Why'd that happen, I wonder."

Her mouth made a scornful *O*. "What's your name?"

"Adam. Adam Shaw."

"Well, Adam, talk about something else." She smiled out of some vagrant mood, running both hands along the ruined line of her hips. "I'm out of cigarettes," she said, a pretty girl again, prettily annoyed at her own foolishness.

I offered her one. She placed it carefully between her lips, bending her head toward mine for a light. When I lit it, her head stayed close. "You're a nice man, Adam Shaw."

"You're an easy woman to be nice to."

"But not a lady."

"Of course you are."

She shook her head. "Not enough of one."

It was as though we were continuing a conversation she had begun with someone else. I took a chance. "I think I know what the problem was."

"What?" She clasped my hand. "What was it?"

"Lydia Cantwell."

Blood splotched her cheeks. "But why?"

"I'm not sure, Joanne."

"Just the goddamned way she walked? That she could have babies?"

She was almost screeching. I shook my head in feigned bewilderment. "I don't know. It was Lydia, though, wasn't it?"

Her cigarette burned forgotten in the hand she waved at her cold, sparkling kitchen. "Hell, it was always her—for the twenty-eight years Dalton's been with her goddamned company. Poor Dalton, he's been waiting and waiting all these years, hanging on with me for appearance's sake until Lydia Cantwell made up her mind."

"How did you find out?"

"He made it too damned obvious," she said scornfully. "It was only later he got sophisticated. The second year he was there they put him on one of her charity things. He was so excited: her the biggest stockholder, he said, and him almost an office boy. He started coming home each night full of Mrs. Cantwell this and Mrs. Cantwell that: how pretty she was, how poised. I only half listened; I'd lost the baby and wasn't all there. All I knew was he was working harder. Then one night at dinner he called her Lydia. I started listening closer. The next night it was Mrs. Cantwell. Then, just like that, he stopped. Never said her name again. That was when I knew."

"Knew what?"

She smiled bitterly. "Why it was so boring for him to touch me. And why he spent nights listening to those speech records so he could talk better."

"Was he seeing her back then?"

"I don't know how you could think about someone so much and not be with them. And he volunteered for every symphony thing she did."

"Then why did you stay with him?"

"He was the boy I loved," she said simply. "The smartest boy in Clio, Alabama, and he was mine. We were going to do everything together." Her hand tightened. "Am I boring to you, Adam?"

She caught me thinking ahead to the next question. "Of course not."

I said it hollow and too late. Her hand loosened. She squinted up at me and then recognition came into her face. I could almost read its stages: who I was; why she had lunged at me that night on the porch; why I was here.

"Joanne—"

"I know you." She stood, backing away. Her festering smile was no smile at all. "You don't want me. You poor stupid bastard, you think Dalton killed Lydia Cantwell."

"Didn't he?" I managed.

"Oh, my God." She laughed shrilly. "And you're Henry Cantwell's lawyer. Dalton didn't kill his precious Lydia. He just did everything else."

"What does that mean?"

Her eyes lit. "I was *there*—the same night he killed her."

I tried to show nothing. "The black man?"

"No." Her smile was unpleasant. "Your precious client, Adam Shaw. Henry Cantwell."

I felt a chill. "How can you know that?"

She stopped to pour a daiquiri, stretching it out. She had all my attention now. "I followed him—Dalton. He thought I was asleep. But I knew who he was running to. I could see him dressing in the bathroom, smiling a little to himself in the mirror. He thinks I can't do things by myself, but I dressed and waited until he drove out of the garage. Then I followed him. To *her* house."

"Mrs. Cantwell's?"

"*Lydia's*," she corrected. "Precious Lydia. I parked down by the road where they couldn't see me, trying to pull myself together in the dark. Ever since he'd met her he'd stopped wanting me and still I'd waited all those years, hoping he'd change, decorating each room so he would like coming home; and now here he was, with *her*. I thought of them inside and me alone in the goddamned car he gave me instead of himself. And then I decided to take every rotten minute of every rotten year and cram them down her fucking throat."

"By killing her."

"Don't you wish. No, I sat and waited, like always. I don't know how long I was in the car, thinking about it. I sat too long. How will I look to her, I thought. She'll laugh at me and Dalton will turn away. I didn't want him to see us together, her like she was and me... I was sitting there crying when Dalton's Cadillac came back down the driveway and left."

"Then it was Dalton."

"Wrong." She was gleeful now. "Lydia Cantwell was still alive."

"Because that's Dalton's story?"

"No." She was circling now around the counter where I sat, waving the drink and cigarette butt and talking with the stagy intensity of an actress at her moment of triumph. "Because I heard her voice."

"You heard her," I repeated. "Through a quarter mile of pine trees and a closed door."

"The door was open." She spoke clearly now, as if anger and excitement had made her sober. "When Dalton left I decided to face her. I got out of the car and began to walk up the drive. There was almost no moon. I had to feel my way by the dogwood trees. Once a branch snapped in my face and I nearly fell. The drive was so steep I started panting. But I kept on and when I got closer the light from her living room helped me see a little. I wanted her. I wanted to spoil her face."

I had stopped doing anything but listen. "I was almost to the top," she continued. "There was a noise. Headlights came toward me from the bottom of the drive. I jumped back. My shoe caught on the edge of the drive and I fell backwards over the hedge and landed on my face behind it.

"When the car passed I stayed pressed down in the grass and brush where he couldn't see me. I could smell the dirt under my face but I didn't move. A car door slammed and I heard footsteps on the walk. Then they stopped. The front door opened. From inside comes a voice: Lydia Cantwell, society and very cool. 'I wasn't expecting you,' she said. And then the door shut behind them.

"I peeked out over the hedge. There was no one on the porch. The car was in front of the garage. But I could see it. It was a black Mercedes—Henry Cantwell's car."

I lit a cigarette, trying to collect my thoughts. "But you never saw this person. For all you know it could have been a woman."

"I saw the car. It was Henry Cantwell."

"Sure it was. You could tell because he rang the doorbell of his own house. He wanted to make things hard on himself."

"I didn't say he rang. I said the door opened."

"Then why did you hear Lydia's voice?"

"She was still up. Dalton had just left."

"How long before? Fifteen minutes? Twenty? Two hours? Maybe you fell asleep in the car. Maybe you'd been drinking."

"He suffered." she said stubbornly. "Like me. So he killed her."

"Of course he did. After deciding not to park in his own garage. I'll tell you what makes better sense. Your husband had an affair with Lydia

Cantwell. Six days ago tonight, with Henry gone, he went to her house. They fought. Maybe he wanted a divorce and she didn't. It doesn't matter. He lost control: I've nearly seen that twice. By the time he got a grip on himself he was alone in the house with a dead woman. So he mutilated her picture, wiped his prints off everything he could think of, and left her there, the victim of a psychotic killer.

"You followed him, and saw him leave. Perhaps you saw the murder. Maybe you heard about it later. But you had him back now. Because if he ever leaves you, you'll tell the police he killed Lydia Cantwell. And that's exactly what you've told him, isn't it?"

"No." Her face twisted in horror—at me, or at herself. "It's not like that."

I rose and walked toward her. "Then it's like this. You killed her."

She backed away, shaking her head with a child's vehemence. "No. That's not true."

"Isn't it? Maybe when he left, you crept up the driveway, just as you've said. Every step in the dark you're thinking about how you lost the baby and how through all the years since, he's wanted her. How you put him through school so he could shuck you for a woman who made you shrink, a woman he wanted like he wanted to be powerful, and someone else. All that churned inside you. By the time you made it to the house, you wanted to kill her. And Henry Cantwell wasn't there to stop you."

"He was," she insisted.

"No. It was Lydia who answered. She was surprised, but she let you in—she'd do that. You were filled with crazy energy, like now. You quarreled over Dalton. Probably you pushed her to the floor and began banging her head. Maybe she just fell that way. But then you strangled her until the tongue came from between her lips. And when that wasn't enough you took her picture and made it ugly."

"You fucking bastard." She stumbled back against the brick wall, knocking the carving knife to the floor. She picked it up, staring at it for an instant. Then she began waving it wildly in front of her. "Don't come any closer," she warned.

I circled until the counter was between us. "Get hold," I urged. "Think."

She looked puzzledly down at the knife. I edged toward her. She glanced up, starting. In one frenzied motion she reached for the blender and flung it at me. I jumped sideways, feet tangling in the barstool as the blender flew past me and shattered against the sink. I fell, palms open to catch myself She rushed forward and lunged at my face with the knife. With one hand I flailed at her arm. There was slicing pain as flesh tore beneath my eye. I fell on my side, arms raised in front of me. She stood with her mouth open. The knife she held had blood on it. Without looking she dropped it clattering to the floor and ran.

I staggered up and ran after her, warm blood down my face and neck. There were footsteps in the greenhouse. The door at its rear was open. Then she was outside running pigeon-toed across the lawn, arms flying upward as she stumbled and fell. I caught up to her crawling forward on her hands and knees, hurt sounds coming from deep in her throat. "You bastard," she was saying. "Look at what I am, you bastard."

She was no longer talking to me, or about me. I walked in front of her to stop her crawling. Her face bent over my shoes as she began weeping helplessly.

"Come on," I said.

She looked up, face shiny with sweat and tears. I reached down. She took my hand, struggling upright. "You're cut," she said blankly.

"It's under my eye. You missed."

Her whole body seemed to wilt and her head lolled. "It was Henry Cantwell," she mumbled. "I saw his car." She turned and began stumbling toward the house.

I let her go.

I walked slowly to the car, handkerchief held to my face. When I looked in the rearview, blood trickled from a one-inch gash. It didn't matter. I was thinking of Henry Cantwell.

TWENTY-ONE

At the emergency room a mustached young doctor in cowboy boots took six stitches and made jokes while a nurse sponged the blood off my face and neck. When they finished I drove to my office, told people who asked that I'd tripped at home, and shut the door behind me without returning a message from Cade that ordered me to call. I felt trapped and shaken.

I was pulling a fresh shirt from my credenza when the telephone rang.

"Mr. Shaw." Mooring's voice was strained. "We're going to need a precise understanding."

"I have one, Mooring. You're a liar, and maybe worse."

There was a long silence. "Meet me at the club," he said finally. "Twelve-thirty."

I hesitated, tracing the stitches with my finger. "Make it noon."

He hung up.

I looked at my watch. It was eleven-thirty. At four o'clock Rayfield would ask for Mooring's name.

I began pacing. But I could talk to no one about Joanne Mooring—except Cade. I would have to meet Mooring.

When I arrived the club was teeming: golfers in bright shirts, overdressed matrons with sullen mouths, bankers come to lunch with borrowers and look into their faces. Parking-lot boys eased long cars to rest, chrome gleaming in the sun. On the far tennis court two figures in white scrambled amidst money-green trees.

Entering, I passed a doorman in spit-shined shoes, coat, and a military cap. Down the hall, in small fussy corners, dowagers played bridge. In the men's grill it was darker and the game was gin, played tightmouthed, for money. A barman brought drinks. Cards slapped and were shuffled again. Dim wreaths of smoke hung over the center table where a steel company chairman, the senior federal judge, a bank president, and the owner of a newspaper held the same four chairs they'd held for years. Their heads butted forward like prows. No one else played, or asked to play.

"Mr. Shaw." At my side was Lewis, the headwaiter. "Please follow me."

He led me out of the grill and down a side hallway. Three years before, when the club president had collapsed on the last tee, Lewis had been a pallbearer. He had always called the dead man Mister. After the funeral, the man's friends came to the club to drink. Lewis had served them. He motioned me through the doorway of a small private room. "In here, please, Mr. Shaw." He made a point of not noticing my face.

The room had green walls and a worn Oriental rug. Mooring sat beneath a crystal chandelier, next to the portrait of some half-forgotten plutocrat. His table was covered in white linen. Two places were set. Lewis whisked out my chair. When he was gone I said, "Isn't this a little baroque?"

Mooring inspected the gash under my eye. "I've hired a nurse for Joanne," he finally said.

"Like with Martha Mitchell?"

He shrugged. "The result's the same. You can't see her."

In the doorway a red-jacketed barman was waiting to be noticed. Mooring's nod summoned him. "Bloody Mary," I said. Mooring ordered Dry Sack. The waiter thanked us and left.

Mooring sat straighter, as if buoyed by the ritual of service. I sensed that he was part romantic: a man who'd redefined himself, selecting the elements of his new persona and the trappings to go with them, leaving his wife earthbound. "You know," I told him, "I've sometimes wondered why I came to despise this place—besides the obvious. It's that people like you find such comfort in it."

For an instant someone else lived behind his eyes; vulnerable and angry. "You're fresh from bullying my wife, Shaw, and in no position to offend."

"I am, though. I'm an Irish Catholic whose father was a cop. Twenty-five years ago you were listening to elocution records. So forget where we are. As far as I'm concerned this conversation's happening in the street. What you told me before was lies. Either tell me the truth about Lydia Cantwell or I go to the police."

Mooring looked at me, expressionless and appraising. A cough came from the doorway. The barman served my drink, then Mooring's, from a silver tray. Mine was tangy with lemon and Tabasco. Mooring sipped his sherry, passing it beneath his nostrils. "There's not much to tell," he said softly. "Lydia and I had an affair. I might be with her now."

"When did that start?"

He ran his index finger down the side of the glass. "Three years ago, whatever Joanne thinks. The details are none of your business. You need to understand only two things. The first is that Lydia wasn't raped." He looked away. "What the police found was mine."

I lit a cigarette, still watching him. "And the second?"

"That when I left, Lydia was still alive."

Laughter came from the hallway, clubmen walking to lunch in pairs. "He's not worth the money," someone was saying. "You could fit the entire Republican party down here into one room and wipe 'em out quicker than the St. Valentine's Day massacre." To Mooring, I said, "What happened that night?"

"I was only there an hour. She was high-strung, but laughing. We celebrated."

"Celebrated what?"

He gave me a quick sideways glance. "Being together. It was hard to arrange."

"Is that what made her high-strung, or was it Jason and the will?"

"No," he said flatly. "She didn't mention that."

"Wouldn't she?"

His eyelids dropped. Scowling, he said, "I'm not sure. Did you draft that?"

"Cade did. And he knows only what Lydia told him: not much."

He took a pensive sip. "I can't help with Jason. That night we didn't talk about him. We made love and said foolish things. Personal things, that's all. We made plans. When I left, she was smiling in the window."

"Or dead on the floor."

He flushed. "I had no reason, Shaw. Lydia was a rare woman—refined, yet real. There are no women like that, now."

The words had the tinny ring of cheap sentiment. I wondered if Lydia were another fine thing he'd wanted, a mirror in which to see himself, the new aristocrat. "Life is unfair," I said with a shrug.

His face hardened. Between his teeth he said, "It wasn't meant like that. She was kind; it wasn't practiced, it just was. There are things I can't explain to anyone. With Lydia I never had to."

"Where did your wife fit in?"

"Badly." He put down his drink. "Most people have two lives, perhaps three. You start as one person, and then—you can't expect a man and woman to keep fulfilling each other, not without children, something to build on." His gaze grew pointed. "Perhaps you understand that."

I shook my head. "Kris Ann's still the woman I want. That's one thing *you* should know: that if I find out who threatened her I won't invite him to the club and quote *Passages*. I'll kill him."

Mooring stared at me fixedly. "Bravely spoken."

"Lunch, gentlemen?" A waiter had slipped into the room and stood at a middle distance. Light from the chandelier made his face shiny. Carelessly, Mooring said, "You don't eat here, do you? You might try the Coquilles St. Jacques."

"Roast beef," I told the waiter. "Medium rare."

"Thank you, sir." He was a grizzled, crease-faced man old enough to be my father. Mooring ordered prawns and the waiter shuffled out, stiff and careful in the joints.

Mooring's eyes had stayed on me through the by-play. "I've had enough condescension now," he said evenly "You think you're different from me. The only difference is that your marriage made things easier. You see, I've known you since you first came here for parties, without ever being introduced. The first dance you stared at the floral display. You were wondering what it cost. I knew that. I knew that your tuxedo tie fastened in back because you hadn't learned to knot one. Your hands kept groping for pockets. When your wife talked to other men, you watched as though one might steal her. You felt out of place. Like me. And like me you kept coming back."

His insight startled me. For a moment I recalled feeling always about to select the wrong fork. "Once I thought Fitzgerald characters were interesting," I told him. "They are—in books."

Mooring lit a cigarette. Narrowly he watched it burn, taking one deep drag with the cigarette still between his lips. "It's ironic. Lydia understood that in you; she used to worry over your marriage, what would happen when you knew yourself. She understood it in me, that it was part of why I loved her. Not her money. Her sense of entitlement. You and I will never have that if we live to be a hundred."

I didn't answer. Mooring was a surprising man. His voice turned crisp. "About your wife. I know nothing of threats. You can accept that or not. But Joanne you leave alone. You're not to come near her or the house. The nurse on duty has instructions."

"You're incredible, Mooring. This morning I got a good look at your wife. She's feverish drunk and violent and crazy from neglect, and all you want is to lock her up."

Mooring's face closed against me. "There's too much you don't understand. I'm not asking your advice. You haven't quite caught on, have you?"

"Draw me a picture."

"I've told you all this so you would understand one thing: you're not going to the police."

"You're forgetting that I know Otis Lee may be innocent. And you or your wife, guilty."

"It wasn't rape, Shaw. That means in theory it could be anyone: me, Jason, Joanne, this man Lee—or Henry Cantwell." He pronounced the name bitterly.

"No one will believe your wife."

His look was keen. "Think about what she told you. She didn't see Cantwell, although that makes the best story. She saw his car. The police say there was no break-in. After Cantwell called Lydia no one saw him until the next morning. Except Joanne. Her testimony could send Henry Cantwell to the electric chair. And that's why you'll leave us out of it and the black man in jail. Because it's practical."

"That's already been done," I shot back. "To Lee's father. You're a bloodless prick and your wife's story is horseshit. If it weren't, you'd be tripping over me to nail Henry Cantwell for killing the woman you were supposed to love."

"Don't judge me, Shaw." Mooring's eyes turned bright and angry. "I hate Henry Cantwell more than you can dream. But Lydia's gone now. I have other obligations—things that don't concern you. There's no one, ever, who can truly judge another person's life, and I won't have you judge mine. All you need to know is that your friend's a murderer. You see," he finished softly, "we *are* at the country club. You've come here, and we've just made a deal."

A golfer laughed in the hallway. Mooring's stare was utterly composed. I stood without speaking, and left.

TWENTY-TWO

I left the parking lot driving too fast until I forced myself to slow down and think. But it was almost by instinct that I stopped at a telephone booth and called Jason Cantwell's.

No one answered. Cradling the still-ringing phone, I checked my watch and read one-thirty. I had less than three hours to decide what I could tell Rayfield. Nora Culhane would have to wait. I drove to Jason's and parked a half-block away.

An hour passed in the heat of the car before the woman appeared, striding loose-limbed with a grocery bag slung on her hip, hair bouncing as she walked. I waited until she was inside the building, then took the stairs up and knocked.

When the door unlatched, her wide, turquoise eyes peered frightenedly through a three-inch crack with a chain across. "I need to talk to you," I said.

She shrank back. "Jason might come home."

"I won't take long. Please, you might save someone from being hurt. Maybe you."

She hesitated for what seemed minutes. Then she unhooked the chain to let me in. She had changed to cutoffs and a thin T-shirt that showed her nipples. Her legs were long and tan, and she reminded me of when I was fourteen and read Erskine Caldwell, and the southern girls of my imagination were ripe and knowing and carried mysteries inside them.

I was older now and hadn't read Caldwell for a while; the girl seemed young.

"What's your name?" I asked.

"Terry Kyle. What happened to your face?"

"Nothing with Jason."

She watched me from in front of the door. I moved away from her to the couch and sat looking up. Softly I said, "There are things about this I don't understand. I'm afraid."

She waited silently. "I'm afraid of Jason," I said with more emphasis. "For you and for my wife."

Her mouth parted. "Why your wife?"

"Before we fought he said things about Kris Ann. The way he said them—how he looked and sounded—was more than getting back at me."

She turned away as if hurt. Then she went to a chair across the living room and sat with the coffee table between us. "He hates you," she said sadly.

I stared at her. "He hardly knows me."

"It doesn't matter." She kneaded one slim wrist with the fingers of the other hand, staring at a half-finished needlepoint cat which lay by the chair. "He has this thing about Kris Ann Cade." She looked at me with unhappy candor. "People are never with the people they want, are they?"

"Not always."

"Not Jason, always. Maybe sometimes. I think with Kris Ann it's just from being messed up when he was young."

"What do you mean?"

She shook her head. "Look, I'm telling you this so you'll leave, okay? It's not good you being here."

"I can't leave yet. There are things I have to know, for my wife's sake and for Jason's father."

"But that makes it worse." Her frightened voice ran words together. "I know 'Old Henry's' your friend and all, but he was no good for Jason—almost shunned him. Jason even used to pretend Henry Cantwell wasn't his real, father, that the real one was a tall man who watched him whenever he went outside, to see that he was safe."

"He told you that?"

She nodded shyly. "He tells me everything."

"How does that relate to Kris Ann?"

Her glance ran to the door and then back to me. "You're all mixed up in it, don't you see? After that fight he told me Henry saw you as a son, not him." The words rushed out now. "It's all a mess. One night when we were smoking dope with the lights turned out he started telling me, like he could only say it when I couldn't see him and he was stoned. About how when he was fourteen, looking at Kris Ann made him feel tight in his throat, all strange. He would think about her alone in his room—like maybe he did things to himself." She blushed. "I shouldn't say that. It's just that he wanted to believe they were close somehow—like she had no mother and he didn't really have a father so they should have each other. But then she did something to spoil it, he said, something about a garden, I don't know what. I've been afraid to ask—you know, when he was straight." She looked at me. "Kris Ann loves you and so does his daddy. So he's got to hate all of you, understand? He can't handle it any other way."

"That doesn't scare you?"

She gazed down at the needlepoint cat, catlike herself: darting eyes clear, then opaque. In a low voice, she said, "Sometimes I hate her, too."

"Krissy's no one to hate," I answered gently. "She's as confused as you or I, only her looks don't ask for help. That makes it harder."

She seemed suddenly not to hear me, but to be listening outside. Footsteps echoed in the tile corridor, moving toward us. We listened like mutes as they came closer and stopped outside. Keys jangled. She turned to me, pleading. I rose, and then the neighbor's door opened and shut.

In silence like a caught breath I asked, "For God's sake, why do you stay with him?"

She sagged in her chair. "He loves me," she said finally. "I'm not from fancy people. I'm no one special. But I can help him. He's not like he seems; the reason his daddy hurt him so is that he's a gentle boy who went begging for love. That's all he needs."

It sounded like a litany of faith. "The Florence Nightingale route is a hard one, Terry."

"What's that?"

"The notion that if you just love someone a little more, ignore what they are, you'll undo things that happened so young that they're part of them."

"But you don't understand." She said it with youthful stubbornness, clinging to what she hoped she knew. Her face—soft, unlined, yet to be written on—was still that of a woman yet to happen. In a fierce, scared undertone, she pleaded, "Let me alone with him. Please, just leave."

"I can't. The night before last, someone left a picture of Kris Ann on my windshield. It was mutilated like Jason's mother's."

She stiffened. "Jason wouldn't have done that to his mother."

"But what if she weren't raped, if she'd slept with someone first: a lover. Jason could have killed her."

"He couldn't have," she insisted.

"Terry, if you were alone that night then he might not only have killed Lydia, he may kill Kris Ann, or you."

She shook her head, looking away. "I told the police he was here with me, remember?"

"Then you may be accessory to a murder."

She stood abruptly and went to the door. "Please, go before he comes home."

I got up, catching her by the wrist. "Terry, he might kill someone. You have to tell the truth."

She turned, frightened, and then her eyes went blank. I heard footsteps again, becoming louder, felt her trembling. When the door opened I still held her wrist.

Jason stood in the doorway.

"Jason. It's all right."

Terry's voice was a thin wire of fear. He looked from her to me almost glassily, flushed and swallowing. I dropped her arm. "Hold on, man."

His face went rigid. He threw the door closed behind him and stalked between us to the bedroom. We froze watching the bedroom door. Jason came though it pointing a black revolver.

It followed me as I moved away from Terry. "I don't like guns," I said in a low voice.

"Jason." She was panicky now. "Don't."

He didn't seem to hear. As he came closer the small black hole of the revolver moved upward toward my face, stopping two inches from my mouth. His black eyes watched me over the gun. Terry moved next to him. "Jason, please..."

His boot jackknifed into my groin. I doubled retching as sickness numbed me and the girl screamed. Then the gun butt smashed my temple.

I was crawling on my stomach through a black hole with white flashes and a wooden door at the end while someone grappled behind me. A girl's voice panted, "Don't shoot him." My head swelled and shrank. With two hands I reached grasping toward a doorknob and wrenched myself up. I couldn't walk. A long dark moment later I fell face first down a flight of stairs, out of the universe.

TWENTY-THREE

I reached in the darkness. My face brushed his overcoat, mildew-smelling. His revolver lay on the closet shelf above me. Teetering on the stool, I grasped the shelf with one hand and stretched. My fingers splayed. The tips felt cold steel...

"Adam!"

My hand fell away as the stool tipped clattering to the floor. I caught the shelf, hanging amidst his clothes. Her fingers clutched the back of my shirt. I lost my grip, fell, landed off balance. Hangers rattled as I stumbled against the closet wall and turned.

Her face was ivory, the blood gone from her lips. Brian cowered behind her. I stood straight. "I have to hold it, Mother."

She began shrieking and then her palm cracked across my face....

Ice water ran down my face and neck. "Can you hear me?" she asked.

I heard myself moan, tasted blood, warm and salty. "Let me take you to the hospital," she was saying.

"Where am I?" The words came slurred to my ears.

"Your car. You crawled here."

I tried opening my eyes. Terry leaned through the window with a rag and a green jug of water, her features swimming.

"No time..."

"Please, you're not seeing me, I can tell. There was this crack when he hit you."

She sounded scared. I rolled my neck on the car seat, trying to focus until I could make out the building. From upstairs a bearded man looked down with his palms pressed on the window. "Get out," I said. "Go to the police."

"I can't. Not now."

White sun cut into my eyes. I propped myself against the wheel and jabbed at the ignition with my key until the motor snarled. The world had shrunk to the size of my windshield, with Terry pleading from the side. Her face fell away.

My car was crawling onto Twentieth Street as horns blasted and my head screamed. In slow motion I drove to the police station, to sleep...

Rough hands shook me. "Drugs and whiskey," he rasped. "You look for poison in your sports car instead of Jesus in your heart."

It was no dream. I raised my head, squinted into the red worn face of a wrinkled stranger with rotten teeth and craziness in his eyes. He stopped waving his Bible up and down. "Give me a hand," I murmured.

I cracked open the door and fell sideways until he caught me. I let my feet slide out, pulling up by his lapels. His breath stank. "So you're who he's got left," I said.

His eyes, clear, white, and glassy, seemed only to see distances. "He's coming, brother."

"Come on," I managed. "Help me inside."

He clutched my elbow as I walked up the

stairs, stopping every few steps, his breathing a low asthmatic whistle. At the top I rested on the glass door. "Thanks."

He looked through me. "He's coming," he wheezed, and teetered away, shouting at passersby.

I walked leaning forward through a long tunnel toward a door I remembered. I opened it, falling. Rayfield disappeared.

I awoke lying on a metal desk with my suit coat folded under my neck and a paramedic watching me. I could smell iodine, felt explosions in my skull. "I fell," I said absently.

The paramedic answered, "You were hit."

"You stupid bastard," said Rayfield.

The colloquy came to my ears with detached lucidity, as when you're prattling at a cocktail party and suddenly hear the sound of your own emptiness so clearly it seems someone else's. But now there was numbness in my feet, nausea, a ringing skull. My crotch felt swollen. "Get me a chair," I mumbled.

Bast slid one over. I pushed off the table and sat. But I couldn't retrieve the pounding of my subconscious, why I awoke believing that I shouldn't be here, that I couldn't tell Rayfield about Jason. Better to stick with Lee. "Listen—"

"Where you been?" Bast demanded.

"Searching—"

The paramedic broke in. "You're concussed, man. You're slurring words."

"He's a stupid fuck," Bast said, "who's going to get himself killed."

"I don't think it was Lee—"

"Who's the gray-haired man?" Rayfield cut in.

"What man?" Then I remembered Mooring.

Rayfield's face reddened. Bast leaned over me. "If anyone's killed out of this, asshole, it's on you."

The place smelled of raw nerve ends. "Better take him to the E.R.," the paramedic said nervously.

"Get Bast out of here," I told Rayfield.

Rayfield's jaw worked. He pulled the ball-point pen from his shirt pocket as he nodded toward Bast. Bast and the paramedic disappeared. A fluorescent ceiling light blinked above me. In the open room silent figures moved at the corners of my eyes. Rayfield seemed distant, on the wrong end of a telescope. He shoved coffee at me. I drank some and lit a cigarette, constructing a small manageable world where I did the same things, smoke and drink coffee. Rayfield's pen began clicking. "What about Lee?"

"He didn't kill me. He didn't rape Mrs. Cantwell..." My voice fell off.

"So you say to let him go." The question was taunting, silken.

I tried to concentrate. "I don't think you can hold him."

"You don't see the mayor, my captain, or all those people who need a killer. Just the idea of who Lee is makes people anxious. Some people want him burned."

My teeth ached. The pen noise was like dripping water. "I don't."

"But you'd do that to protect Henry Cantwell."

I couldn't answer. I righted myself and tried reaching for my jacket.

"You know, I've wondered." He said it behind me, musingly. "I guess the worrying over your wife was crap."

I turned back to his long, speculative look. The look and something new in his voice kept me there. He placed a chair with its back to me and straddled it leaning forward, eyes curious and disdainful as he said quietly, "You're queer, aren't you?"

It was like falling in a dream. I wasn't sure where I was or how the fall would end. "Aren't you?" he spat.

"Just graceful."

"No, you don't look queer. But you can't go by that." His silent stare gauged me until he seemed to decide something after a long while. "You really don't know, do you? He's got you running like a rat in a maze, getting beat up and lying for him, and he hasn't told you."

"Who? Told me what?"

"Henry Cantwell."

"What about him?"

Rayfield smiled slightly. "He's a faggot, Shaw."

"Bullshit."

"Seven years ago," he spoke over me, "the vice squad raided a gay motel. Your good friend Henry Cantwell was in bed with a sixteen-year-old boy. He likes them young,

Shaw; he just doesn't like getting caught. He was crying when they brought him in."

I closed my eyes. "Who told you this?"

"I saw him. He was begging—it would ruin him, couldn't they understand—weak, like a fairy." His voice thickened. "It made me sick to watch him. He shivered while they read his rights and told him he had one phone call. He got up, pacing in a little circle like he couldn't decide. When he reached for the telephone his hands were shaking.

"It was over in an hour. Someone called the captain who ran vice. The records were destroyed. Cade walked into the station, looked around like we were dirt, asked the captain for Cantwell, and dragged him off without speaking. Cantwell wouldn't even look at him. But the boy was a stray and Cantwell had money. It never made the papers, never went to court. It never happened. Except it did." His voice shook now. "I hate queers, Shaw. But even worse I hate Cade and Cantwell buying us like whores. It won't happen twice. This isn't some sweet little boy getting corn-holed and some vice-squad politician. It's a murder. It's mine."

There was thin sweat on his forehead. From my subconscious welled the reason I hadn't turned in Jason. The room shimmered as I stood, said, "See you, Lieutenant," and tried moving toward the door.

"Where were you?" he called out.

I didn't turn. "Nowhere."

His pen clicked behind me.

TWENTY-FOUR

A slim, silent black man gave me a sideways glance as he walked past the house. I knocked again, resting my hand on the doorframe. The porch was cool, but the dirty, sweet honeysuckle smell made me sicker. I took the deep, rhythmic breaths I used while running. My ears echoed with their sound.

The door opened and then Etta Parsons' mouth. "We need to talk," I said.

"Why?"

"Because you've known about Jason Cantwell for twenty-seven years and told no one. Now it's time."

Her surprise became shock. I stepped in front of her. "Look, whoever killed Mrs. Cantwell threatened my wife. If anything happens to her..."

She backed stiffly from the door to the living-room couch without answering or dropping her gaze, and sat. She looked smaller, older, less today like Lydia Cantwell than a lone black woman strip-mined of dreams. Through the sepia gloom, she asked, "What do you want?"

"The truth about Jason, from the beginning."

Her eyes moved sadly to Lydia's picture, as if saying that it was only she who had lived to know the end of things. "I don't see it matters now."

"It matters to me. I think Lydia's murder

began long before she died, perhaps with Jason. Or don't you give a damn?"

Her face toughened. "They've arrested Otis Lee."

"Yes, and maybe he killed her. Maybe that's a chance you'd like to take."

The sound of my own hypocrisy echoed in the room. But only I heard it. Her hardness dissolved in doubt. I had the sense of a long ago secret, hoarded inside until its sadness was hurtful to the touch. More gently, I asked, "Jason isn't Henry Cantwell's son, is he?"

She looked at the picture. Then, slowly, she nodded.

My knees were buckling. I sat heavily across from her. "How do you know that?"

Her legs were crossed, thin shoulders drawn in. "It's all complicated," she finally murmured. "I came to the Cantwells' after she'd married him, when I was just past being a girl, like her. Clifton—the one I'd meant to marry—he was killed in Korea." She paused, swallowing, and her words came faster. "After that I didn't know what I'd do. My godmother got me a place with the Cantwells because she'd been maid to the family. It was such a big house I was scared when I came there, not knowing my duties, my mind still with Clifton. At first I didn't see much and I don't know about before, except what she told me later."

"What was that?"

"Nothing to start with. It was more a feeling things weren't right. Oh, they talked some;

every night I'd bring them Manhattans in the sitting room after he'd come home. But something was left out. You know how a man watches a woman when she's new to him—sort of follows her with his eyes—like the way she's made, or even that she's there, surprises him?"

I nodded, for a moment almost smiling. "I think so."

"Well, Mr. Cantwell wasn't like that."

"How was he?"

"I don't know," she said, "I guess close to cowed, like when he talked to her his eyes would slide away and mornings sometimes he'd even look down when he saw me, like he was fixing to apologize." Etta spoke in a rush now, as though speech were catharsis. "I remember once they were in the dining room, talking real low, and then she got up from the table and left him there. He went to the liquor cabinet for a bottle of brandy. I saw him staring in at his library with the bottle in one hand, like he couldn't decide what to do. Then he just stepped inside and closed the door behind him. I should have felt sorry for him, he seemed so lonely. But I saw what was happening to her."

"What was that?"

"It was like she was falling apart. She was pretty and so young." Etta spoke the word feelingly, almost in anger, her hands becoming small fists. "She should have been laughing, going out with someone who wanted her, not wasting in a dark house, day after day and year after year just drying up, not being loved or touched. It's a waste that should happen."

My head was pounding. "Sure, now. It is."

Etta nodded fiercely. "She'd walk from room to room, looking around like it was all strange and she was a prisoner. You don't have to be in jail to be in prison: I already knew that. She began staying in bed until he'd gone. One morning I brought breakfast to her room, hoping she'd eat. She was still in bed, holding a man's framed picture in both hands. She looked up and gave me a funny smile, like, 'It's no use pretending, is it?' " Etta's own smile was slight and sad. "That was the first time she really noticed me—*me*, not a maid. After that we began to talk."

"Do you know who the man was?"

"She never said, but I think maybe a man from Grangeville. From the picture he was pushing forty, good-looking except for his eyes: clear enough to see through and cold as a snake's. It chilled me to look at them. But all she told me was that she'd run from loving him, that he was part of her but evil and that he wanted to put her on a shelf away from people to make up for things he couldn't have. It didn't make sense, all of it. But, I think he was the reason she married Mr. Cantwell."

"Did she say that?"

"She just said she married him thinking he'd never lie or hurt her, and then moved her shoulders like she'd been wrong. She didn't say it angry; it was sadder than that, and surer. A few days later she started going out."

"In what sense?"

"Disappearing." Etta's eyes turned vague

until I guessed that Lydia Cantwell had become more real than me or where she was. "She'd be gone three or four hours and then come back late afternoon jittery and absent-minded, like she was part scared and part somewhere else. I started making tea to settle her down. She'd never liked it but she got to taking it at the kitchen table where she would look out the window. She'd ask me to sit with her and then start talking about all sorts of things, wild almost, everything except about where she'd been or who she'd seen. Something in her couldn't say that. I never asked. I didn't want to press things."

I said nothing. But silence and my face gave my thoughts away. "Things were understood," she insisted. "Oh, they'd have their Manhattans and weekends they might give dinner parties for his parents or the Sumners or Cades, and she'd smile or even laugh, like nothing was wrong. But when I served them drinks I could tell how alone she was. *I* was the one who really saw her."

"You, and at least one other."

Understanding came into her eyes. "Yes," she said coldly. "One."

"When did you learn that?"

Her lids dropped and she placed her palms flat on the couch, speaking without emphasis or inflection. "One morning as soon as Mr. Henry was gone she dressed in a hurry and left. She was out longer than normal—five, six hours. I was dusting the staircase when she burst through the door looking flushed and half-crazy.

Right away I ask if she wants tea. She flings down her red silk scarf, runs past me up the stairs, and slams the door behind her without answering. I wanted to go up after her. But I couldn't. I just dusted." Etta's eyes were still hooded, her flatness of speech lending the trancelike quality of literal recall. "At four o'clock she came to the kitchen where I was, and says, 'I'd like tea now,' real quiet, like she's sorry. I put one tea service in front of her. She looks up at me, then toward the other chair. 'Please,' she says.

"I sat down with my cup. You could see she'd been crying but her eyes were dry now. She looks at me very steady and says, 'I'm pregnant.'

"She doesn't say anything about Mr. Henry. She doesn't have to. 'What will you do?' I ask.

"She looks sad. 'I don't know,' she says. 'It's all so hopeless. He's married; I'm married. I'm not even sure I want him. He was just there.' "

" 'What does he say?' I ask."

"She looks out the window. 'He loves me, in his way: at least I'm part of a life he's wanted. But it would be impossible for him at work, and his career has really just begun. He knows that.'

"I can't think of what to tell her. After a time she says in a low voice, 'Etta, it's like I'm being punished.'

"The way she looks and sounds I feel like shivering. 'Why would you be punished?' I ask.

"She shakes her head. 'For many things.'

"I feel so bad that without thinking I reach

out to touch her hand. As soon as I touch her I feel like it's wrong and pull back. But she just looks at her hand, smiling a little.

"We sit like that across the table, neither one of us talking. Then we hear Mr. Henry coming through the front door. She looks at me and says very quiet, 'Thank you, Etta.' Then she stands, sort of squares her shoulders, and walks out to meet him.

"I stayed in the kitchen. She said something to him and then I heard the library door close. I waited, pretending to work. They didn't come out for over an hour. Then the door slid open and she called out that her and Mr. Cantwell would be having their Manhattans. When I brought them to the sitting room, they were in their same chairs, talking polite, like usual, except he was so pale. 'Thank you,' he says, and she smiles and tells me, 'You should go home now, Etta. It's late.' It was always strange how she could do that. From her face I couldn't have told anything at all.

"I thought about her all night. But when I came back the next morning she was still in her room. When she finally came down I was in the kitchen, polishing silver. Her hair was just so, and there was powder beneath her eyes, as though she were hiding circles. She looked hardly alive, more like a doll. 'I'll be staying home now,' she said.

" 'Is that what you want?' I asked.

"She stared out the window. 'We've come to an understanding.' I didn't say anything.

Then she looked straight at me and said, 'You're the only one who knows, Etta.' And then she asked for tea."

Etta's face had begun fading in front of me. "Did the man try to see her?" I managed.

"I don't know. Right away she shut herself in, reading up on babies, picking names, trying to be the best mother she could after Mr. Jason was born by smothering him with love. She saw the father only once I'm sure about, when Mr. Jason was about to turn six. It was afternoon and I was in the dining room and she was upstairs. The telephone rang. When I picked it up, she said through the extension, 'That's all right, Etta, I have it,' sounding real nervous. I didn't know who was calling. But a few minutes later she was dressed and hurrying out the door. Two hours later she came back looking tired. She sat down in the kitchen and said, 'He wants to marry me.'

"She didn't need to say who. 'Can you?' I asked.

"She shook her head. 'Not now,' she answered, and for a long time after there was only the birthday presents."

I rubbed my temple. "I don't understand."

Etta blinked as though she had forgotten that, her glance moving from piece to piece of the Cantwells' hand-me-down tables and chairs. "He made her do that. Just before that same birthday she gave me ten dollars and asked if I'd stop on my way across town to get a toy gun for Mr. Jason, one of those that shot caps. She said she hated them but the father said if he couldn't have her or a son he'd at least be part of his birthday. She told me it was something that had to be. I wish it hadn't. Mr. Jason always liked guns too much."

I shrugged. "It wouldn't have mattered. Take them away and a kid just makes one with his finger and pretends."

"Well, it wasn't always guns," she allowed. "But every year until his fifteenth birthday, she'd hand me money—his money, she said—and tell me what present he wanted to give."

"And after that?"

"It just stopped. She never said anything about it."

"Did she ever say who it was?"

"No," she said firmly. "She never would have done that."

I took a deep breath and asked, "But you know it was Mooring, don't you?"

Etta's face was cold. She looked down at her skirt, smoothed it, and nodded curtly.

"How?"

Her voice turned scornful. "Because he called once or twice, just before she started going out, even came by once on his way home—to drop something, he said, when I could see he didn't need to and just wanted to stare at her. He looked awkward, out of place." Grudgingly she added, "She seemed to like him and I guess I could see why in the state she was in. He was good-looking enough."

"But that's not all of it."

"No." She said it quickly, as if embarrassed. "Three years ago he started turning up again. It was like she didn't care about the secret anymore. She'd run to the door every time he came. I felt strange. We'd gotten older together, caring for the house and Mr. Jason, and I hadn't seen her act like that since before he was born. She looked younger. I didn't like how he'd gotten so smooth but to her it didn't matter. It was a second chance, she said: Jason was grown, for worse or better, and she didn't want to be with Mr. Henry anymore."

"Was she divorcing him?"

"She never said." Her forehead creased. "One day Mr. Mooring and her had a long talk out back and after that she stopped leaving the house to meet him. He still sneaked by—she was still glad to see him—but they acted more careful.

"It was like that the last time he came. He dropped by the day after the fight with Mr. Jason, just before she went to see Mr. Cade. He was there maybe fifteen minutes. They talked out back looking real serious and then he went his way and she went downtown. She told me she had an appointment to see Mr. Cade and that I could leave."

"But you don't know what she and Mooring talked about?"

Etta looked at me gravely. "I never saw her again."

In the silence that followed, my head filled with metronomic pounding. Finally, I asked, "Who do you think killed her?"

She stared at me. "I guess Otis Lee had reason," she said evenly. "And he watched her all the time."

"Would she have let him in?"

"I don't know."

"But she would let in someone she knew, like Mooring. Or Jason."

"I don't see why Mr. Mooring—"

"But you do see Jason, don't you."

Etta looked back at Lydia's picture. After a long time she said, "Lord knows she tried. But all that caring didn't seem to matter at the end. He had a terrible temper and Mr. Henry always pretty much ignored him. And they'd had that fight. Still, it would be so wrong. I mean, she gave up everything for that one child."

Until the end, I thought, and even then, when she wanted more, she had never quite made it. "Did she ever ask you to go with her if she left Mr. Cantwell?"

Etta's head snapped up. "She didn't have to. I was the only one who really saw her."

But did she see you, I wondered. Etta read my thoughts. "She understood me," she said sharply. "She understood about Clifton. She gave me part of her own life to make up for that."

Her words were tense, angry. I realized what she had sought from me was not release from secrets, but something more: an affirmation that the service to which she had given her life was not just that of a maid. They had been friends, she said, but what she meant was that was all she had.

"I know," I told her. "That was why I came."

She nodded fractionally. I rose, feeling dizzy. "Thank you for helping," I managed.

She didn't answer. My part of witness was over. As I silently left, she smoothed her skirt again, still staring at Lydia's picture.

Henry Cantwell opened the door. His head seemed to get smaller, then larger. "Good Lord, Adam, what have you done?"

I steadied myself. "I got pistol whipped by Jason Cantwell. You know, the son who isn't yours."

Henry blanched. "What happened?"

I told him curtly, then snapped, "I need your phone," and passed him in the doorway. From behind he said thinly, "I'll be in the library."

I went to the kitchen, sat by the window at the table with two chairs, and called Kris Ann. "Where are you?" she asked somewhere beyond anger.

"Henry's." There was no way to explain. "I'll be home right after. Lock the doors and don't go anywhere."

"Whatever," she said coldly. "I can always call Daddy, can't I?"

"Krissy, I don't think Otis Lee killed her—"

She hung up.

For a moment I sat listening to the dial tone. Then I stood, got my balance, and walked to the library.

TWENTY-FIVE

Henry sat in his chair. On the table beside him were a snifter of cognac, his half-glasses, and the copy of *War and Peace* he read for consolation. "Should you begin fearing death," he had told me once, "pick up *War and Peace* and after a time all that will melt away." That much was familiar. But the way he looked had changed, and the way I saw him.

"How did you know?" he asked tonelessly.

I lit a cigarette and gazed down at him. He wore a three-piece suit with his father's gold chain across the vest. His eyes, shiny and translucent, stared back with shamed insistence.

"Rayfield told me part. He enjoyed that."

Henry winced. "And what did you think?"

"That I've never known you."

His mouth opened, closed, opened again. "Adam, we—my feeling for you isn't because—"

"Oh, God, Henry."

"I mean, you're almost a son."

I took a deep, harsh drag. "Then I can see Jason's point."

He shut his eyes. "Sit down, please."

I didn't move. His eyes opened. "Sit down, damn you. I won't have you hovering like that."

I took a long time sitting. Wisps from my cigarette twisted between us, then disappeared. Twilight and his reading lamp cast thin silver in the room. "Is it—what I am?" he asked.

"Don't make it so easy on yourself."

His eyebrows raised. "You think that's easy."

"Easy, and not the point."

"You're hurt then," he said gently.

"Don't be sentimental. There's a black man in jail who maybe shouldn't be. I've taken on Cade and Rayfield and Mooring, been beaten up by Jason, put my marriage in jeopardy and now Kris Ann, and you've been content to let me do that, not knowing the truth. I'll get that now if I have to shake it out of you."

He raised a hand to stop me. "Adam, please—"

"*Hurt* is a trivial word, Henry. I want to know what you're really after. Your marriage was a fraud and you don't give a damn about Jason. I'm a cat's paw you've played against Roland."

"Has that been too hard for you?"

There was sudden steel in his voice. Softly, I answered, "Not too hard."

"I hope not." He spoke without apology. "Because I couldn't tell you."

"Just Roland."

"There were reasons for that." I shrugged my indifference. "Please," he urged. "Hear me out. I'll explain as much as I can."

I sat back to light a second cigarette, watching him. His chest looked small, his breathing shallow and rapid. In pale light the skin of his face—too slack beneath the eyes, drawn tight across his cheeks—made him look like a dying man. He stared fixedly away. "That boy I was with wasn't the beginning, Adam. I'd had those feelings—wanting to

245

touch and be touched—long before, from when I was young. They made me sick. I tried believing I wasn't like that. My father, Roland—they were the men they wished to be. There was no one I could tell."

I rubbed my forehead to fight the ache inside, and for a moment Henry was Eddie Halloran, smiling, listening, telling no one, winding up dead. "I married Lydia hoping to be different," he went on. "There was someone else, I knew, but we had things in common, and I thought somehow..." His voice flattened out. "The wedding night was a disaster. I was what I had feared. Afterwards she lay awake in her pink nightgown. I could hear her breathing. Finally I couldn't stand it. I told her about the feelings. It was as though she went into shock. She began shaking her head, saying, 'Oh, God, no,' over and over and asking why, why had I married her. Then she broke down. When I closed the door behind me she was still sobbing.

"The next morning I couldn't face her. Neither of us—it just went on like that. We talked of annulment, finally. It wasn't fair to keep her but I didn't know what to do. I was so damned afraid of being found out. Then she told me she was pregnant. It was odd: I was shocked and then that wore off, and I was relieved. I had something to forgive now, too, and she needed me." Henry paused, finishing in a hollow voice, "And God help me, I knew people would think it was mine."

He looked up—for a question, something to

keep him going. I just watched him. His face fell and he lapsed into a drone. "Lydia made it easier, in a sense. I asked who the father was. She tilted her chin in that pose she had, sitting right where you are now, and told me never to ask again. When we stepped from this room, the lie began, and grew until it cut across all our life. We were faithful in our way: she played the gracious hostess and I the contented husband and father. But there was little between us except appearances and less between me and Jason. She mothered him as if to say, 'Look: here's someone I care for.' But when I looked at him, I saw my failure: the weakling, the one who'd let down his wife and father, the closet homosexual." His voice was bleak. "And still I wanted to know how that would be.

"For years I wondered, playing out my part. I'd never—I'd never had a man, never had sex with anyone. The evening it happened I was driving back from a business trip. The boy was thumbing by the shoulder of the road: a tall, slim boy in blue jeans. I stopped for him. He was hungry and dirty and needed money." Henry's voice turned raw. "When I put my hand on him, he didn't move. My throat was tight. He was young and empty-looking. I drove to a motel with a smirking nightman. It was dirty and there were stains on the sheets. But that blank-faced boy was exactly what I needed.

"At the moment they burst through the door I was the happiest I could remember. And then they were pulling us apart and calling me an 'old queer.' It was like being trapped inside someone else's body. I rode to the station in the back of a prowl car with the boy chewing gum and a fat policeman in between. All I could think of was to be free. When we reached the station they took the boy somewhere and dragged me inside. I never saw him again.

"When they booked me I broke down, begging. They just looked away, all except for that policeman, Rayfield. He was staring at me from a corner like I made him sick. He wouldn't stop." A purple vein throbbed in Henry's temple. "I imagined our friends looking at me like that. I saw Roland's face, the contempt in it hardening. It came to me then. Of all of them, Roland was the one I'd sell my soul to keep from knowing. And only Roland could help."

"So you called him."

He nodded dejectedly. "He fixed it. I don't know how. I didn't want to. I was just grateful, then."

"And later?"

"Later, it was done."

I was silent. Henry's eyes raised from the floor. "You do understand about not telling you, at least a little? I'd failed with Jason, and you at least respected me. It didn't seem relevant to Lydia."

He leaned forward as though reaching. I ground my cigarette as smoke died in acrid curls, lit another, and said, "Did you kill her, Henry?"

He went white. "I suppose I deserve—"

"Because Joanne Mooring says you did."

"That's insane—"

"Specifically, she says she waited here that night spying on Lydia and her husband. She swears that when Mooring left Lydia was still alive. So she started toward the house to confront her. And then, while you say you were sixty miles away, your black Mercedes turned up the driveway and scared her off."

Henry seemed to shrivel in his chair. Faintly he inquired, "Why hasn't she gone to the police?"

"That puzzled me until I learned about Jason. If Mooring's his father all that would come out. And Joanne drinks. The police might not believe her and suspect Mooring instead. Not bad reasons. The one I believe is more complex. For years Jason received anonymous birthday presents from his real father. Suppose Mooring wants to protect Jason. Perhaps he thinks that if the police learn that it was he who made love to Lydia, they'll suspect Jason of killing her. Jason wouldn't have to be Oedipus then. Just a murderer."

Henry's hands twisted together. When I finished, he looked up, mumbling as if it didn't matter, "But she lied, Adam."

"How would you know?"

He flushed. "I never left Anniston. I was with someone that night.

"With whom?"

His gaze was level. "A man."

"A man," I repeated.

He nodded. "Yes."

"If that's true, then you lied to Rayfield."

"I suppose I did."

"You suppose. Does Roland know?"

"He knows."

I felt the pain in my skull leeching strength from the rest of me. "And he sat there with Rayfield and let you lie."

"I'd do anything to hide this," he said miserably. "That was something Roland already knew."

"You lie to the police, to put yourself closer to the electric chair, and Roland watches."

Henry's hands trembled. "You talk about something you don't understand. I'd go to cocktail parties, pretending to be happy, and all the time I'm hoping, looking for someone whose eyes don't slide away. Furtiveness becomes a way of life."

"That's no answer."

He looked across at me. "I'd found someone, Adam. A man with a wife and three children."

I pulled out a cigarette and began tamping one end on my wristwatch. "Who is he?"

"I can never tell that."

I looked up. "Rayfield would find that convenient."

"It doesn't matter." For a moment Henry's face was almost serene. "I love him," he said simply.

I lit the cigarette and smoked half of it. Night had fallen. Henry sat in a circle of lamplight as if cornered by darkness. Finally I said, "Tell me what happened, leaving out his name."

"You won't try to find him, Adam."

"I won't even assume that he exists."

"Then you don't believe me."

"Just tell it," I said angrily.

Henry checked his cuffs and tie knot with quick, nervous gestures. "There's not much to tell," he said reluctantly. "We'd arranged to meet. He told his wife he was going on a trip. I got the room and called Lydia to say I was too tired to drive home. I'd used that excuse before; she knew what it meant. Usually she treated it with weary, almost tolerant, contempt. But this time she was intrusive, tense sounding. Who was I with, she asked. When I wouldn't say, she grew angry. There was something we had to discuss, right now. Couldn't it wait, I asked. She hesitated, then said, 'It's waited too long already.' But I didn't want to know. I just wanted to get off the phone." His voice was hoarse. "I just wanted to be with him. So I told her I'd be back in the morning and hung up."

"Then you never learned what she wanted."

He shook his head. "Jason and the will, perhaps. But I didn't return to find out. If I had, she might have lived."

"And now you wonder."

"Yes." He spoke intently. "But there's something more. I have this terrible sense of buried connections, that what's happened to all three of us—even Lydia's death—is entwined with what I am. I have to know, Adam."

251

In the bad light his face seemed etched with guilt and questions. I wondered how much of him I knew, how far the hidden parts had taken him, how much good there was between us. "There was a girl once," I said, "in Florence. I was there for two weeks on a college tour, with money I'd saved working. It was good and it wasn't. I got a *pensione*, spent most of my time at the Uffizi and the like. I saw the paintings. Then, the evening before I was to leave, I looked out my window to the alley below which led to a *piazza*. The sun was setting and for a moment before nightfall the walls of the city were dusty pink. It became dark. I was turning away when I saw her through a window across the alley. She was slim, with long dark hair like Kris Ann's, though I didn't know her then. She was packing. She began to undress, carefully folding her things in the suitcase, one by one until they were all folded. I watched her. When she was through she came naked to the window and for a moment looked out at the city, as I had. Then she pulled the blinds.

"The next day I looked for her in the *piazza*, hoping to buy her a glass of red wine. I never found her and at noon our bus left for the airport. Perhaps I wouldn't have recognized her. But I always wondered."

Henry listened, thoughtful. "It's different," he said when I was through.

"Perhaps."

"I have to know," he repeated. "Maybe none of this has ever meant anything. Maybe life doesn't. But a man has to live as though it does. I have to. Especially now."

"Why me? Why not Roland?"

"Because I trust you." He looked at me directly. "And because you need answers, too."

I shrugged. "I guess we'll see."

The depression in his face seemed to ease. "You believe me then, Adam."

"We'll see." I stubbed my cigarette. "We'll see what I do."

I got up without waiting for an answer. My legs were rubbery, my head light. I felt foolish, surprised. Henry rose, reaching for me. "You're pale, Adam. Let me drive you to the hospital."

I waved him back. "I need to get home to Kris Ann. Just stay there. Please."

He slumped, arms falling to his sides. I got to the library door, hesitated, then turned, propping one hand in the doorway. He watched me in the dimness. "Men," I said. "Jesus, Henry, how did you get stuck with that one?"

He shook his head. "I don't know, Adam. It just was."

I nodded slowly. When I turned to leave he was reaching for *War and Peace*.

I awoke panicky with the sense of lost time. It was dark. Seconds passed as I recognized my garage, replayed the surreal drift of the drive home, a collage of strobe-light beams, curves that shifted and distances that shrank abruptly, leaping shadows. The luminous blue of my

253

wristwatch became numbers again. I relaxed; I had lost perhaps fifteen minutes.

I got out, moving from muscle memory through the garage and into the backyard. The night moved. Fluorescent moonlight yellowed the grass and oaks and the pathway of mossy stones leading to the sunroom. Its windows were dark. Inside the house was total darkness.

Stumbling from stone to stone I ran toward the house, slipping, falling palms forward on the slippery moss of the stone in front of me, smelling its dankness. Crablike, I pushed at the slimy rocks and then the whine came and bits of rock flew into my face.

The second bullet struck the tree behind me. Kris Ann, I thought frenziedly. I came up running off balance with the third shot, headed for the sunroom window. Ten feet, five feet. A fourth shot. Arms across my face, I hurtled through the window amidst a hail of shattering glass and hit the floor, blacking out for the last time.

TWENTY-SIX

I awoke staring up at the antique fan. Stinging cuts covered my hands. The house was dark and silent and no one stood over me. I couldn't remember Kris Ann's Audi parked in the garage.

I got up.

Glass crunched beneath my first step. The step took too long. My brain was a box of light unable to send signals through its walls. Inside the box I knew someone could kill me, but my feet were stone.

I took a slow second step. My head felt melon soft.

The third step was easier, and the fourth. I got used to the numbness and to making noise that they could hear.

The living room was empty.

I stopped to let my eyes adjust. In the dining room ahead, moonlight caught the hard polish of mahogany. Its corners were stained by darkness. But when I went there nothing happened. The windows were cracked open and through the screens came cricket sounds in a chorus of rising and falling, moving like the night had moved. The lot next door, tangled and overgrown, was full of them. I realized that the shots had come from there. Still I heard no footsteps but mine.

I edged to the kitchen door, back to the wall until my head turned the corner.

Nothing. Nothing but two barstools at the counter, a coffee cup and dirty ashtray, thin shadows on the wall. Slowly, silent now, I moved to the drawers for a carving knife.

It was smooth, balanced in my hand. I began reaching for the light switch, then stopped. Light would help them.

A pen clicked behind me. I froze, heard nothing, felt nothing except fear that tricked the brain. Fear now at the base of my spine and between my shoulder blades. The sound of my own steps came to me from some great distance.

Suddenly I was tripped, falling forward, losing the knife. My palms hit as it clattered across the tile. I turned on my knees to fight.

Kris Ann's shoes lay where I had stumbled. The knife slid against the far wall and stopped. I was dead if they heard me. I crawled sweating toward the knife, grasped it, rose again.

Still nothing.

I began up the dark staircase to the bedroom, breathing harder. Perhaps they would be there. I moved faster to the second floor, hurried down the dark hallway past empty bedrooms, toward ours. It was dark. I gripped the knife tighter, found the light switch, pushed down.

Our bed was made and inside there was no one dead or living. I went to Kris Ann's nightstand and opened it.

The gun was missing. "Kris Ann," my brain began chanting, faster and faster in a terrible rhythm. I went down the hallway to the stairs, holding the knife in my left hand, feeling and not feeling the smooth banister. "Kris Ann..."

Footfalls. I was trapped in mid-stairway. No trick of the nerve ends but footfalls moving from the kitchen below me toward the dining room, real as the acid in my mouth. Coming closer.

A shadow moved into the alcove. I raised the knife.

Something clicked. The lights turning on.

Shock as the knife dropped from my hand. "Thank God," I blurted. "You're all right."

I told them about Jason. Bast took notes. Rayfield asked questions. He seemed backed away from me, just a policeman, and his thumb stroked the pen without clicking it. I didn't tell him about the Moorings, or Henry's lover. Jason used a gun, I said: it had to be him.

Rayfield shrugged without comment. When I ventured that it couldn't have been Lee, he answered coldly that I was wrong: my friend Nate Taylor had sprung Lee an hour after I had left. There wasn't enough to hold him, Rayfield added: they'd just wanted to see what I'd do.

I stared at him. "Like get shot."

This time it was Bast who shrugged. "If that's what you want," he said, and closed the notebook. Kris Ann watched in silence.

They went. A bespectacled doctor and two nurses came and went, leaving Kris Ann and me alone. Everything—the walls and sheets, even the bed frame—was white. Kris Ann still wore her white tennis dress. "You shouldn't have left," I said. My voice sounded tinny. "He might have shot you."

"I was too angry to wait." She looked away. "And I had the revolver."

"So you could drill Jason Cantwell at fifty paces."

"Yes." She didn't smile.

I watched her. She sat against a cinder-block

wall, the right strap of her dress blood-speckled from helping me to the car. "Next time," I said, "just tell me to fuck off. Something simple."

She said nothing. After a moment she rose and took a cool rag from the nightstand, running it across my face. Her finger gently traced the stitches beneath one eye. "What's happened to us, Adam?"

I tried smiling. "You cheat at back-gammon—"

"The baby?"

"Krissy, stop—"

"I mean it's not just coming here and Daddy, is it?"

"Not now." I reached up, my fingers disappearing in her hair. She closed her eyes.

"I don't know who you are."

I looked away. "When my father died I stopped thinking about that. My mother needed someone and I was there. Then she wanted a lawyer—someone who wouldn't desert her by being killed—and I became one. I don't know—I don't like talking this way."

"But why?"

"Because words don't make any difference. You string them all together and in the end people define themselves by what they do."

She shook her head. "Word games, Adam. There's too much we never say."

I looked up again. "Like what happened between you and Jason Cantwell?"

She stiffened. "What do you mean?"

"The way you avoided him at our engagement party, how afraid you are. Roland giving you that gun and how desperate you were to keep it. You've been trying to tell me ever since Lydia was murdered, and I haven't listened."

"He killed Lydia—"

"What happened in the garden, Krissy?"

She looked startled. In a muted voice, she said, "It doesn't matter now."

"Krissy, you've been threatened and now I've been pistol-whipped and shot at. It matters."

She stared at a spot beside my head. "All right." She said it bluntly, angrily. "He tried to rape me."

"How?"

"How do you suppose?" When I didn't answer, she spoke hurriedly, getting it over. "One Sunday when I was sixteen Daddy took me by to visit after church. Sometimes he'd do that. That day Henry and Lydia got to talking with Daddy, and Jason said why didn't we go out back. He was talking too fast and wouldn't look at me but I thought it was mostly shyness. I didn't know until it was too late."

"Easy," I said. "I know that. Just tell me what happened."

Her eyes were wide with memory. "Is this really necessary?"

I took her hand. "Yes. It is."

"If you want, then." Her voice was harsh. "We were walking across the lawn toward the back. I was chattering on about people we knew, anything because he was so awkward. We got away from the house and then he stops and turns to me with his hands in his pockets. His face is contorted and then he starts talking so fast to the ground that at first I hardly heard him. It was insane, things he'd dreamed up. We're close, he keeps saying, he knows I must feel it, too. He looks so twisted up and lonely that I feel sorry for him, as if I'm his mother or something. I begin telling him it's all right, sure, we're friends and can talk. 'But I love you,' he says, and begins coming toward me with this strange expression. His eyes were so dark.

"I knew before he touched me. I looked around but couldn't see the house for the pine grove we were in, like he'd wanted. He began kissing me. I said, no, it wasn't like that. He just shakes his head and then he's pushing me against a pine tree. He's too strong. His hands are up my skirt and I start wriggling and begging him not to. Then his fingers came inside me. I began screaming." Her voice fell off. "No one had done that before."

"It would matter anytime—"

"I was still screaming when he got my pants down. I hurt inside and no one could hear me. He kept panting, 'Fuck me,' and pushing his fingers deeper in me with the other hand on my throat. I began punching and kicking and then suddenly his fingers came out and he was bent over holding his groin and looking up at me wide-eyed like I'd hurt his feelings. I was bleeding where he'd touched me. 'Kris Ann,' he moaned, and reached out for me. I ran into the house."

I felt sick and angry. "What happened then?"

She breathed out and her voice became less strained. "I told Daddy I didn't feel well and wanted to go home. Lydia looked at me strangely but Henry got me some soda water and then I left with Daddy. On the way home, I told him."

"What did he say?"

"Nothing. All the way home he stared straight ahead. It was his face." She looked down at me. "It's the same face you have for him sometimes: so filled with hate that I almost believe you could kill him. His eyes were like diamonds. And the quiet. The way he was quiet scared me almost worse than Jason. It was like he felt too much to speak.

"When we got home he sat me down across from him and began asking questions in a voice that never changed no matter what I told him. He made me tell him everything. I don't remember him even blinking. He must have seen the way he frightened me because suddenly his face changed and he put his arms around me and began telling me things would be all right, that he'd take care of it."

I reached up. There were chill marks on her arms. "You frighten me now," she murmured.

"No need. It's just that it still matters. It matters to you."

She shook her head. "I learned better, with you. It wasn't like that and mostly I forgot."

"What did Roland do?"

"He sent me away for a couple of weeks, but

he never really said what else. I do know that the Cantwells never brought Jason by again and that somehow he was kept pretty much out of my way. I saw him once or twice a year; Birmingham's a small place and sometimes you have to get by. But he always looked away. It just died."

But now I knew it hadn't. "Does Henry know?"

She looked thoughtful. "He must. I'm sure Lydia did, because for a while she seemed embarrassed, almost oversolicitous. But no one ever mentioned it. I knew it wasn't *their* fault, and if anything they were kinder to me than before. It seemed better to pretend it hadn't happened."

"But it did." I shook my head. "Why didn't you tell me—at least after Lydia was killed?"

She gazed at me steadily. "Because I was afraid of what you'd do."

"Jesus—"

"Adam, look what you've done *without* knowing."

"Yes. Get shot at. Ever since I found Lydia I've heard nothing but lies and secrets and half-truths, and now it's you and your father. I'm sick of it."

Her eyes still held mine. "I'm sorry, Adam. I thought it was best."

I realized that my feet and legs felt numb, disconnected from my nervous system. I closed my eyes, almost floating. More softly, I said, "I'm sorry, too. For everything."

She took my hand again. A nurse appeared

262

with something to swallow. Kris Ann promised to stay. In five minutes I was asleep.

I dreamed, but not of Jason. We were in Paris, four years prior. It was spring and Kris Ann sat on the porch of the *pensione* with a view of the Tuilleries up a narrow side street of small shops, a patisserie, sidewalk cafés. Her dress was white and simple. She still held herself carefully from the baby, as if her body were strange to her. In the dream I knew that later she would exercise and her shape would return, but now she was pale and thin and stretched and emptied out.

I brought our breakfast, black coffee and croissants. The croissants were flaky and soft. When I told her that, she nodded but took nothing. Sun crept down the side street as she stared out and beyond to where tourists walked at a relaxed, almost ceremonious, pace among the hedges of the Tuilleries, as though it were Sunday even for them. Coming down the alley a plump Frenchman with a poodle and newspaper whistled to himself. She watched it all gravely, disinterestedly. "What will happen," she asked, "in time?"

Her face hadn't moved from the street and her monotone made the question no question at all. "Nothing," I answered. "Or the same things. We'll have the same quarrels and joys and disappointments, and food will cost too much and I'll keep on loving you. I'll still like sex in the morning, you'll like it at night, and sometimes I'll come home at noon to work out a compromise—"

"Seriously."

"Seriously, I didn't marry you to provide an heir."

Her voice was still flat. "Then why did you?"

"Because I love you. It's that simple."

"But you wanted a son." She said it accusingly, or self-accusingly.

"I did, Krissy. So did you."

"But he was the only chance we'll ever have." She turned to me in wonderment. "When they told us that I watched your face before I even thought of me. It was like you were listening to a weather report. I spent three days crying. You never cried."

"I can't cry, Krissy. I never could."

Her eyes blazed. "Damn you," she said fiercely. "Damn your father for getting shot."

I reached her as she started sobbing and held her to me, face buried in my shoulder. "Too early," I said softly. "It's okay, baby, it's all right. I brought you here too early, that's all." Her shoulders shook with sobbing. "It's all right," I wanted to say now. "A son just has to be a boy. There's no magic in being *our* boy." But when I awoke, Kris Ann was gone.

She returned in the morning with two books I liked. I didn't tell her about the dream.

They weren't allowing visitors, she said, just her and the police. But friends called and some of my partners. Nora Culhane called, trying to sound angry about being stood up, trying more seriously for a story: I referred her to the police, and did that with all the reporters who called after. The Kells called. Cade called saying he'd hired private police to guard our house; I didn't thank him and he didn't ask how I was. Nate Taylor called, but when I asked him where Lee had been last night he didn't know.

Then Henry called.

He sounded tense. "They won't let me visit."

"They're like that. I'm no worse than when you saw me."

He paused. "What I said, about going on: I want you to stop."

"I'm not sure I have that choice anymore."

"Adam, this is my responsibility. It always was. I realize I never should have involved you. Please, believe this is for your own good."

"Not until we've talked."

"We'll have time. Just take care of yourself and Kris Ann."

"Henry, there's something I have to know—"

"Goodbye, Adam. Rest." He hung up.

I held the phone for a long time after.

Kris Ann returned with the doctor. There was no fracture, he said: I could go home Monday if I remembered that a second blow to the head could cause brain damage. Kris Ann promised to remind me.

I kept wondering about Henry, and Jason.

But Rayfield had Jason now and I was hurt,

fearful of the wounds and hatreds I felt reaching from the past toward Kris Ann and me. They gave me another pill.

Then Rayfield called to say Jason was out free.

TWENTY-SEVEN

"The girl swears Jason was home all night," he said Monday morning, "and their neighbors don't know different."

He sat flatfooted in the armless chair, thumbs gripping his notepad like a hat he didn't know where to put. Burst veins like faultlines in his eyes made him look sleepless and volatile.

"What about the gun?" I asked.

Rayfield put the pad in his lap and began rubbing the tips of his fingers. "She says she made him drive to the Cahaba River and throw it in."

"So you let him go."

He looked sharply up. "We booked him for assault. If you'd told me the truth downtown we'd have pulled him in with the gun and you wouldn't have been shot at. Assuming it was him."

"Jesus Christ, forget the gun. The will is good enough now."

Rayfield stood. "Oh, it's the will that killed her. It's just not Cantwell's boy." He walked

266

to the end of the bed. "Let me tell you what I think happened. Lydia Cantwell had a boyfriend she wanted to marry. Cantwell knew, or guessed. For years she'd been his cover and now he stood to lose both that and her money. Then, the night he called from Anniston, Mrs. Cantwell told him about the will. It came to him: by killing her before she signed that will, he could pin it on the boy. So he drove back that night and strangled her. It all fits. He's got no alibi, he lied about the phone call, and there's no one in town believes Cantwell gave a shit for his son. All you have to do is think about how he could use that will." He leaned forward, speaking intently. "I'm almost there, Shaw. All I need is her boyfriend's name."

It hit me with the force he had intended: Rayfield had Henry Cantwell one witness from a death sentence, with me in between. Find Mooring, I thought, and he had Lydia's lover, Jason's father, and the final proof that would convict Henry Cantwell: Joanne Mooring to say Henry had come home that night. "I'm curious, Lieutenant. Why did Henry shoot at me? I forget."

"Because you know the boyfriend or some other detail that convicts him. It's good you're starting to think about it."

I shook my head. "It doesn't compute. I was coming from his place the night I was shot at. I'd just seen him."

Rayfield leaned still closer. "Cantwell was alone, Shaw. Nothing to keep him from following. He's a crack shot, you know, and what with you blacked out in the garage he'd have time to see the lights weren't on and set up in the bushes next door. It's a perfect blind."

"It's perfect bullshit."

"You know it isn't. He killed Mrs. Cantwell, played you off against Cade, and then threatened your wife when you got too close. Who did you see the night before you found her picture? Who did you see again the night before you were shot at? What did you tell him that can't come out?"

I said nothing. "You want your wife killed?" he kept on. "By the time we cull all of Mrs. Cantwell's friends for gray-haired men it may be too late. But you can stop it. Just tell me who Lee saw visit Mrs. Cantwell. Lee's not lying, is he?" His voice rose. "Tell me, Shaw. Tell me before that fairy kills you, too."

His face was rapt and excited. I felt cornered. In a low voice I answered, "You might be better off looking to your own fears."

A sick, trapped look drained the keenness from his face. "You're obstructing justice," he said tightly. "Withholding evidence, lying. I can have you disbarred."

"Maybe."

"It's your last chance. Make me leave the room without her boyfriend's name and I start working on you."

I shrugged.

In the instant before leaving he looked almost

lonely. Then he straightened and walked out, closing the door with fearful gentleness.

Kris Ann smiled behind me in the bathroom mirror. "Like what you see?"

"Not particularly." For a moment my image had blurred. I squinted, shaking my head, and my features reappeared. The stitches were gone, leaving a thin scar the doctor said would turn white. But the bruise near my temple was blue and yellow and still swollen enough that my left eye was half-closed. I didn't mention the blurring. "I take it Henry hasn't called."

"No. Should he have?"

"I guess not."

"How do you feel?"

"My head's kind of light."

"You're home now," she assured me. "You can relax." But when I'd finished toweling off and followed her to the bedroom she was loading Cade's revolver. She took it with us to the living room, secreting it behind a vase on the mantel. Cade's bulky rented policeman paced the porch outside.

I listened for the telephone.

Kris Ann brought two mineral waters. "I think you should talk with him."

"Henry?"

"Daddy. Maybe if you discuss this face to face..." Her voice trailed off.

I got up and began pacing with the policeman on the other side of the window. "How good was Henry with guns?"

She looked at me curiously. "Good enough to teach me, remember? Jason, too."

"I've got to see him."

Her eyes widened. "Jason?"

"Henry."

The policeman's footsteps sounded from the porch in monotonous rhythm. Kris Ann looked silently up at the mantel. In a flat voice she said, "So now you think it's Henry."

"I just need to talk to him."

The telephone rang.

Kris Ann went to answer it. "Oh, hi," I heard her say. "He's fine, just resting.... No, Daddy's not here. I think today's his board meeting.... Yes, he's up.... You're sure?.... All right, just a minute."

She reappeared in the living room. "It's Clayton," she said almost sadly. "He says he has to see you."

The taxi dropped me in front of the fifty-year-old building I thought of as Henry's bank.

The Cantwell-Alabama Bank and Trust was a cement-pillared structure with marble floors and oak-paneled rear offices of which Henry's was the largest, a commodious rectangle with high ceilings, a brass chandelier, and a green rug so deep it muffled my steps like a prowler's.

He wasn't there. Neither was any piece of him—plaques or portraits or family pictures—except the sense of a man passing silently through. I wasn't sure why the room made me sad. I didn't stay to think about it.

I stopped in the wide marble lobby as customers passed and employees in white shirts or blouses glided around me at such a uniform pace they seemed run by remote control. I'd wanted enough to find Henry, imagined it so clearly, that I seemed unable to do what I had come for.

"Adam."

I turned to see Clayton Kell hurrying toward me. "I'm sorry," he said. "You look terrible."

"I'm okay. It sounded important."

"It is."

I trailed him to his office, a windowless square he'd worked years for, sitting while he shut the door behind us and reached for ice in the small refrigerator he hid in his credenza with a fifth of bourbon. He filled two glasses, slid mine across the desk, took a hasty gulp of his, and blurted, "It's all a mess."

I stopped the drink an inch from my mouth and watched him until he stammered, "Adam, the police were here."

"What did they want?"

"They had a warrant. There was nothing I could do. I tried calling Roland and he wasn't in. Henry either—he just hasn't been around—"

"For Christ's sake, Clayton, spit it out." I caught myself "Look, no one's saying you fucked up. Just tell me what happened, okay?"

"All right." He nodded silently, repeatedly. "Okay. It's just that Rayfield—" He looked up and said, "Lydia's bank account is total hash, Adam. It's all wrong."

271

"How wrong?"

"Eight hundred thousand fucking dollars."

"How could that be? You're computerized, you get daily balances—"

"I don't know." He slammed down his drink. "I mean, I do and I don't. They made me go through the records and it's gone."

"What records? What did they show?"

He pushed a low stack of papers at me. "I copied what they took."

"Good."

"The top one's Lydia's last statement of account, all right? Now the earlier ones show that for years she kept her balance at around a million—"

"Just lying around at six percent?"

"Christ, Adam, I'm not her investment counselor. Henry is. That's the problem." He jabbed his finger at the top sheet. "Look here. On March fifteen, there's an entry showing that Lydia's account was debited eight hundred thousand dollars. Now she could have withdrawn that much, though I don't know why she'd want to. But there's no withdrawal slip, not a goddamned thing with Lydia's signature to show she got the money. I know. Rayfield made me go through them twice. There has to be a slip. Money doesn't leave here without one."

"Or shouldn't."

He nodded, collapsing in his chair until his chin doubled into folds and his small round belly strained his shirtfront. His face sagged with the unexpectedness of it. "What about the auditors?" I asked. "You've got a daily audit. Wouldn't they pick this up?"

"No." Clayton wiped his face. "What they look at is whether the records for all our accounts square with the cash we actually have on hand. That part's okay; Lydia's statement shows eight hundred thousand dollars withdrawn and we've got eight hundred thousand dollars less money. The problem is that the money went out and there's no signed withdrawal slip. The auditors don't check slips. It would take too long."

Clayton took off his glasses, wiping an imaginary smudge. My head began to throb. "Let me ask you something, Clayton. You don't keep people's money segregated, right? I mean, you don't have some special place for Lydia's and another for mine and Krissy's."

"Uh-huh."

I reached for my glass and drank, the whiskey burning down. "So," I finished slowly, "what really happened is that eight hundred thousand dollars of the bank's money disappeared and Lydia's statement of account kept the auditors from catching on."

Clayton's cheeks blotched. "What are you saying?"

"Clayton, how many people know about this?"

"Just us. Why?"

"I think someone's embezzled eight hundred thousand dollars."

His mouth fell open. "Who?"

"Who could alter Lydia's account statement?"

"The computer programmer, clerks—I suppose anyone at the bank. Hell, I could have. But to do that to cover embezzlement wouldn't work. Lydia—the customer would raise holy hell as soon as we mailed out her interest statement. She'd open that sucker and—" His lips stopped moving.

"Unless she were dead," I finished.

"Oh, my God."

"We can't let this out."

"We've got to." His voice rose. "There's Rayfield, reports to the Feds—"

"I mean just until we get to Henry. Maybe there's some reason. We can't go running off."

"Sure." Clayton nodded and dabbed his forehead. "Sure." The word fell emptily into the long silence that followed and then Cade walked in.

TWENTY-EIGHT

When he saw me Cade stared in anger and surprise. Then he limped to a chair in front of Clayton. From his pallor the shattered hip was hurting.

"Well," he demanded, "what's the problem?"

The question was for Clayton, its rough edge for me. Clayton hung between speech and the dread of speaking. "There's eight hundred thousand dollars missing on Lydia's account statement," I cut in, "and no withdrawal slip."

Slow comprehension leeched the anger from Cade's face and voice. He turned to me. "Do the police know?"

"Yes. And Henry's out of pocket. Clayton tried finding him and couldn't."

"You've told no one else, Clayton?"

"No, sir. I wanted your advice."

"Then I'd better see the account statement."

Clayton passed the single paper, and Cade gripped it tightly in front of him while he scanned. "Rayfield's got that," I told him.

"Good God." He looked up at Clayton. "Adam and I need to talk somewhere. Please, you just stay put and don't say a word to anyone. We'll be back."

Cade led me down the hall toward Henry's office. It was past five and the bank was empty, but Cade shut the door before taking Henry's chair. He leaned over the desk, staring moodily past me, fingers drumming silently, uncharacteristically, on the glass top. "You're wondering why I never told you about Henry."

The irrelevance of that surprised me. But I nodded, saying, "At least I'd have understood the tension between you and Rayfield."

"It was Henry's place to tell you, not mine."

"So you let him lie."

"This isn't ethics class," he said sharply. "When Henry told me he'd been with a man we were in the library, with Rayfield waiting outside. He swore he'd perjure himself before giving his friend to Rayfield. What was I supposed to do, come out and tell him Henry was going to lie? I couldn't abandon him, not then, and knowing what I knew I couldn't turn him over to someone else. It was a dilemma. My one hope was to get the questioning done with and then keep Rayfield away until he found another suspect. Besides"—Cade paused, speaking slowly now—"you're not sure this man even exists, are you?"

It hadn't been irrelevant at all. "No," I answered. "But Henry told you about his lover that morning, not later. That argues he didn't make it up."

Cade smiled without humor. "You assume that Henry was too shocked to lie. That's your flaw, Adam. It's fatal in a lawyer to be so tangled in his own emotions that he can't think like someone else. Think like Rayfield. His Henry Cantwell is a clever man who killed Lydia and then reappeared the next morning ready to play a part. His Henry spins sympathetic lies about loyalty to a friend to make his failure to confide in you sound noble. Rayfield's Henry Cantwell ruined the lives of both Lydia and Jason to conceal his own sexual transgressions. Rayfield's Henry is a virtual schizophrenic."

I felt sick. "And yours, Roland?"

He slumped for a moment, trapped-looking and for once intensely human, worry eroding the hard angles of his face. "I don't know anymore. I think about Kris Ann..."

I was almost sorry for him. Reluctantly, I said, "There's something worse."

"What could be worse?"

I told him about Joanne Mooring.

As he listened, Cade's fingers stopped drumming. His eyes became intent, expressionless. When I finished, he drew himself up, took an audible breath, and asked, "She saw him?"

"No. His black Mercedes.

Cade stared at me. Then he murmured, "That's enough for Rayfield," paused with his hand over his forehead, and added, "So you think Mooring's the father."

"That's right."

"Did you tell all this to Henry?"

"I'm afraid so."

Cade began rubbing his temple. "It's too much," he protested. "Do you appreciate in all of your busyness that I've known Henry Cantwell for over forty years?"

"I appreciate that, yes."

"Do you?" he lashed out. "Do you know what you've done? You've trapped your own client so that Rayfield can break him like an egg. By now Henry's a desperate man."

I felt too weak to argue. "Clayton's waiting," I said tiredly, "and we're getting nowhere."

Cade flung out his arm. "Then tell me what to do, why don't you. Your Mooring discovery puts me in a hopeless conflict. One client, the bank, is out eight hundred thousand dollars which it appears that another client, my friend, murdered his wife to conceal."

"To believe that, Roland, you have to believe that Henry strangled Lydia, set up

Jason, threatened Kris Ann, and shot at me—all because he's a thief, which is as incredible as the rest."

"Who else, dammit. Show me who. Otis Lee, Mooring, Mooring's wife, even Jason—none of them could take this money. Only Henry could and then keep that from Lydia. Say she did want a divorce. The first thing she'd do is take stock of all her assets. If he'd stolen her money, and not told her, he could never let that come out. Think what he might do—"

"We have to talk to him."

Cade shook his head. "But that's where the conflict is. Until now I've looked at this like he's innocent. Now I have to consider, what if he confesses? We're barred by the attorney-client privilege from telling the bank."

"But we can't be sure there's a conflict until we talk to him."

"God." Cade looked at me resentfully. "I need time to think what to do."

"Maybe the morning," I tried. "We can think overnight and see him then."

"It won't work. Clayton can't hold off telling his board that long."

"He told us. If we ask him to keep quiet until tomorrow, then we've assumed the burden."

Cade leaned back. "That would leave the night to figure how to handle Henry, and maybe by noon tomorrow we'd know what to tell the bank."

"Right."

"Very well." Cade began snapping decisions. "We'll see Henry tomorrow morning, at his place. I don't want anyone else around. And you're to come with me. I may want a witness." He snatched the telephone, stabbing out numbers.

"What's this?"

"Henry." Cade's mouth was a tense line as he held the phone out so I could hear it ring. "Not in." Then there was a click and Henry's voice, thin and reedy and faraway sounding, said, "Hello."

Cade clamped the phone to his ear. "Hello, Henry. How are you feeling?... Good." I watched Cade maneuver his face to match the smoothness of his voice. "Adam and I are here at the bank. He's found something, and we both think it's important we meet with you tomorrow morning, early."

Cade began listening. I wondered how Henry felt and sounded. Cade was telling him, "It's better at your place." He listened again, nodding, then casually answered, "Eight will be fine. Bye, now," and hung up. Henry would never imagine Cade's hand shaking as it put down the phone. His forehead glistened with the beginnings of sweat. "Eight o'clock," he said tiredly. "God, I hated that."

"How is he?"

"I don't know." Cade shook his head. "I just don't know."

"Think he'll call one of us tonight?"

"If he does we can't talk to him. I want both of us there, especially me." He looked up at me, bursting out, "It's you who's made this disaster, letting Henry manipulate you until you've built a case against him by accident and then baited Rayfield into coming here to finish it."

"Look, Henry asked me to help."

"Did he? Or did you force him to pretend to want that while trying to scare you off with Kris Ann's picture and then gunshots, so that he could ask you to stop helping for your own good. Think—you're not clever enough. Not once since the killing has he told you anything you haven't forced out of him. He's maneuvered you until he couldn't anymore—"

"Save it, Roland. This is hard enough."

Cade looked incredulous and then his face became blurred in front of me. "Do you think I like it?" he was saying.

My skull was a blinding ache. I blinked once, saw Cade again. "Clearly not," I answered. "But whether that's on Henry's account I wouldn't know."

Cade gave me a long, wintry glare before asking, "Now what does that mean?"

"You probably hate Jason Cantwell more than I do. More, even, than you hate me."

He stared until he was sure what I meant. "She told you?"

"Yes. I understand now why you gave her that gun. It would have been simpler to tell me about Jason."

"*That* was between *us*." Cade's fist crashed down on the desk. "Damn you, you're like a

280

skin graft, stuck where you don't belong. For two cents I'd rid us both of you—"

He stopped, eyes narrowing as I stood, dug in my pocket for two copper pennies, clinked them in the cup of my hand before I tossed them underhand so that they hung for an instant above the desk, fell, hit his chest, dropping silently on the soft rug. "They're yours," I said. I turned my back and went to find Clayton.

By the time Clayton dropped me off it was dusk and I was having trouble with balance. I passed the guard on my porch without speaking. Kris Ann's face as she met me was a double image. "Are you all right, Adam? Let me call the doctor."

I leaned in the doorframe. "No need. I'm just tired."

She took my arm. "There's a problem at the bank, isn't there?"

Something in her voice made me turn. "Henry called," she said reluctantly. "He sounded upset."

"I'd better call him."

Her face became one, then two, then one again. "It can wait until morning," she urged. "You look like a ghost."

I stared past her from the hallway toward the kitchen telephone. It was a blur. I put my hand on the railing and walked slowly upstairs.

Henry never called back. After a time I feel asleep. But in a dream my father died again, and only Brian wept.

TWENTY-NINE

Cade knocked before eight, grim-faced and hostile, staring over my shoulder at Kris Ann. We drove to Henry's without speaking.

This morning I saw clearly. Sunlight fell through the pines like yellow dust. A slow wind stirring their needles felt like wetness hovering and the dogwood were wilting or fallen and smelled faintly of decay. A bird called. No one answered when Cade rang the doorbell.

We stood with hands in our pockets, waiting. After a moment Cade began pounding the door. I went to the garage and saw the black Mercedes through the window, and Lydia's Lincoln. Cade kept pounding as though transfixed. When I came back and said, "Their cars are here," he jabbed angrily at the doorbell without answering.

I began circling the house.

I saw nothing through the left front window but an empty living room. Cade hit the doorbell again. I went around to the side.

Henry's library window was level with my chin. I edged through the bushes and hydrangeas, stretched but could see only part of the room: the standing gold ashtray, the chair where I often sat, but not Henry's chair. His copy of *War and Peace* lay facedown on the floor.

I went to the rear of the house, more quickly now. The lightheadedness returned.

Double glass doors led from the patio to the

living room. They were locked. From the front Cade's hollow pounding came again.

Decorative stones lay scattered in the garden. I snatched one and tossed it through the windowpane nearest the doorknob.

The sound of shattering glass made me flinch. I reached to turn the knob and stepped inside. Cade rang the doorbell with the staccato bursts of a madman.

I went to the library.

Henry slumped in his chair, staring out.

The book lay at his feet, and near that the revolver. Dried blood came from his mouth where the bullet had gone. There were blood and brains and fragments of skull on the chair and the shelves behind it and on one corner of the blue Miro. The reading glasses were in his lap and his arm had fallen over the side of his chair. He still wore his cardigan sweater.

His hand was white and cold-feeling. Time stopped as half-forgotten fragments tumbled through my mind: "Hail, Mary, full of grace... The Lord is with thee... Holy Mary, Mother of God, pray for us sinners now and at the hour of our death."

It was quiet. Cade had stopped ringing.

I dropped Henry's hand and stared at him. His gray eyes seemed frozen in eternal disappointment.

"Why?" I asked him.

Cade rang the doorbell again. I turned away, walked slowly to the front door, and opened it.

Cade stood back, surprised. "He's in the library," I said.

Cade brushed me aside. I sat on the front steps.

Time passed. Things happened that I half noticed and didn't care about. Two police came, like before, and, like before, a team with doctor bags. They glanced at me and hurried on.

Then Rayfield came. When I followed him mechanically he looked away. But when he looked at Henry Cantwell there was pity on his face, and something like relief.

From around me came now-familiar noises: orders, doors opening, footsteps. "Just blew his fucking brains out," someone said.

My brain began screaming.

I went back to the steps and sat. Someone stood over me. I gazed stupidly up.

Cade's face was filled with hate. "I hope you're satisfied, Adam." His voice was barely controlled. "Because you as good as pulled the trigger."

I sprang up.

From the side, Rayfield moved quickly between us, snapping, "Drive him home," at Bast. But as Cade stared past him there was still only hate.

THIRTY

The next two mornings I went to the firm, burying myself in trial strategy. I avoided Cade. When word seeped back that he had asked that I be fired, I did nothing except work harder. The dizziness came and went.

The media were full of Henry's suicide and guilt: "The quiet man who exploded," wrote someone who had never met him. Otis Lee left town unnoticed. Mooring's role remained hidden.

The second morning, Cade began meeting secretly with senior partners. There was nothing I could do, or cared to do. I was drafting a motion to throw Nate Taylor out of court when Culhane knocked on the door.

"Aren't you returning phone calls?" she asked.

"I've got nothing to say."

She leaned in the doorway, considering me. "You look awful," she said seriously, paused, and then asked, "How is your wife taking it?"

I couldn't explain Kris Ann's face when I told her: not shocked or even bewildered, but like that of a hunted animal. And then without speaking she had walked upstairs and closed the door behind her. "He was our friend," I told Culhane now. "So was Mrs. Cantwell. Kris Ann's life was threatened. It's hard for us to talk about, or even know what to feel."

"Still, there must be things you want to say about him."

"Only to myself."

Her look wavered between hesitant and bold. "It's not your fault," she finally said.

"Sure. I know."

She shook her head with a small, doubting smile, and was gone.

I stared down at the motion. Halfway through the fourth page I flung my pencil against the wall and went to the police station.

Rayfield and Bast sat stirring coffee, torpid and diminished-seeming, like actors without roles. "What do you want?" Bast demanded.

"To be certain it was suicide."

"Suicide," came his sardonic answer, "or self-defense."

"Even without a note?"

Rayfield swiveled to stare at a window blocked by venetian blinds. "Two-thirds don't leave any," Bast said.

"It's hard to believe that Henry Cantwell would do that."

"Well, you'd better get used to it. Suicides are tough to fake. You have to get every detail right: the victim's fingerprints not only have to be on the trigger but the cylinder. Cantwell's prints were on both, his wound was a contact wound like suicides have usually, and the bullet looks to be from the same revolver that was fired at you."

"Was it registered to Henry?"

In profile Rayfield's jawline worked. "Look," Bast said, "Alabama's full of unregistered guns, especially over fifteen years old, like Cantwell's. They didn't start registering them until after Kennedy was shot. The first one, that is."

"Then you're not troubled that he used a gun you can't trace."

Bast shrugged. "Not really. There were no strange prints in the house and no one had broken in. Plus, for a murderer to get everything right, Cantwell would have to be a very cooperative victim. It's time to start living with it. Henry Cantwell stole his wife's money, then killed her and tried to kill you. You're lucky to be alive."

"But someone could have—"

"Let it be," rasped Rayfield. His face, still turned to the window, was slate gray. "He killed himself, now let it be."

Bast rose from his chair to stand between Rayfield and me. "It's done with," he said.

His voice was final. Nothing remained except Henry's funeral.

Cade and I went, separately, Cade because Henry's sister had asked it, me for reasons of my own. Kris Ann stayed home. "I can't go," she told me. "I can't resolve this yet." She had said almost nothing else about Henry. But there was still a strange alertness to her, a sense of watching and listening, and the revolver remained hidden on the mantel. I had decided to give her time, and to go to the funeral alone.

It was sparsely attended. The people who knew Henry Cantwell had fallen away, leaving reporters and Clayton and scattered others, blinking from the afternoon sun as they entered to sit by themselves. I chose the front row. The funeral party gathered at the back of the church. Behind Henry's casket his sister and Roland Cade followed four pallbearers who seemed to lean outward in silent dissociation. In the far corner stood a short, balding man I didn't know; a relative, I supposed. But when they began rolling the casket toward the altar, he hung back watching it, and I forgot him.

They came slowly down until they were next to my pew and for a moment frozen in time Cade's stare riveted me across the rolling casket. And then it was past and Cade and the rest were sitting, and the funeral began.

The clergyman mumbled the prayers in haste. An air of sad embarrassment settled on the mourners and when the service was over and the casket gone, they left quickly. I stayed, not following to the grave. The church emptied and it was silent, and I lost track of time.

The quiet turned oppressive. I stood finally and began walking up the aisle.

The balding man remained at the rear of the church. I passed him without speaking and went outside.

Jason Cantwell waited on the steps in front of me. "I've come for you," he said.

The reporters were gone and there was no one else near. Jason's face was sullen and defiant. "It's not time," I answered. "They're burying him now."

He shrugged. "It doesn't matter. He was never my father."

"He was never anyone's father, and Kris Ann was never yours to have. It's past and all in your mind. Let us be."

He shook his head. "It isn't settled."

He was moving closer. "Don't do this," I said quietly. "You've no gun now."

He flushed. "I don't need one."

"Then I'm telling you, Jason—once. This is nothing you want to happen."

He stopped, searching my face, and then took one slower step forward. I waited.

There were footsteps behind us. We turned. The bald man stood framed in the door of the church, as if to call us back.

Jason stared at him, and then, slowly, his face became irresolute. I moved to pass him on the steps, stopping so that our shoulders brushed and our faces were inches apart. "It's over," I said softly. "Touch Kris Ann and I'll kill you, sure."

His face went rigid. I waited, letting the moment pass between us. Then I went down the steps without looking back.

I walked to my office and sat alone with the door closed and no lights on. Through the window a late afternoon sun died slowly among the high-rises of the city, its cast in the room thinning to light and shadow. I didn't move.

The rap on the door was so soft and tentative that I had to listen before saying, "Yes?"

The door opened. The man from the funeral

peered in. He was round and owlish in his glasses, one hand jammed awkwardly in a pocket. "Mr. Shaw?" he asked.

I stared at him. "Who are you?"

His smile was more nervous tic, shy and self-hating. Then he closed the door behind him and said simply, "I'm Henry Cantwell's lover."

THIRTY-ONE

I watched him across the room. Finally I asked, "Why are you here?"

His mouth twitched again. "Henry spoke of you often."

"But why now?"

"I had to trust someone." He looked down. "You see, we were together that night. The only person Henry killed was himself."

"Oh, my God."

"You see how it is, then." He said it almost tenderly.

"Yes," I murmured. "I see."

He walked to a chair in front of my desk and grasped it. "I could have come forward. But he knew how afraid I was. I'm a banker in Anniston, with a wife and three teenagers who know nothing of this. I couldn't face becoming a different sort of man."

For a long time I just looked at him. "How did it happen, you and Henry?"

"We found each other, that's all. For two years I thought I loved him. But not enough." He shook his head. "Perhaps I was too hurt."

"Hurt?"

His eyes were small and tortured. "Before the night she was killed I hadn't seen Henry for over two months. When he called I scrambled for any excuse to get away. We were together all night. At six o'clock I got ready to sneak out. Henry took my hand and began talking very fast. He couldn't see me anymore, he said. He loved me, I should never doubt that, and this was for my own good. I was shocked. Why, I asked him. He kept shaking his head and saying he was sorry, that he'd wanted us to have one last night and could I understand that. But I didn't, I couldn't, there was no reason and he looked so miserable. I wanted to stay and make him tell me why. But," he smiled bitterly, "it was nearly morning and getting light outside. I drove away."

I ran a hand across my face. "What's your name?"

He hesitated. "Calvin Bayles."

"Did you ever see him again?"

"No." Bayles' face seemed almost to decompose. "I called him when I read about his wife. I asked if he was all right, if things were too hard. He said no, that you were helping him. I hardly listened. What I really wanted to know was whether he'd exposed me to the police. I hung on the line, afraid to ask and afraid to hang up. He knew. 'Don't worry,

Calvin,' he said, very quiet, 'you'll be all right, too.' Then he hung up. I almost cried. But after that I didn't talk to him until the night he died and then I let him down again."

Bayles' fingers were white I on the chair. "Look," I said. "You're not alone in caring for Henry, or deserting him. Just tell me."

He gave me a strange pitying look: sadness and community and comprehension. "This last will hurt you, too."

"Then that has to be."

Bayles' voice was raw. "The night he died, Henry called me at home. He'd never done that before. I took it in the den so no one could hear. I was angry at him for calling there but when he began talking his voice trembled so much I forgot that. He said that my name might come out now, that he couldn't help it anymore, but we were all tangled up in things at the bank he couldn't explain. I didn't understand any of it. Please, I begged him, please protect me. He said he'd tried to, that he'd called you, but you hadn't called back and probably weren't going to and he had nowhere else to turn—"

"Oh, Jesus..."

" 'Do anything,' I told him. 'Please, anything else at all. Please, if you love me.' For a long time he didn't answer and I thought maybe he was crying. Then he said, 'Forgive me,' and the line went dead. The next day I saw his picture in the evening paper. He was gone."

We faced each other across the desk. Bayles

said hoarsely, "I pushed him to it. I was his last chance and he shot himself to save me."

I closed my eyes. "Why tell me this now, when he's dead?"

"You were part of it, too. I want you to know what I did."

My eyes opened to his strange expectant look. "For what? To share the guilt? I've earned that. But you'll have to find absolution somewhere else. I don't qualify to give it."

He flushed. "That's not what I want. You can decide whether the police should learn what I've told you. Henry's dead, I know. But if it will help clear his name I won't run from him anymore."

I shook my head angrily. "I won't play God. You passed that buck to Henry and he's dead. I won't decide for you what kind of a man you are."

He shrank back. "Please..." The word died on his lips.

"God help him," I mumbled.

His shoulders sagged. "I loved him."

I turned away. "Go home," I finally said. "I'll do what I can. Just go home."

He was crying now, his "thank you" close to a whisper. He paused as if searching for other words, found none, and shuffled to the door. He turned there with a last silent look of pity and thanks and then disappeared into the long corridor. I listened until his footsteps made no sound.

The firm was almost empty now. The receptionist had left and the phones had stopped ringing. Two silent janitors drifted by like ghosts with dustmops. I sat motionless.

After a long, time I reached in the drawer for my father's darts. I threw them mechanically, retrieving and throwing again until my mind was washed blank. Then I sat back and reviewed everything I knew about Lydia's murder, and everyone involved, from the beginning. When I finished my hands were shaking.

I held them in front of me until they stopped. Then I picked up the telephone and called Clayton Kell.

THIRTY-TWO

At eight the next morning I met Clayton at his office. The papers I'd asked for were stacked on the desk in front of him. "Maybe," he said carefully, "you can sort of explain this, so I can pretend to know what I'm doing."

"Pretend to who? You're a bank officer, we're your counsel."

He frowned. "Roland's our counsel."

"Then you'd better tell me straight out."

"All right." Clayton paused to rub the bridge of his nose. "Roland called after Henry shot himself. He said that until reports were made to the feds, we should say nothing to anyone except him or people he sent. He specifically mentioned you." He looked embarrassed. "Somehow he managed to float across the notion that you were on the way out."

"Then I need your help."

He looked down at the stack of papers. "What do these have to do with Henry's suicide?"

"I won't know until I see them. Please, it's important to me.

Clayton grimaced. "You're buying trouble, Adam."

"No," I said flatly. "It's a favor I'm asking. Really."

Clayton hesitated, searching my face. Then he pushed the papers across the desk.

The top packet was headed "Loan File: Rue Napoleon Center." I began reading hurriedly through its pages. "At the cocktail party you said this got the bank into trouble. How?"

Clayton leaned back in his chair. "Okay," he sighed. "Three months back this man Broussard came to us wanting a loan for Rue Napoleon Partners. They'd bought an area of old warehouses in New Orleans and were renovating it as condominiums and a shopping mall. The project was going bad; the area's shabby and they've had overruns on construction that left them cash-short. Their problem was that they'd borrowed several million already and without more money from us they'd have to stop building. If that happened they'd be forced to sell the property at less than they'd borrowed, and paying back the rest might have wiped out Broussard and his partners. So it was a salvage loan and I didn't like it."

"Why'd Broussard come to you?"

"He came to Henry. That bothered me, too. Broussard's a 'new South' hustler, one cut below nouveau riche. I didn't understand why Henry wanted the business." He winced. "It turned out there was a lot about Henry I didn't understand."

I finished the first file. "This says the bank loaned. Broussard four-and-a-half-million dollars on January sixth."

Clayton nodded. "Henry pushed it through over everyone's objections. Our only collateral was the property. As I said, that's no collateral: if Rue Napoleon Partners were forced to sell it they couldn't have paid off what they'd already borrowed, let alone us. About two weeks after we made the loan a federal bank examiner came to audit our loans and said the same thing. He gave Henry a choice: nine hundred thousand dollars more collateral, or nine hundred thousand dollars less loan. Henry looked ill."

"Which way did he go?"

"There wasn't any choice. They had no more collateral. We had to reduce the loan by nine hundred thousand dollars."

"What did Broussard do?"

"It's in the next file. He threatened to sue on the grounds that we'd committed the extra money and then ruined him. That went on for over a month. Henry became totally irrational, tried everything to save the loan and couldn't. But Broussard never sued and the partnership's finishing the project. Maybe he found money somewhere else."

I lit a cigarette. "I think he did, Clayton."

Clayton's face went slack with comprehension. "Lydia?"

"The sequence fits. Look: in early January Henry brought Broussard to the bank and got him a loan you should have never made. Late that month the examiner forced you to reduce it by nine hundred thousand dollars. For over a month thereafter, Broussard fought to get the loan restored and Henry tried to help him. They gave up in early March. And on March fifteenth Henry stole eight hundred thousand from Lydia's account."

"So you're saying that Henry had a cut in Napoleon Partners, and was bailing himself out."

"That's consistent with what he did. Do you have papers showing who the partners are?"

"No." Clayton frowned again. "Henry was supposed to get those, and never did."

"Then I'll try to find out."

He shook his head. "What difference could it make? Henry killed Lydia and stole the money, and now that he's dead his reasons don't matter anymore. You should be looking to Roland and your job, and to getting it together with Kris Ann before it's too late."

I stood. "I'll be all right, and Krissy, too. Just don't tell anyone what I've asked you. Not yet."

Clayton's round, troubled face gazed up at

me. "Rennie and I like you both, Adam. Why would I make this worse?"

I nodded. When I closed the door to return to my office he was still staring after me.

A clean copy of the motion waited on my desk. I sat, reading and not seeing, and then snatched the telephone to call Nora Culhane.

She wasn't in. I left messages and spent the day waiting.

She returned the call around five. "I'm surprised," she said.

"I need your help."

"Why?"

"Your boss, people at the station—they can't know."

"You sound crazy, Adam."

"Look, are you interested or not?"

"Yes, okay—off the record. What is it?"

"I think I know why Henry Cantwell stole the money."

"Go on."

I explained what I learned at the bank. When I was through she asked, "Why are you telling me this?"

"I want you to fly to New Orleans."

"For what?"

"Go to the parish recorder's office and check the name and address of each partner. Make copies. Do whatever you have to do to find out who they are. After that you can use the information any way you want."

"Why can't you do your own errands," she said tartly.

"I can't leave now. There's something else I have to do."

"Then if you want my help, be honest. Does all this relate to Lydia Cantwell's murder?"

"I'm not sure. It depends on what you find."

"Adam, the station can't send me unless I at least tell them something."

"Get sick then. Charge the ticket and I'll pay for it."

"You're serious."

"Yes."

"Then let me think about it." She hung up.

I paced and smoked cigarettes. An hour later she called to say that she would fly out in the morning. "I hope you find what you're looking for," she said.

THIRTY-THREE

Kris Ann was quiet that night, the deep and inward silence of someone brooding on a hard decision. She glanced at me occasionally, distant and thoughtful. I tried reading until she picked up her sketches of the children she taught, done to distract her since Henry's death. She began drawing with deft, short strokes, lips parted as they were when sleeping, so that she looked always about to speak, or even smile. I watched her, remembering how I'd watched her seven years before, memorizing her movements and expressions so that I could hold them in my mind like photographs. She had known that, and it had quickened her smile and the things she did in my apartment. She had cooked and I cleaned and she spent her spare time painting and reading the books I liked then, Joyce's *A Portrait of the Artist As a Young Man* and essays by Camus, talking about them later. "It's strange," she once said of Camus. "I don't think he's sure why he hopes for so much, or even if he should. But he does." I had smiled then. We were going to Washington....

The next morning I went to Maddox Coal and Steel.

Mooring's office was at the end of a carpeted hallway lined by pictures of foundries, open hearths, and blast furnaces. A short-haired woman in her forties sat next to his closed door. "Do you have an appointment?" she asked.

"No. But tell him Adam Shaw is here. I think he'll see me."

She frowned, pressed the intercom button, and said, "There's a Mr. Shaw outside." Her frown deepened and she hung up looking betrayed. "Go on in," she said.

Mooring sat at his desk. His drapes were drawn, his office spare, neat, and dark. "What is it?" he asked.

"Our deal is finished."

His lids dropped. "You wouldn't be here,"

he finally said, "if you didn't want something."

"I've got two questions. I want the answers."

"And if I won't give them?"

"Then I'll help the newspapers grub through your affair with Lydia Cantwell until you wish it had never happened."

He looked up at me, curious and almost detached. "What's in that for you?"

"The pleasure of it."

His eyes flickered. "That's unnatural."

"It's natural as breathing. Push too many people too far and one of them is going to watch you, and wait. It's my turn."

He folded his hands on the desk in front of him, appraising me. "All right," he said at length. "I'll listen to your questions."

I sat, leaning forward over his desk to ask quietly, "Whose son is Jason Cantwell?"

Mooring looked away. Finally, he said, "I've never known."

"That's hard to believe."

He turned back. "Why, because you think he's mine? He couldn't be. She had someone else then, I don't know who. If she hadn't it might all have been different. But then the most I could do was be around her. Being *with* her was something I grew into."

For the first time he spoke with feeling, as if seeing the pattern of his life. For a moment I thought of Kris Ann. "Then how does it seem now?" I asked. "The rest of it."

Mooring watched my face, pondering whether to answer. "It's a habit," he said at

301

length. "I've gotten used to who I've become. But you didn't come to ask that."

"No. I didn't."

"Then tell me your other question."

I lit a cigarette, still watching him carefully. "Did Lydia ask Cade to get her a divorce?"

His face stiffened. Then he nodded, once. "When?"

He winced. "Just before she was killed."

"You mean the afternoon she went to see him."

"Yes.

"Is that what you visited her about, just before she left?"

"Yes." He looked at me steadily, miserably. "I was leaving Joanne."

"Why didn't you tell me that before?"

"At first I thought you knew. I was sure you'd come to the house because Cade had told you. When I realized you knew nothing I was amazed and then I began thinking it was better you didn't. After I called Cade I was convinced he was acting to protect his client and perhaps others from needless hurt, and that you were irresponsible. And"—Mooring's voice fell off—"there was no point in hurting Joanne, now."

"Did you believe she had killed Lydia?"

"No." Mooring shook his head. "That would be too grotesque. I don't think she could, even with what I'd done. I just didn't want—after Lydia died, the only thing left was simple decency. I owed her that."

He grimaced at the sound of it. I took a deep drag of cigarette smoke. "About Cade: are you sure she actually told him?"

"He didn't say so exactly." Mooring looked as though a sudden light had hurt his eyes. "But she must have. When I came back that night Lydia was a different woman. Her first smile seemed to come from deep within her, and then all at once she was smiling and crying and leaning against me. When she looked up, her face was streaked with tears. I brushed her cheek, and asked, 'Is this what I'm getting?' She shook her head. 'It's just that I'm free,' she answered, and then she told me I made her feel delivered to herself, after being lost. I couldn't imagine how I'd done that. But I felt delivered, too. She was all I'd ever wanted." Mooring turned from me. His voice was thick. "She wouldn't lie, Shaw. Not about that."

"No," I said quietly. "Lydia wouldn't lie."

He didn't move. "Why do you want to know this?"

"That doesn't concern you, anymore."

'Then I've answered you now." His profile was utterly still. "Please go."

I let myself out.

His secretary peered up, ready to pass the messages spread in front of her. "Hold his calls," I told her. "Just ten minutes or so."

She looked at my face, and slowly took her hand off the telephone. I went to my office and waited for Culhane.

It was mid-afternoon before she called.

"Where are you?" I asked.

"Here. Home."

"Already?"

"I was done by eleven. I got a twelve-thirty plane."

"You should have phoned from there."

She hesitated. "I could have. I didn't want to."

My head was pounding again. "There's no problem, is there?"

"I got what you asked for, the partners' names."

"And?"

"Adam, there's one of them you're not going to like."

"Who? Cade?"

"No." I heard her inhale. "It's your wife, Adam. Kris Ann Shaw."

THIRTY-FOUR

Culhane lived on the second floor of a two-story building in a complex twenty minutes from town. As I drove there the skies lowered and darkened and then light rain spattered on my windshield and the road turned slick and shiny. It was raining harder when I knocked on her door.

"You're wet," she said awkwardly.

I stepped into her living room: white walls and sliding glass windows opening to a porch where Swedish ivy hung. Culhane stood to one side, watching me, her expression stiff and cautious. "You'd better show me the papers," I said.

She was still for a moment. Then she went to the kitchen and brought back a small pile of Xeroxes. The top paper was headed: "Napoleon Partners—Certificate of Partnership," with signature lines for five partners. The last name was signed in a small, careful hand. The *i* in *Kris Ann* was looped. "Is it hers?" Culhane asked.

"It's hers."

She looked small and serious. "I'm sorry, Adam."

"No need. It's nothing you did."

"But you still love her, don't you?"

"At least the idea of her. Maybe that was never fair."

"Please, tell me what this means."

"It means that Henry Cantwell didn't kill his wife."

She stared. "Then you're going to the police."

I shook my head. "This is mine to do, Nora, like the story is yours. Surely you see that."

She stood taut. "Call Rayfield. You've already been hurt. You're begging for something worse to happen."

I handed her the paper. "Then you'd better keep this for your story."

"For Christ's sake, Adam, don't you see what you're doing?" I started for the door. She grabbed my arm. "Damn you, you're acting out the case that killed your father."

Her face when I turned was pale and intense. "Just...where did you dredge up that?" I asked softly.

"It's so fucking obvious. The chances you've taken, this obsession to prove who killed her—it's more than saving Henry Cantwell or your wife. It began making sense when Rayfield told me how your father died. So I got the clippings from when it happened and then called police who knew him. They told me everything. It's incredible. He was thirty-two, like you are now, and a homicide lieutenant. The wife of a policeman—your father's closest friend—was found raped and murdered. Your father was assigned to the case. He found out that the dead woman had been sleeping with a police captain named Tyrell, a man he'd never liked. His friend's wife had broken it off—"

"I know the facts, Nora. He was my father."

"Then let me finish. For almost a year your father tried to prove Tyrell had killed her, until they hated each other. Tyrell spied on your father and tried to have him busted. Each time Tyrell interfered, your father documented that, for evidence. It became obsessive. Tyrell stopped doing anything but worry about Kieron Shaw. Your father never got a warrant: Tyrell was over him, and made sure of that. But when your father was very certain, he went to Tyrell's house alone to face him. He told Tyrell what he had. Tyrell pulled a gun and shot him through the heart. They sentenced Tyrell to life. Your father was buried, with photographers and newsmen everywhere. His picture ran in all the papers. You look exactly like him." Culhane's eyes were sad and knowing. "Adam, you're not doing this for Henry Cantwell. The man you've done this for was murdered twenty years ago. You've given him too much already."

I waited. "Are you through now?"

"Yes."

I opened the door. Then I paused, turning back in the doorway. "You left something out, Nora. Things I haven't let myself remember for years. My father was a good and decent man. He never made a promise—no matter how small, or how busy he was—that he didn't keep. He never lied, and hated lies and liars. We played baseball. He was tall and slim and had this way of looking at people, even the priest, that said he saw them through their words. He was proud. He even walked proud into Mass, kneeling so quick and graceful by our pew that he was up in an instant. He seldom smiled, but when he did it was bright and sudden, and without knowing it he made people want to be like him. We—my mother, Brian, and I—lived on his strength. And when he died, my mother found her strength in hating him for that, and Brian in God, and I became someone I was never meant to be and made a mess of Krissy's life, and now that's mine to face. But there's the other thing."

Nora looked up. "What's that?" she asked.

"My father was right. Tyrell killed the woman."

"Oh God, Adam."

I touched her cheek. Then I turned and walked to my car through the rain, to find Kris Ann.

The skies had turned black and slantwise rain battered my hood in the metallic beat of the night seven years ago, when I knew how I'd begun to lose her.

We had come back late from a movie and parked at the end of Cade's driveway in a cocoon of rain and darkness, not wanting to go in. Thin vapor from our breathing glazed the windshield. Through it, the house was vague and dark and massive, its single light a blur of yellow from Cade's bedroom. Kris Ann and I slid down in the seats, faces turned to each other, debating whether she would come to my room again. "But it's unnerving," she said, "like making love in a fire drill."

I grinned in the dark. "It develops intense concentration and singleness of purpose. Someday our children will be banging on the bedroom door demanding water, and we'll have either learned to concentrate or else—"

"Our children," she smiled, "are one thing. My father is something else."

"He is that."

Her smile faded. "What are you going to do about his offer?"

"I don't know. We've been planning on Washington, after all. Of course it's a fine firm and a better start in some ways: more money, a good practice if I make partner. I suppose our life might be easier."

308

"What about that apartment in George-town we were going to find?"

There was something in her tone I couldn't place. "It still sounds good. I just wonder whether Birmingham might have more of a future for us. And it is where you've grown up."

She looked away. "Of course Daddy's here," she said slowly.

"I've thought of that. The other way you wouldn't see him very much." I smiled. "For-tunately, once we're married he won't be sleeping next door. What do you think?"

She turned to face me. "It's up to you, Adam. Please, just think about what you really want. I need to know that."

I nodded. "Then I'll consider what your father said."

For a long time she was silent. "If you like."

She sat straighter, facing toward the wind-shield so that her face was in shadows. The rain beat down. "Let's go in now," she said abruptly. "I'm getting tired."

She didn't come to my room that night. The next morning she said nothing about it, nor in all the years since, living in the house her father bought us....

When I got there, Cade's car was next to hers.

THIRTY-FIVE

I parked and circled the house to the front. Rain soaked my clothes and hair and ran down my face. I reached the porch, slowed, and went noiselessly up its rain-slick steps.

Cade and Kris Ann were framed in the living room window, close together on the couch, their backs to me. Cade talked urgently, index finger jabbing his palm. Kris Ann's face in profile was strained and attentive. Their lips moved, but on the other side of the glass I heard only rain beating on the canopy and the steps and the leaves of trees. I moved to the front door, opened it, and walked inside.

Cade stood quickly. Kris Ann turned pale. "I know about New Orleans," I told her.

Her mouth opened. Cade moved between us, eyes hooded and watchful. I looked past him. "We're going to the police, Krissy."

Her glance moved between us. "For what, Adam? Why?"

"Lydia Cantwell's murder."

She shrank from me in horror. Cade was still, almost expressionless, watching me with his back to the mantel where Kris Ann's revolver was. "We have to go," I told her softly.

Cade's voice was tight. "I can't let you do that, Adam."

I shook my head, speaking to Kris Ann. "I've got no choice, Krissy. Maybe you can explain to Rayfield why you got home so late

310

the night Lydia was killed. But now I know that Henry never left Anniston, and that the black Mercedes Joanne Mooring thought she saw in the Cantwells' drive was a navy blue Audi like yours."

"Adam, that's not right—"

"I wish it weren't. From the time I started looking into Lydia's murder you tried to stop me—for Roland's sake, you said. And when I wouldn't, I found your picture on my windshield. You're an artist, after all."

"You can't believe that."

"I can't believe you. When I asked you to leave town you refused and tried persuading me to quit. The night I was shot at, you'd switched off every light in the house, your revolver was missing, and you were out. When you came home the revolver was in your purse. This partnership finished it. You hid that from me, damn you, and now Henry and Lydia are dead. I'm giving you to Rayfield."

I moved toward her. Cade's face as he stood between us was hard, determined. "I won't permit this. They'll try Kris Ann for murder."

"They'll do that anyhow. The news people know about Napoleon."

Cade stared at me. "Then you sent the Culhane woman."

"That's right. By nightfall Rayfield will be here looking for Kris Ann. It's already done."

Kris Ann looked to Cade, pleading. He stepped forward. "You've ruined everything, Adam. I always knew you would. God, how I hate you."

"For what, Roland? Finding Lydia's murderer?"

"You're such a fool." He shook his head. "Sweet Jesus, to have lived through this for seven years and remained so stupid."

"Not quite so stupid."

A strange smile of contempt turned the ends of his mouth without touching his eyes. "But you are. You see, Kris Ann didn't kill anyone."

I stopped to face him as he awaited my answer. After a moment I said simply, "I know."

Cade stared at me in the long silence that followed. I broke it, speaking softly. "I counted on you, Roland. You do love her, in your way."

Cade's eyes widened as if admitting light. Kris Ann bolted up, staring wildly at both of us and backing away until we formed a triangle, the couch between us, Cade to one side. The mantel and gun were still behind him. "How did you know?" he finally asked.

"Bayles came to see me."

"I wouldn't have thought that."

"Love is strange. But then you know all about that. It all comes back to the three of us: you, me, and Kris Ann."

Cade's head tilted. "How long have you wanted me for this?"

"I suppose since the beginning, on some level."

"Why so soon?"

"I started sensing the connections. You've hated me ever since Kris Ann brought me home. At first I tried believing you were a protective father. I didn't want to face the fact that we were rivals. The job offer, the house, the talks with me—all these were ways of keeping Kris Ann for yourself. She knew that, inside. I didn't, or didn't want to." I turned to Kris Ann. "I never wanted to be a lawyer, so how I did it never really mattered. Maybe I was dazzled by things I'd never had. All the time you wanted me to take you away from him. You sensed how unhealthy it was. Instead I used you as an excuse and kept you here. God help me, it was you I wanted, not the rest."

Her face was blank and wounded. She shook her head, over and over. "But look at what you've done—"

"Please, Krissy, understand what *he* did. Roland meant to destroy our marriage. Over time he planned to cut me down in front of you and then wean you with money until you didn't respect or need me. But he invested badly. Another man would have given up. Your father is a different sort of man. He learned Napoleon was in trouble and promised them financing in return for a share in your name. He didn't have that kind of money himself. But Henry had the bank's money and Lydia's, and Roland knew that he was homosexual. My guess is that he put detectives on Henry until he found his lover. Then he threatened to expose the other man unless Henry arranged a loan. The details aren't important. What I have to know is why you took that partnership."

"It was a present from Daddy," she burst out bitterly.

I shook my head. "Why didn't you just tell me?"

"It was between me and Daddy. I thought maybe it would hurt your pride. I didn't know about Henry—"

"It was *ours*," Cade cut in. "You don't need to explain anything."

I turned. "Then you can, Roland. You can tell her about Jason."

Cade turned to her, face suffused with blood. I went on. "Ask him, Krissy. Ask him if you have a brother."

They faced each other in terrible silence. Then Cade nodded mutely, and reached toward her. She recoiled, crying out, "Why, Adam? Why do this now?"

"Because we have to face the truth or there's been no point to any of this. Your father was young when his family lost their money. It humiliated him. He despised Henry for his 'weakness,' and for what he had. So piece by piece he took what was Henry's: his father's affection, his place at the firm, and then Lydia. Roland wanted her and had her, and she had a son. But they couldn't marry because of the scandal it would cause and perhaps for fear he'd lose you. After your mother died he proposed. Lydia refused and denied him Jason, but it was you who paid the price. He became fixated on you, pouring all his hate and disappointment into keeping you his—"

"Stop." Cade's face and voice filled with torment. "How can you know anything of me?"

I turned to him. "Before Henry died you told me that I couldn't think like someone else. You were wrong. I've learned to think like you. You'd taken Henry's place but now he had your son. At first you tried to reach Jason through Lydia, forcing her to buy Jason presents. But Jason grew up warped. When he tried to rape Kris Ann the conflict tore you apart: *your* son, touching the daughter you wanted for yourself. It ate through you until you hated all of them. Did you ever tell Henry, Roland?"

"Why should I have? He was *our* son. Henry was a weakling."

"So you destroyed him."

"I warn you, Adam."

I shook my head. "Krissy has to see what you are. You blackmailed Henry for more than just money. You enjoyed it. When Broussard's loan was reduced you forced him to use Lydia's money to cover the difference. You hoped she'd never find out. But she was in love with Mooring. She must have despised coming to you. But you knew the Cantwells' finances and could minimize the involvement of outsiders. In a way she began her own murder. The will is a fake, isn't it, Roland?"

He nodded reflexively. "How did you learn that?"

"It has to be. When Lydia came to your office you must have found out she'd fought with Jason and that only Mooring knew she was asking for a divorce. You would have asked when she intended telling Henry and learned

315

she wasn't expecting him back that night. You knew a divorce would uncover your blackmail of Henry. Everyone would learn what you are—me, your partners, even Kris Ann. You couldn't let that happen. So when Lydia left, you had your secretary type a new will to cover Lydia's reason for coming. But you had a second purpose. You could use it to revenge yourself on Jason.

"Late that night you called on Lydia. She let you in: after all, you were Jason's father. But she was set on Mooring. All the years of hate and jealousy overwhelmed you. I wonder what she felt when she realized you meant to kill her, and how—"

Kris Ann's hands clutched her throat. In one continuous motion Cade leaped to the mantel and whirled on me with the revolver. "No," Kris Ann screamed.

Cade turned to her. "He means to put me in prison. I can't let him live to see that." His voice became rhythmic, compelling. "Please, baby, you have to choose. How can you think he loves you? He used you to get my money, left you here alone when he thought you might be harmed. Now he's accused you of killing Lydia to get at me. He knew I loved you. Everything I've done was for you. He used you—"

"Tell her the rest, Roland."

"Stop," she screamed.

"Please, baby—"

"Tell her how you strangled Lydia."

Cade started toward me with the revolver.

"She'll choose, in time. She'll understand what I did—"

"She'll understand what you are. You took Lydia's picture and mutilated it with her dead at your feet hoping the police would think her killer was insane, like Jason. It was no deception. You're more psychotic than Jason ever dreamed of. You liked killing her."

"No." Cade's voice was anguished. "She looked so *new*. All those years I'd wanted her, her elegance, even her distance, and then she says she's free at last—free of Grangeville and all of Henry's secrets, and ours—"

"Maybe she was just happy, Roland. She'd almost made it."

He shook his head. "She insulted me. When I began moving toward her she started to beg, told me she'd do anything to please me as long as she could have Mooring. It was all for *him*. She was crying when I touched her." His arm raised until he faced me over the sight of the revolver.

"It's no good. You can't believe Kris Ann will forget watching you kill me. You'll go to the electric chair."

Cade's mouth was a harsh line. "I'm going either way. You've seen to that. At least now you'll die first and I'll have time alone with Kris Ann, to explain—"

"Daddy—no." Kris Ann ran to him, grasping his free arm and falling to her knees. "Don't do this."

She looked up. Cade reached to stroke her

hair. "Do you choose me, baby? I want you to choose me."

"Don't touch her, Roland."

Kris Ann's eyes closed. Her face was white and frozen. Cade kept the gun on me as he stroked her hair and the back of her neck. "She's mine, Adam. There's nothing you can do to stop me now."

I moved toward him. "Let her go."

"No." He shook his head. "Not again."

"Then let her hear first. You can't be afraid, not the way you've maneuvered me."

The gun didn't move. Only the keenness of his look disclosed interest. "So you understand that, too."

"I understand it all. You gave me the will so that I'd be the one to find Lydia. You knew I'd give it to the police to protect Henry. The will provided them Jason as a suspect and you an excuse to force yourself on Henry and control me. You counted on that: you'd run my life for seven years. And you wanted one last contest with Krissy as the prize."

Kris Ann covered her face. A close volley of thunder exploded, rattling the windows. I talked through it. "It began falling apart when Henry came home. You knew he would be gone that night, but you must have been sick to find out *where* he had been, and with whom. So you helped him lie, knowing—as he did not—that Bayles' exposure would reveal you as the murderer.

"Rayfield made it harder. He hated you and knew Henry was gay. Then they discovered Mooring's semen. Rayfield didn't know whose it was, but you must have. You were almost caught. But your interest and Mooring's were identical: he didn't want to be uncovered and although he didn't know why, you couldn't withstand it. For twenty-eight years since, you changed the course of his life, and he never knew."

"When *I* uncovered Mooring I wanted to protect Henry. So like a fool I hid what I knew from Rayfield and protected you instead."

Wind and rain began howling on the porch behind me. Kris Ann wept at Cade's feet. His stare over the gun sight was filled with rage and loathing. I spoke faster. "Henry and you were locked in a terrible contest. Henry didn't want Bayles exposed and you'd concealed the link between your blackmail and the murder by covering her divorce plans with the fake will. But he had enough suspicion to ask me to investigate and enough guts to insist on that to you. It wasn't my favor to him. It was *his* favor to me. We were friends—"

"Likes attract," Cade said contemptuously. "The weak and the envious."

"I don't envy the strength it took to mutilate Krissy's picture." Her face raised from her hands. "That was him, too," I told her. "All through this he's tried to make me afraid of losing you to a murderer, or to him. I didn't know that they were the same man."

Cade looked down at Kris Ann. His gun wavered slightly. I calculated the distance between us. "Please," Cade was saying. "He

319

never cared for you. I proved that with the picture."

She rose, looking from Cade to me. Reason—cold and certain and unforgiving—came into her face. "You bastards." She turned to me. "Both of you. I've been the battlefield where you could prove who was the biggest man—"

"Baby, I had to show you he didn't care—"

I began moving toward him. "Bullshit, Roland: by then I'd found Mooring. You were trying to save yourself. When I talked to Joanne Mooring, I began closing in on you, except that I didn't understand what she was telling me. Instead I suspected everyone: the Moorings, Otis Lee, and finally Jason. You were willing to sacrifice Lee and I was caught between Lee and Henry. But when Rayfield told me about Henry's arrest and then Henry admitted what had happened I was closer yet. How did you find out fast enough to shoot at me?"

Cade still watched Kris Ann. "Coincidence," he said absently. "I called Kris Ann right after you did and found out where you were."

"And then you waited in the vacant lot the way you told me Henry did."

He nodded. Kris Ann stared at him. "But people's lives. Lydia's and Henry's. Ours."

"Baby." Cade's voice was soft, crooning. "You're the only one who mattered. The rest..." He looked back to me.

I stopped six feet from him. "The rest were

320

expendable, like Henry. When Clayton told me that Rayfield had found eight hundred thousand dollars gone from Lydia's account, all I needed was to lean on Henry until he told me who Bayles was and what you'd done. You knew how close I was: when you talked about Henry—how trapped and desperate he must feel—you were talking about yourself. I swear it, Roland, even if I could forgive you the rest I can never forgive what you did next. You maneuvered me into giving you time to think while believing I'd bought time for Henry. Then you went to work. You implied that he had no lover. You blamed everything you'd done—Lydia's murder, Krissy's picture, your shots at me—on Henry. You had to break my faith in him for just a few more hours. You succeeded. I didn't return his call that night. God damn you, I could have saved him.

"The appointment you made wasn't for eight the next morning. It was for eight that night. You made sure he never called again. It wasn't suicide, Roland. You killed him."

"No, Adam." Cade's smile flickered eerily. "You killed him, by not calling. When I put the gun in his mouth he just looked at me. He wanted to die."

"But you're insane." Kris Ann's voice was broken. "To kill Lydia and Henry. To think that was for me—"

"There's more, Krissy. Roland planned to use Henry's murder to have you for himself He meant to burden me with guilt and have me fired. He was in the clear now and had the partnership to give you. I was to be the irrational ex-partner. That was the choice he meant to give you. You were going to be his." I began moving toward Cade. "You killed my friend, Roland, but I survived. I'm taking you in."

"No." Cade raised the gun, bracing his shooting wrist with his left hand. "That's one thing you will never do."

Kris Ann reached toward him. "Daddy—"

"I have to." Cade straightened with an insane ravaged dignity. "Perhaps it's better that you know what I've done for you. Now you can truly choose."

"Don't make me." She reached out for him. "Please."

"There's nothing else left." Cade squinted, aiming at the center of my face as I moved closer. "You have to choose now." His finger tightened on the trigger.

Kris Ann lunged as he fired.

The gun jerked upward. Cade stared at me, astonished, amidst falling plaster. Kris Ann fell past him in the bullet's echo. I jumped.

My head drove into his stomach and knocked him against the mantel. He bounced back, cracking his gun on my skull. I doubled, stunned, hugging his waist tightly as his momentum pushed me backward and my knees collapsed and I pulled him down on top of me. As we fell my arm lashed up at his wrist and knocked the gun to the floor, and then Cade landed on me with his full weight, fingers grasping my windpipe.

They tightened, shutting off air. There was ripped tissue in my mouth and the taste of blood. Rhythmically, he began smashing my head on the floor. My skull exploded. His face, intense and rapturous, broke into pieces in front of me. Then it went dark and there was only his sweat and weight and panting, the sourness of his breath, iron fingers as I choked for air. My left hand flopped on the wooden floor, touched steel, groping. The trigger curled against my finger. His thumbs pressed toward the back of my throat. My hand closed. In a blind reflex I jammed the gun between us and fired.

His fingers dug fiercely. I gagged, and then they twitched and loosened and I swallowed air, raw and tender in my throat, and retched it up. There was light. Cade's face was inches from mine. His eyes seemed great with surprise, a last, profound disappointment. They made his expression softer, almost gentle. "Lydia," he murmured, and then they went blank, and he was dead weight, and his face fell against my shoulder.

His body trembled. I lay down the gun and pushed him off me. He flopped on his back, staring emptily at the ceiling, a dark stain near his heart. Kris Ann was crawling toward us. I couldn't speak. There was no rain or wind or thunder.

In the aching, awful silence I got up and stumbled toward the telephone. I turned in the hallway. Kris Ann kneeled over Cade, tear streaked, holding his head in her hands. Her hair fell across his face.

I went to the telephone and told them to send Rayfield.

When I returned, Kris Ann was chattering at Cade, crying and asking him why. Blood trickled from the corner of his mouth. I let her go until she wasn't speaking or sobbing. Then I went to her side.

"They're coming," I said softly.

She looked up at me. Her eyes were burn-holes. "You had to kill him, didn't you?"

"Krissy, it's time now." I reached out.

She turned away. When I took her hand it was lifeless. She didn't struggle, or help. I pulled her up and led her to the porch as she looked back at Cade.

It was quiet outside, and cool. The rain had stopped, and there was the shine of wet-ness on the grass and the fresh smell of ozone. Sirens wailed in the distance, coming closer. Kris Ann wept. I pulled her to me. She was stiff in my arms, resisting. My eyes turned wet, and then I began silently to cry, for Henry and Lydia, and for my father, for what I had done and all the things between us Kris Ann and I would have to face.

She shivered. I held her close.

X